ALICE WOOTSON

Ready To Take a Chance

ARABESQUE®

ISBN-13: 978-1-58314-807-5
ISBN-10:   1-58314-807-8

READY TO TAKE A CHANCE

www.kimanipress.com

Printed in U.S.A.

To the readers who let me switch gears and take them through a range of plots from suspense to comedy, I thank you for your loyalty. To Kicheko and Evette for their patience with me, to the National Basketball Association for providing the excitement of the game, and lastly but most importantly, to my family, especially Ike, for coming along on this exciting ride.

Chapter 1

"I'm sorry to stick you with this, but I have to go home." Shana apologized to Paula for the third time in two minutes. "I thought I could make it." She wiped her forehead. "I—I guess I should have stayed home, but I promised the team we'd have track practice after school." She grabbed a tissue from her shoulder bag just in time to cover a cough. "Will you announce that I have to cancel?"

"I'll take care of it. Go."

"I know the other teachers won't like missing their prep times this afternoon. I hate it when it happens to me." She leaned against the wall beside Paula's desk. "I'm so sorry."

"Quit apologizing and go home. I'll tell Mrs. Simms when she gets in. I got you covered." She waved her away. "Now go before you give me what you have and you know this office can't possibly operate without me." Paula leaned closer and frowned. "You look terrible, what my grandmama would call 'death warmed over.' I don't know how you managed to do it, but you're pale and flushed at the same time. Are you sure you can drive home okay? Do you need somebody to take you?"

"That's just what you need. Two classes to cover instead of one." Shana took a deep breath and covered up her cough. "I can make it. I don't have far to go. I'll creep home taking the small streets and then crawl into bed when I get home." She coughed again. "Maybe I'll just lie on my hall floor for a few days before I crawl into my bed." She tried to smile, but it was interrupted by a sneeze. "In a little more than a month I'll be back here and I'll drag the month of May with me."

"Don't even try it. May has to wait to do its thing until after April is finished, and March is still here. You better be back way before then. You know Murdock School can't function without you any more than it can without me."

"Sure." Shana managed a weak smile which was quite an accomplishment since it felt like her fever was melting her face. She walked from the office at a pace a snail could beat.

The bright late March sunshine covering her as she made it to her car did nothing to make her feel better. It wasn't that she preferred the bitter rain and snow flurries that had squatted over Philadelphia and played tag for a week before it had decided to saunter off. She was just too sick to care.

"I can't believe this. I managed to avoid the flu that circulated in December and the strain that showed up in January," she muttered as she drove from the parking lot. "Philadelphia was hit hard, but that was to be expected. I managed to avoid it, then." She caught a sneeze just as she turned onto the street. "Getting the flu at the end of March is worse."

Everybody was trying to hold on until winter was over and make it to spring. In a few weeks, the earth would sprout and bloom and grow, and she was feeling like death was pounding on her door telling her that the end was here.

She inched her car along Greene Street as if she were in rush-hour traffic on the expressway instead of on a nearly deserted street. She lifted her hair from her neck and turned the air conditioner up high in spite of the light snow flurries drifting down. She wished she lived in the next block instead of two miles from school.

Finally she eased her car into the driveway on St. Martin's Lane and frowned.

"What's Elliot's car doing here? I hope he didn't catch what I have. We can't have both of us sick at the same time."

She took a deep breath and forced herself out of the car by imagining herself snuggled in her bed. That was the only way she could get her body to move. The sun had completely fled and a gray blanket covered the sky, matching her gray mood. The bare white-wicker porch furniture had lost the blue cover she had placed over it in November. She didn't have the energy to care. Maybe next week she'd be able to fix it. Or next month. If she lived that long.

She unlocked the heavy carved wooden door and pushed it open.

"Elli…" She never finished his name.

Soft music drifted down the stairs forcing her words to stay inside of her. Nina Simone's husky voice crooning about love filled the wide downstairs hall and squeezed against her. Elliot's voice, joined with a giggle from someone else, led her upstairs as she followed the music. The sounds bounced off the polished oak floors.

Uh-uh. She shook her head and the pain reminded her why she had come home early. A new kind of pain joined it. *Oh, no way. I must be hallucinating. He wouldn't dare.*

Slowly she climbed the stairs, clutching the banister as if afraid it would collapse if she let go.

She had spent a week the summer after they had moved in carefully stripping and finishing the hardwood staircase. She had done her best to make it inviting.

Laughter skipped along the stairs, oblivious to the effort she had put into the staircase. Maybe she had made it too inviting.

She swallowed hard and tightened her leg muscles

so she could stay on her feet. The flu had nothing to do with the weakness in her legs right now, nor the feeling inside her that felt as if a fist were wrapped around her stomach and squeezing.

She reached the second-floor hall and stared, but she wasn't looking at the bentwood rocker beside the bookcase under the window. Right now her ears were more important than her eyes. Muffled sounds skipped from the bedroom. Two voices. Coming from her bedroom.

She swallowed hard again and leaned against the wall. She didn't want to move, and not because of the flu. She didn't want to think. She wanted to wait until the sounds went away, as if they had never happened. Then she took a deep breath and pushed open the door.

She felt as if she had stumbled into a soap opera.

"What—what are you doing home?" Elliot sputtered, pounding at her head worse than her headache. He sounded as if she were the one at fault.

"I'm the woman who lives here. Remember?"

Shana stared at the bed as if she needed more time for the image to etch in her mind. As if she would ever be able to erase it. She glanced at the young woman on her side of the bed.

She had seen the young blonde before. Here in this house. Elliot had invited this woman, Ingrid, his graduate assistant, to their open house last Christmas. Shana hadn't known the welcome she had extended to Ingrid had included her husband and her bed.

Ingrid's glance slithered away. She pulled the top sheet under her arms.

Funny, Shana thought, though there was nothing funny about the situation at all. *She's modest in front of me but not in front of my husband.*

"Fancy meeting you here, Ingrid." Shana's voice was stronger than she would have expected it to be.

She stood straighter when what she wanted to do was run down the stairs and find someplace to curl up into a ball until this all went away. She took a deep breath. She certainly couldn't curl up in her bed. It was already filled to capacity.

"Mrs. Garner…" Shana's stare kept the rest of the woman's words from coming out.

"I think that, since you're in my bed with my husband, we should be on a first-name basis. Don't you?" Her stare hardened. "Did you ace this test, Ingrid?"

"Shana." Elliot scrambled from the bed and groped on the floor beside it for his pants.

"You've got it all wrong, don't you? I'm not the one you should cover up for." She threw her words at him and coughed. Nothing was heavy enough for this situation.

"Shana, listen."

"I hear you. Your actions are talking for you. How could you? How dare you?" Her stare pinned him. Then she looked away.

Her gaze went to the crystal angel on the dresser; well within reach. Her hand tightened. Then she loosened her fingers. Elliot wasn't worth the angel. He wasn't worth spit.

She stared back at this person she thought she knew as well as she knew herself. She took a deep breath, coughed, then freed her next words. "Now I know what 'action speaks louder than words' means." Tears choked her, trying to get out, but she refused to release them. Maybe she would later, but not now. Not in front of these two. "Don't tell me this isn't what it looks like. That's exactly what it is."

"I'm sorry. I…"

"Yeah, you are. A sorry piece of trash." She took a deep breath and let it out slowly. "You should be glad—" she said through clenched teeth "—glad that I'm not a violent woman. Glad that I don't think you are worth going to jail over. I've already wasted too much of my life on you." Although she didn't want to, Shana blinked.

Elliot squirmed. Then he reached to her.

"Let me explain…."

"Don't you dare touch me. Not now. Not ever again." He pulled his hands away and Shana continued. "It might be interesting to see how you try to talk your way out of this, but I don't want to hear it. I don't want to hear anything from you ever again."

She heard her voice rise. She felt as if she were watching a scene in a play—a new play with an old plot. She forced her voice back to where it would be if she hadn't just found her husband in her bed with another woman.

"What I *do* want is for you to take the rest of the trash and get out of my bed, out of my house and out of my life."

"But—"

"The only 'butt' in this is yours and Blondie's and I want both of them out of here. Now." The spike in her temperature had nothing to do with the flu. She coughed again. "I'll give you fifteen minutes. By the time I get back I want you both gone. If I thought it was feasible, I'd tell you to take the bed with you. You two obviously enjoyed it more than I ever did with you."

Shana turned from the room. The symptoms that had made her come home came back almost immediately. She forced her legs to carry her downstairs and into her car.

She got as far as the supermarket parking lot three blocks away and found a spot at the edge. The shock, the hurt, the betrayal bubbled to the surface and mixed with her tears. She was glad it was the middle of a weekday and the lot was almost empty. She needed to be alone. She swallowed hard. She'd have a lot of time for that. The rest of her life. She didn't bother to wipe the tears. More would just come to take their place. A while later she sat up and wiped her face.

When was the last time she and Elliot had had sex? She frowned. He claimed that he was under a lot of pressures at work. Today she saw exactly what kind of pressure he meant.

I put my needs on hold for him. What a fool I was.

She wiped more tears, but didn't move from the car.

Chapter 2

Laughter from three kids on the way to the store pulled Shana from her misery. School was out.

If I hadn't gotten sick, I would just be coming home. If I had decided to stay in school and fight the flu today, the house would have been empty when I got home. I never would have learned about Elliot's extracurricular activities. If I had just not... She shook her head. *Was this the first time?* How many others of the young women he came in contact with at the university had been in her bed?

A shudder rippled through her. How many of the young women Elliot had introduced to her had he had affairs with? She shook her head. *I'll bet they all had a*

*good time laughing at dumb, naive Shana. What if I
hadn't found out? What if today had never happened?*
She shook her head again. *No. No what-ifs.* She wiped
her eyes. *How could he? How dare he? That pig...* She
took a deep breath. She shouldn't insult pigs. Pigs never
did anything underhanded. They didn't try to hide what
they were. They didn't care who knew that they wal-
lowed in the mud and filth. She took a deep breath, then
drove home.

No sounds greeted her this time when she opened the
door. No laughter. No deceiving voices slipped down the
stairs. She let out a deep breath. This time her arrival
was expected.

She went upstairs. Without looking inside, she closed
the door to what had been her bedroom and went down
the hall to the guest room that she and Elliot had planned
to change into a nursery when she got pregnant—when
the time was right.

She sat on the bed. This room would stay a guest
room, now.

*Did I do something wrong? Why had Elliot turned
to another woman?* She swallowed hard. *No. This isn't
my fault. He always blames me for whatever goes
wrong, but I'm not taking the weight for this. This is definitely on him.*

She forced her mind to stay in the moment as she
pulled off her slacks and blouse and crawled between
the sheets. At last she could give in and curl into a ball.
Tears, one from each eye, slid down her face and

dropped to the pillow. Nothing stopped them, so two more followed. Soon her pillow was soaked.

She waited for her tears to extract the hurt from inside her and wash it away. She was still waiting when she finally drifted off to sleep.

Shana opened her eyes. She had slept for hours, but it was still daylight and Elliot was still her cheating husband. She sat up, and for a few seconds wondered why she was in the bed in the guest room instead of her own bed. Then reality came back to her with a jolt.

Her head felt as tight as an overinflated balloon and just as fragile. She wanted to roll over and go back to sleep until things were back to normal, but she made herself get up. The old normal would have to be replaced with a new one.

She went down the hall and hesitated when she got to her bedroom. She took a deep breath and coughed. Her cough reminded her why she had come home early and, therefore, stumbled into a future far different from the one she had expected. She took another deep breath and went inside the room.

The bed looked just like a normal bed. It didn't look important enough to cause the end of a marriage.

She went to the closet that spanned one entire wall. For too long she stared at Elliot's clothes. She thought of performing her own variation of the scene from a movie a year ago. Elliot certainly deserved it as much as the guy in the movie had. But Elliot didn't own a sports convertible and burning of any kind outdoors wasn't allowed in Philadelphia.

She took an armful of his clothes from the closet, went downstairs and opened the front door. They'd make unusual decorations draped over the shrubs growing against the house and on the other bushes lining the front walkway. Or maybe they could be a new kind of covering for the gray cement sidewalk.

She stared a minute longer. Then she closed the door and dropped the clothes onto the hall floor. She looked at them, then got a box of trash bags from the laundry room.

Elliot belonged in one of the bags, but she'd settle for putting his things in them instead. Trash's trash belonged in a trash bag.

She went upstairs for another load. The flu kept reminding her of its presence: coughs, chills and fevers took turns trying to stop her, but determination won.

"Just a little while longer," she whispered. "Then I'll sit down, I promise." Her words were followed by a fit of coughing.

She bent over and held her sides to wait for the coughing to stop, but her head felt as if her brain were crammed against her skull, so she straightened up again. *Which was worse, aching sides or an about-to-burst head?* A toss-up, she decided when her lungs got tired of coughing. She wished the flu would fly away.

An hour later, she looked at the trash bags lining the driveway. They reminded her of the piles of trash that had accumulated all over Philadelphia during the last sanitation workers' strike. These bags bulged just as those had, looking as if they were filled with treasure. She let out a hard breath. Just more proof that looks could be deceiving.

Her stomach reminded her that she had missed lunchtime, but she ignored it. She had to make a phone call.

Another hour later and after much persuasion to get him there, the locksmith handed Shana the keys to her new locks. She leaned against the door as his truck pulled away. A few hours down and the rest of her life to go.

She was hungry, but she forced herself to go out. She had an important errand to run; one that wouldn't wait.

It didn't take long for her to finish her business and leave the staid old bank building on Germantown Avenue. As she crawled into the car, she was glad she didn't have to walk any farther. Slowly, she drove home.

She was still hungry, but she gave up the idea of food. It just wasn't worth the effort to fix it.

She started for the stairs when the doorbell rang. She closed her eyes and leaned against the banister. Maybe whoever it was would go away. She didn't know who was there, but it wasn't Elliot. He wouldn't just ring and wait. He'd pound and demand to come in after breaking his key off in the new lock.

"Open up, Shana Garner. I know you're in there. Paula said you'd be too sick to be anywhere else."

Shana smiled at the voice of her best friend.

"Okay, Martie." She stifled a cough. "Just a minute."

She went over to the door and, after fighting with the stiff new lock, opened it.

"I've got the cure for what ails you right here." Martie held up a large jar.

"That isn't chicken-noodle soup, is it?" Shana pushed the door closed and turned the dead bolt.

"Not just any chicken-noodle soup." Martie rubbed her hand slowly over the lid. "If I marketed this soup, it would make Campbell's pull their soup off the market. I made it from a family recipe handed down through generations." She started for the kitchen. "Come on. I have something here that's better than the whole shelf of medicine in the supermarket's cold and flu department."

"I'll try it, but I doubt if it will help."

"You gotta have faith. Sit there." Martie led her to the chair at the end of the table.

Shana leaned her head on her arms and watched as Martie fixed the soup. It was nice to have someone care about her.

"Here you go. Through the magic of microwaves, ready in no time." She sat across from Shana. "Go on. Eat," she said as Shana just stared at the bowl. "A chicken sacrificed her life for you, and I slaved over a hot stove after I got home from school. The least you can do is show your appreciation."

Shana forced herself to take a taste. Then another. Soon her bowl was empty.

"More?"

"No, thanks. That's more than I expected to get down."

"Are you sure it's just the flu? From the looks of your driveway, you've been cleaning for weeks. Maybe you're just tired out."

"I put those out today." Shana blinked hard. "After I got home."

"You couldn't stay for the other half day of school, yet you came home and did some major spring cleaning? What was so urgent that it wouldn't wait?"

Shana stared at the table in front of her as if she would find written help in explaining to Martie what had happened. She felt her eyes fill and shook her head, but that didn't stop the tears from forming a pool on the table in front of her.

"Hey. What is it?" Martie reached across the table and grabbed Shana's hand.

"Elliot was here when I got home." She wiped her face. "I swore I wasn't going to cry again." She wiped her eyes again. "He's not worth it."

"Tell me."

After starting and stopping and interrupting her story with hesitations and more tears and an occasional cough, she told Martie what had happened.

"That pig," Martie said when Shana had finished. "How could he?"

"I already called him a pig." She sighed. "I decided that pigs don't deserve the comparison."

"That's his stuff out there?" Martie pointed to the driveway.

"Yeah."

"Want a match?"

"I thought about it. I decided that Elliot already caused enough pollution in my life." She stood. "Want to help me take the bed apart and put it out there with the bags?"

Martie laughed. "Think you can manage?"

"Oh, yeah. I might collapse afterward, but I'll manage."

Together they worked. Anger gave Shana strength. The addition of a hammer to knock the bed apart didn't hurt. She just pretended that she was hitting the offending part of Elliot's anatomy.

As Martie helped her drag parts of the bed downstairs, Shana swore she'd never again let a man get close enough to hurt her.

"That's it," Shana said less than an hour later as she piled the dirty linen on top of the bed and stood back. A few snow flurries drifted over the bed and the matching dresser and chest that she and Martie had placed beside it.

The furniture was so heavy that it had been a struggle getting the pieces down the stairs even with the drawers out, but she and Martie had managed. The effort was worth it. She didn't want anything left in the bedroom to remind her of what Elliot had done. The image was stored securely in her memory without any reminders. She hoped the memory was deep enough so it wouldn't escape too often. She stood outside the door, but in spite of the cold, she didn't go inside. She stared at the bed which looked like an extralarge pile of trash. "I wonder how long it will take for him to try to come home."

"You mean, what used to be his home," Martie corrected.

"Yes." Shana shook her head. "Things weren't perfect between us but I never thought they were this bad." Her eyes were filled with tears when she looked at Martie. "We've been married for thirteen years. No fire stays hot for that long, no matter what you do." She sighed. "I thought he had some feelings left, though. I thought our marriage had just settled into a comfortable groove." She swallowed hard. "I guess to Elliot it was a rut." She blinked. "I still have feelings for him." She sniffed. "Or at least I did until this afternoon." She let out a deep breath. "I guess the feelings were only on my part." She frowned. "We—we shared a bed, but we might as well have been sleeping in separate rooms for…" She paused and frowned. "Nothing happened in that bed for months." She looked at the parts piled in the driveway. "At least not between me and Elliot. Who knows what activity took place when I wasn't home." She blinked hard. "I was the only one practicing monogamy."

She stared at the stuff lining the driveway once more, then turned her back on the evidence of Elliot's presence in her life and went back inside.

Chapter 3

The phone was ringing when Shana and Martie got back inside. *Probably the worm himself,* Shana thought as she locked the door. As she picked up the phone, she tried to decide if worms deserved comparison to Elliot any more than pigs did.

"Mrs. Garner. This is Ingrid." Shana steeled herself. Then she gave thanks that the woman was not within reach. She doubted if she could have kept her hands to herself again. She turned her attention to the woman who insisted on disrupting her life even more.

"I already gave. Not at the office, though. Here at my home. On second thought, I didn't give. You took."

"I'm sorry you had to find out about me and El that

way. But if you'd have given him a divorce when he asked, that wouldn't have happened. We would be married by now. I don't understand why you want to hang on to him when he doesn't want you."

Ingrid's whine sounded like the yowling of a cat in heat. Maybe that was a true explanation. Shana set her jaw, but she didn't hang up. She believed in giving a person enough rope. She hoped Ingrid put it to the use for which it was intended.

"I mean," Ingrid continued, oblivious to what Shana was thinking. "You're not that old. You can find somebody else. Some men like older women. Why don't you just let El go? I wouldn't want a man who didn't want me."

Shana plopped into the chair beside the phone table. She exhaled a hard breath. Maybe it would cool her off. Maybe not. She didn't care. She twisted and untwisted the phone cord pretending it was a scrawny, pale neck. Then she let out a slow easy breath. She even smiled slightly at what she was going to say.

"I didn't give *El* a divorce for a very good reason. He never asked me for one. Evidently he doesn't care enough for you to marry you. I had no idea he was fooling around. What was that you said about not wanting a man who didn't want you?"

"That's not true. El said you threatened to make it messy for him." Ingrid's voice had taken on a harder, more grating whine. "He said you'd make him lose his teaching position and he's so close to tenure. He said—"

"I don't give a pretty kitty about what he said. Who are you that I would want to lie to you? You can have him and with my blessings. I'll cut him loose as soon as possible. I can understand why you're in such a hurry. In ten years you'll be my age and thirty-five is over the hill, isn't it?"

"Why would El say you wouldn't give him a divorce if it isn't true?" A puzzling note joined the whine.

"You're a grad student. You must have earned *some* of your credits the old-fashioned way. Think hard about it and I'm sure you can come up with an answer."

Shana gently placed the phone down. No sense punishing it. It was just the carrier.

"What was that about?" Martie stood beside her.

"Ingrid wants me to stop giving Elliot a hard time about giving him a divorce."

"What?"

"She said he told her that he can't marry her because I won't give him a divorce."

"You believe her?"

"Oh, yeah." Shana nodded. "I believe her. Elliot probably did tell her that I won't free him." She sneezed. "Elliot is a lying, cheating animal. A new species. Human development took a step backward with him. If I could, I'd divorce him tomorrow, wrap him up in a package and tie a pretty bow around it." She coughed. "On second thought, forget the bow. I'd probably wrap it around his neck and pull it tight."

"He'd deserve it." Martie went to the stove. "Let me

make you a cup of tea. A cup of tea always makes you feel better."

"It will take more than tea this time."

"Okay, then. First we deal with the flu." Martie lit the burner under the teakettle. "Then we deal with your life."

They were on their second cups when the phone rang again. Had Ingrid finally figured it out?

"We have to talk." Elliot didn't waste time with *hello*. That was fine with Shana. The word *hello* gave a sense of civility and she was still a long way from feeling that toward Elliot.

"No, we don't."

"You're blowing this out of proportion. It didn't mean anything."

"Did you tell that to Ingrid?"

"What do you mean? What does Ingrid have to do with this? I mean—" His words were cut off by Shana's laugh.

"Man, you are a real piece of bad work. Enough of this. Come get your things."

"What do you mean?"

"There's a lot of not understanding going around today. Maybe the city added something to the water. Speaking of water, your things are in the driveway. They're in trash bags where you belong with them. You'd better get them before the snow flurries turn to rain."

"Are you crazy?"

"Not anymore. I'm saner than I've been in a long time."

"You can't do that with my things. I live there, too."

"Not anymore you don't. And as for your things, I

already did. If I forgot to put something out, just drop a list in the mail slot. If I agree that it's yours, I'll put it out and you can pick it up the next day. When I'm not at home, of course. I don't want to see your lying face. Besides, you're good at doing things when I'm not at home."

"Look, Shana, baby…"

"No, no, no. You've got it all wrong, *El*. It's 'Ingrid, baby,' now."

Shana didn't wait for a response to this last statement. Instead she hung up.

"That didn't feel as good as I thought it would," she said to Martie as they went back to sit at the kitchen table.

She traced swirls on the place mat with her finger. She had bought the mats when she and Elliot had gone to Jamaica two years ago. Back when they'd been in love.

She gathered the mats into a pile, meaning to get rid of them. Then she looked at them and put them back in place in front of each chair. She liked these mats. She wasn't going to lose them, too.

"But you got through it." Martie patted her hand. "That's what's important."

"Yeah, I did and it is." Shana nodded and sat up straight. "Talk to me. Take my mind off things. What happened after I left school today?" She frowned. *Was that just today?*

Martie told her about some of the reports the kids in her science classes were working on, trying to put as much of a humorous spin on it as she could.

"Tina tried to convince me that watching BET

would qualify as a science project. She said she could report on the environment of the performers. Then Herman, figuring that Tina was on to something, said he was going to do a report on rap music. I told them they both had until tomorrow to write a one-page paper defining science."

Shana tried to laugh at the funny parts of the stories, but she was having trouble even smiling. Laughing wasn't a close possibility.

The conversation slipped to other things including the weather. It was after eleven when Martie cleared the table. "I'm spending the night," Martie said when Shana yawned.

"Thanks for the offer, but I may as well get used to being alone." Shana finally managed a smile. "I'll be all right."

"You're sure? I can go home and get what I need for school tomorrow and come back."

"I'm sure."

"You really sure?"

"Positive. I'm going to crawl into bed and sleep away what's left of this day." Shana stood and Martie did, too.

"Okay. I'll be going. After all, *some* of us have work tomorrow." Martie hugged her. "I'll stop by tomorrow after school. I'll bring food."

"Maybe my taste buds will be back in service by then."

"They weren't too bad with the chicken soup today."

Shana waited at the door until Martie backed her car down the driveway. Then she turned out the porch light and climbed the stairs in the too-quiet house.

She sighed as she walked down the upstairs hall. *At least the flu no longer seems important. This Saturday I go bed shopping. I will reclaim my room.*

Chapter 4

"Okay, okay," Shana said as the ringing of the phone shrilled her awake. She groped around the nightstand, then remembered she wasn't in her bedroom.

She rushed down the hall and picked up the phone from the floor in her old bedroom where she had put it.

"I'm here, I'm here."

"Girl, I was about to hang up and you would have missed an award-winning performance," Martie said. "Turn on the radio news station. Quick. Gotta go. Lunch is almost over."

Shana shrugged and put down the phone. She turned on the clock radio and sat on the floor beside it.

She was used to Martie's now-and-then cryptic

messages. Most of the time they weren't worth the time and effort, but she'd humor her like she always did.

"...scandal in the faculty department of Barton University. Elliot Garner, noted English professor, has been accused by a graduate student of sexual intimidation and misconduct."

Shana was glad she was sitting. She didn't need to add an injury from falling to her already big problems. She scooted back and leaned against the wall. The reporter continued in a voice that sounded as if she were reporting the biggest story of the decade.

"Ingrid Alderdice, Professor Garner's graduate assistant, filed a complaint of sexual misconduct with the university this morning."

The reporter's voice was replaced by loud sniffling. Then Ingrid's voice whined on. It was so unlike the one she had used over the phone with Shana that she sounded like a different person.

"He—he…" She sniffed. "Professor Garner said that he'd use his influence to keep me from getting my degree if I didn't…" Ingrid's voice broke at just the right place. "He said if I didn't…" Her sigh drifted from the radio as if it were weighted down with a ton of stones.

Shana could picture Ingrid batting her eyes that were green only by the miracle of contacts. *What else wasn't real?* Shana's sigh was as heavy as Ingrid's was.

Ingrid's body was real. Shana had seen that for herself. Nature might have had some help in strategic places, but Shana hadn't been close enough to look for telltale scars. She shook her head. She had been close enough, though. Close enough to see that her marriage was crumbling. Too close.

I should turn off the radio. I shouldn't care what happens to Elliot. Why can't I have more control over my feelings?

She forced her attention back to the story. She shook her head and listened to the lie flowing into the space that she once shared with a husband.

"If I didn't…" now Ingrid's voice choked "…you know." Sobs punctuated the end of her words.

"How long has your affair been going on?" the reporter asked.

"It wasn't an affair," Ingrid snapped. "He took advantage of me." What had happened to the tears and the pitiful little voice?

"All right," the reporter quickly corrected. "How long has he been…" The reporter hesitated. "Uh, taking advantage of you?"

"Since last semester."

Shana gasped and leaned her head back against the wall. *Way before she had welcomed Ingrid into her home, Elliot had already done so.* Shana shook her head. *And I didn't have a clue.* She blinked. Her stomach felt as if a vise were clamped around it and somebody was tightening it. *Ignorance is only bliss until you learn the truth. Then it can tear you into little pieces.*

Regardless of the effect the story was having on

Shana, the reporter let Ingrid continue and Shana kept on listening.

"Why didn't you go to the authorities earlier?"

"I—I was afraid he would ruin things for me. He could have destroyed my whole future, you know."

Shana was grateful when Ingrid's voice disappeared and the reporter's voice came back on. That had to mean that it was almost over.

"We attempted to contact Professor Garner," the reporter said, "but he hasn't returned our calls. We also attempted to speak with President Dixon of Barton University, but he declined to comment."

Shana turned off the radio and slowly went to the kitchen. Part of what she had just heard—the last semester part—kept repeating in her head.

When she got to the kitchen, she sat in the first chair she could reach. It wasn't her usual chair, but it was better than falling to the floor.

She breathed deeply, hoping the oxygen would replace the stupidity in her brain.

Since last semester. She released a slow breath. *I don't know Ingrid's plans for the future, but unless they include acting, she's ignoring a sure thing.*

Shana opened the teakettle and stuck it under the faucet. She forced her attention back to the news story. Water flowed over the sides and into the sink. Shana stared at it as if trying to figure out what was going on. Then she turned off the water.

The radio in the kitchen was off, but it grabbed her attention as if it were a television. She shook her head, then set the kettle on the stove and turned on the gas. As she waited for the water to heat, her mind went back to Ingrid.

Elliot was a lot of things, but he was not the type to use any kind of force to get a woman. She believed that he might use persuasion when necessary to get his way, but he wouldn't have to resort to even that with most women.

He had always attracted them. Shana chewed on her lip. She had often thought that somewhere there was at least one man without pheromones because Elliot had more than his share.

She used to be flattered. After all, he had all of these women leaping at him, often in front of her, but he was only interested in her. At least that was what he had told her. Evidently he used lies, too. But not the lie that Ingrid accused him of. Elliot was in the doghouse, but Shana knew he wouldn't have done what Ingrid accused him of. This was Ingrid's own version of what a woman scorned would do.

The kettle whistled and she filled her cup. She shook her head. Naive *isn't the right word to describe what I used to be.* Stupid *is more accurate.*

She sat sipping her tea and thought about yesterday's phone call from Ingrid, glad she didn't have to decide whether or not to tell anybody about it. She didn't have any proof. She shrugged. *This was Elliot's mess. He got into it on his own, with help from Ingrid, of course. Let him get out of it by himself.*

The phone rang and she answered it. A reporter tried

to question her, but Shana gave the standard "no comment" and hung up. After two more such calls from other reporters, Shana decided to let the answering machine do its job.

She went into the living room and stared at the television as if it were on. She took a deep breath. Her eyes no longer burned from the flu. Her fever had been replaced by a chill that wasn't associated with illness.

Her flu had been chased away be Elliot's infidelity. It was as if fate had decided that she could only take on one problem at a time. She sighed. She wished fate had taken the bigger problem away and left the flu. She had experience in dealing with the flu. She went into the living room.

She had started to doze off in the huge recliner when she heard Elliot's voice on the machine. She thought for a while, then she picked up. *May as well get this over with.*

"Shana, do you know what you did when you talked to Ingrid?"

"Sure I do. I told her the truth. I told Ingrid that she can have you."

"You've ruined me. I was supposed to get tenure in September. I'll never get it now. You know the academic world's attitude toward bad publicity."

"Evidently you forgot and you're the one who needed to remember."

"I'll never get tenure now. It was all worked out. An increased class load was in the plans. Now suddenly the department head is talking about cutting faculty. Me. I'm now 'excessive faculty' and it's all your fault."

"Sure it is. Entirely mine. It's all my fault that you were rutting around with Miss Ingrid Victim. I shouldn't have come home unexpectedly. I should have called first to see if you were using our bed."

"Stop being ridiculous. You know Ingrid doesn't mean anything to me."

"And I know this because…" When Elliot didn't fill in the blank, Shana continued, "I've never before seen or even heard of anyone showing disinterest the way you did."

"I'm coming home. We'll discuss this like two adults."

"I told you—this isn't your home anymore." She swallowed hard. "But you'd better come get your stuff. It's still out there cluttering up my driveway. When you do come, remember to call first. I don't like surprises anymore."

"We have to talk."

"That's what we're doing now." She sighed. "Go to Ingrid, Elliot. I'm sure you can find a way to persuade her to change her mind. You always were good at persuasion. Offer to marry her. That's what she told me she wants."

"I can't marry her. I'm married to you."

"It's too late to remember that now." She sighed. "It's too bad that it takes longer to get a divorce than to get married. I think that should be reversed, don't you?" Shana shifted in the chair. "On Saturday I'm buying a new bed for my bedroom. That will be a good time to get your stuff out of my driveway. Your bed is out there, too, and the rest of the bedroom set. Maybe you and Ingrid can use it at your new place." She swallowed hard. No way would she let him hear her cry. "On Monday I'm going to start divorce proceeding."

"You'd throw away thirteen years of marriage over a little thing like this?"

"Flirting with other women is a little thing, and I don't even like that. How many others have you had in my bed?"

"You're being ridiculous. They didn't mean anything."

"'They,' huh? As in plural? Does Ingrid know she wasn't the first side dish that you sampled?"

"She's not important. None of them were. You can't divorce me. I won't let you."

"After the little news story that you starred in today, I don't expect to have a problem with any divorce judge. Besides, then you can marry Ingrid. That will shut her up. She can go to President Dixon and tell him that she lied. That she was…" Shana took a deep breath. "That she was a willing partner and that you two are getting married." She took another deep breath and let it out slowly. "Elliot, I really don't care what you do anymore nor with whom you do it."

"If I come home, together we can convince the president that Ingrid is lying and I won't have to marry her."

"What do you mean *we?* You're not listening to me. But then you never did much of that, did you?"

"Don't do this to me, Shane. I need you."

"I'm not doing anything to you, with you, nor for you ever again. This doing is all yours. And as for need, your needs change with your whims. Go need Ingrid. Or somebody else. Anybody else. Just not me. You don't have the right to need me anymore. Leave me alone."

"You can't keep me away. It's my home, too."

"Not anymore. I was grateful when Mom left me this house. I never dreamed how much more grateful I could be."

"If I lose my job over this, it will be your fault. I'll fix you. I'll…"

"Goodbye, Elliot."

"You'll be sorry. I better not get fired because of you. You better not destroy my career. If you had been better in bed, I wouldn't have had to turn to somebody else." His sharp words bit into her skin and swiped at her chest, but she didn't let him know. "If you—"

Shana hung up. The phone rang right away.

"Don't you dare hang up on me. I—"

Shana hung up again, but immediately took the phone off the hook and laid it on the table. She shook her head. *No more hanging up on you, Elliot. No more of anything with you.*

Shana flicked on the television. Maybe somebody else's troubles would take her mind off her own. Maybe it would help her forget the sting of Elliot's last words.

He had never said anything about her lovemaking before. He had acted satisfied. She swallowed hard. But then yesterday she had discovered exactly how good he was at acting.

A few minutes later, after flipping through the channels, she turned off the TV.

If somebody wasn't in bed with somebody else's spouse, they were planning to go to bed with somebody else's spouse, or talking about revenge on somebody who'd cheated on them, or confessing to the talk-show world that they had cheated or been cheated on. *Didn't anyone think about anything except sex anymore?* She went into the kitchen to make another cup of tea.

Elliot's behavior was the norm according to the soaps and the talk shows. He would fit right in with either. What happened between us would make a good story line. Maybe it has already been used. She blinked hard. *It certainly seemed more like fiction than reality.* She shook her head. *I'm the one out of sync.*

She stirred her orange-spice tea but she didn't drink it. *What was Elliot going to do? The only thing he knew how to do was teach.* She shook her head. *Uh-uh. Not true.*

He knew something else. He knew how to cheat on her. He knew how to hurt her deeper than anyone ever had before. *After what he did to me, I can't care about him.* She hoped she could find a way to quit caring. She needed to use it fast. She couldn't keep her anger going forever, and she knew that, when it disappeared, pain would move in. She sat at the table. By the time she picked up her cup, her tea was cold. She hadn't taken one sip. Along with thirteen years, she had wasted one good tea bag.

Chapter 5

At three-thirty the doorbell rang and Shana knew it was Martie. She quickly opened the door. It would be good to have some company besides her thoughts.

"So. What do you think about Elliot's chickens going home to roost?" Martie walked to the kitchen and put the bags she was carrying onto the counter.

"What?"

"That's something my grandma used to say." Martie waved her off and shrugged. "'Chickens coming home to roost.' 'What goes around comes around.' Same thing. Let's see if I can put it into 'city-ese'— What do you think of Elliot's payback?"

"You know Ingrid lied. You were here when she called me."

"So? Elliot lied, too. That evens things out, don't you think?"

"I guess so." Shana shrugged. "I'm not sure he deserves to have his career ruined, though. Ingrid knew what she was doing. She probably threw herself at him. Women make a play for Elliot all the time. Most of them didn't even care when I was right there with him."

"Elliot didn't have to catch her," Martie said. "He should have realized that thinking done with the brain is more reliable than that done with another part of the anatomy."

"Yeah." Shana shrugged. "Still…"

"You feel sorry for him."

"I have…" She shook her head. "I *had* a lot of years invested in him. He was my first real love. We were going to have a baby next year." She swallowed hard. "Do you know that next week will be our thirteenth anniversary?"

Martie had to lean close to hear this last sentence. "I guess the number thirteen deserves its reputation." She patted Shana's hand. "If this had to happen, it's good it was before you got pregnant. Nothing is harder on a kid than divorced parents." Martie blinked hard and stared at the wall. Then she shook her head and looked at Shana. "Look. You'll find somebody else. Somebody who will make you forget Elliot."

"I'm not looking for a replacement. I thought I could trust Elliot and look what happened. I can't count on having good judgment. It's obvious that I don't have any. Besides, I'm not one of those women who have to have a man in her life to be complete. I'll do fine on my own." She stared at her hands and focused on her wedding ring. "I just have to get over Elliot."

Martie leaned closer. "You're not thinking about taking him back, are you?"

"The only place I'm taking Elliot's butt is to divorce court. I can't have somebody in my life whom I can't trust, and I'd never be able to trust him again." She shrugged. "It's just going to be hard getting used to his not being around."

"I can understand that."

"I don't want to talk about Elliot anymore. Tell me about school."

"Girl, you'd better hurry back before the flu destroys the rest of your brain. If you're asking for news about school, you're in worse condition than I thought."

"I'm coming back on Monday. I already told Paula." She sighed. "I'm not looking forward to facing everybody, though. The ones who won't come right out and ask me about what happened will look at me with questions on their faces." She shrugged. "I guess the sooner I get through that the better." She opened one of the bags that Martie had brought. "The food smells good. What did you bring? I'm hungry."

"Sounds like the old Shana is back. Is this a late lunch or an early dinner?"

"It's three meals in one."

"I won't fuss about you skipping meals. I know you had a good reason. Besides, I'm too hungry. The yogurt that I had for lunch is long gone. I'm suffering from the three o'clock saggies."

"Saggies?"

"Honestly, girl, you have to keep your vocabulary current. You know how you get tired at this time of day? Right after school?"

"Of course. I just never heard it called 'the saggies.'"

"It has to have a name. Why not 'the saggies'?"

Shana shrugged as she set the table. She didn't have an answer. Lately, she didn't have answers to a lot of things.

She sat down, but she didn't feel much like eating anymore. *I hope I do justice to this food. I can think of better diets to be on. The Cheating Husbands' Diet shouldn't even be counted as one, but that's what's messing with my appetite now.*

She reached for the roasted chicken and took a drumstick. Then she took a dollop of coleslaw, but put it back. She stared at the chicken on her plate as if waiting for it to shrink to a size she could manage. When it didn't, she picked it up. They ate in silence, but her thoughts were shouting at her.

"You're coming shopping with me tomorrow, right?" Shana said as she put her empty plate in the sink a while later. She had eaten more than she had expected, but not as much as she usually did. The flu was not the only reason. She shook her head and put the top on the roasted-chicken container.

"I wouldn't miss it. I get to go shopping and I don't have to spend a cent." Martie stacked the salad containers and put them into the refrigerator. "Have you decided what you're looking for?"

"Anything except light oak."

Shana thought of the headboard resting against two of the bags containing Elliot's life with her. *He'd better come get them. I don't need reminders staring at me whenever I go out.*

"I can understand that." Martie nodded. "When is he coming to get his things?"

"Not soon enough."

"You talked to him."

"I talked at him. It's never a dialogue with Elliot if you're not saying what he wants to hear." She looked at Martie. "He called after the radio report. He wants to come back. He said he loves me."

"And what did you say?"

"I said the *d* word."

"The *d* word?"

"I don't mean *dear* or *darling*. *Divorce* was the word of the day. He passed right over it as if it wasn't there." She blinked. "He blamed me. He said if I had been better in bed, he wouldn't have had to go elsewhere." She let out a hard breath. "He said it would be my fault if he loses his job."

She didn't tell Martie about Elliot's unfinished threat. He always said things like that when he was angry about something. She poured more tea.

"Are you sure we can't call him a dog?"

"Yeah. All of the dogs that I've met have been nice."

"Okay. We'll think of something appropriate." Martie leaned back. "So. How's the flu?"

"I think it was scared away by this Elliot mess."

"At least that was good for something."

Shana laughed for the first time since she had come home sick. Surviving didn't seem so impossible any longer. She stirred sweetener into her tea.

"Hey." Martie pointed to the clock on the stove. "Turn on the television. We don't want to miss the news." Shana glanced at the clock.

"It's too early. You know I set the clocks five minutes fast so I won't be late."

"That's okay. We can catch the end of *Oprah*. Maybe she has a guest who will give advice for situations like this."

"I don't need anybody's advice. I know what I'm going to do. I'm dumping Elliot." She shook her head. "I've already started the process. The proof is in the driveway. More proof is in my new bank account."

"Huh?"

"I closed out the joint accounts before Elliot could. He probably figured he could talk me into letting him back so he left them alone." She frowned. "As for watching television for suggestions, I never could understand taking advice from a stranger. I mean, if you have all the facts of your situation and you don't know what to do, how can you expect a stranger to know what's best for you?"

"If everybody felt like you, a lot more folks would be out of jobs besides Elliot."

* * *

At four fifty-five, Shana turned on the television and sat back. Oprah's guest was wrapping up his advice for parents whose children were discipline problems. He didn't sound as if he had children, much less had ever been around any for any length of time. Then the local news came on.

The television reporter could have borrowed the opening from the radio reporter heard earlier. The opening music alerted the viewer that the program was starting and the leading news story was announced. Elliot would probably make the headlines in the local section of the morning newspaper, as well.

Then Ingrid came on. Her blouse looked as if it came from the trunk with Shana's grandmother's clothes stored in the attic. It was even complete with an old brooch. If Ingrid had worn gloves, the only skin visible would have been her face, and half of that was hidden by the tissue she used constantly to wipe her eyes.

"I—I believed him when he said he would destroy my career if I didn't…" Her voice trailed off into sobs. She managed to wipe her eyes and flick her hair at the same time.

"I wonder how long she had to practice that to get that right," Martie said.

Ingrid continued. "I—I looked up to him. I respected him." She batted her eyes at the camera. "He is so much older than I am, you know."

Elliot will love that, Shana thought.

Ingrid sniffled, but it was done delicately and with good taste. "Before I knew what had happened, we were sleeping together."

"She's good," Shana said. "I know she's lying, yet I almost believe her."

Martie nodded. "It's too bad they don't give Emmys for people starring in news stories. And I doubt if much sleeping went on."

After stating that neither Elliot nor the university president was available for comment, the reporter found another story.

Shana turned off the television. News about anything short of a nuclear attack on Washington by aliens from Venus would be anticlimactic for her.

"Are you sure you're going to be all right?"

"Yeah. I'll be fine. I—"

The phone rang. Shana started to answer it, but changed her mind. She didn't feel like talking to anyone right now. The answering machine took over.

Shana recognized the name of the reporter who sounded as if she were reading from a teleprompter. It was the same woman who hadn't been interested in doing a story when the Murdock School track team had won the match in competition with other eighth graders in the district.

Before she hung up, the reporter repeated her number three times as if she expected Shana to return her call.

The phone rang again right away as if somebody knew exactly when the reporter had hung up. It was a different reporter this time, but the message was the same. Shana intended to do the same with this message. No question about it. Scandal sold a whole lot better than good news about kids.

She had a fleeting thought of competing with Ingrid for the Starring-Role-in-a-News-Item Award.

I could wear a long black dress, loose of course, and find a large black hat. With black flowers. A thrift store should have something like that. If I look really hard I could probably find a black silk handkerchief, too. That would complete my in-mourning-for-a-dead-marriage outfit. Or maybe I should dress like one of the pictures in a sexy clothes catalog? That would show everybody how crazy Elliot was to choose somebody else over me. Or maybe I could...

"Shana? Are you okay?" Martie nudged her. Shana shook the fanciful thoughts away.

"I'm fine. For a few seconds my imagination took over."

"You got to watch that. I don't remember you allowing it to be in charge since the time you decided to roller-skate in the dorm hall at Cheyney during our freshman year. You know what happened then."

"Oh, come on. Mom had just sent my skates. I had to see if I could still skate. I still think Dean Jackson overreacted."

"I'm glad it wasn't a motor scooter your mom sent. No telling what Dean Jackson would have done if you had been caught doing wheelies in the hall. One thing you can believe is that you wouldn't have a degree from Cheyney or any other college in the state." Martie shook her head. "I was there and I still can't believe you did it." She laughed. "To get back to the present. What time tomorrow?"

"I figure ten o'clock will be late enough for you to be past the grumpy stage when I come pick you up. I'll still call before I leave here just to make sure you're civilized."

"I'll pick you up. I know your tendency to be early. I'll need every minute of sleep I can get."

Martie left and Shana urged her to take the leftovers.

Then Shana sat in the living room. The phone rang and she turned off the ringer. Next to go was the volume on the answering machine. For good measure she turned on the cartoon channel. She'd have to sit through countless cereal, junk-food and toy commercials, but at least she didn't have to worry about the news coming on.

At eleven o'clock she turned off the television. She didn't need another news program. She had watched enough news to last her forever.

She checked the doors to make sure they were locked, but she didn't look out to the driveway. She didn't need anything to remind her of what had happened yesterday. She shook her head. *How could one day ago seem so far in the past?*

Chapter 6

"Where are we going?" Martie asked after she and Shana were in Shana's car. She covered a yawn and fastened her seat belt. She had driven over to Shana's house, but she still wasn't fully awake.

"Ethan Allen and if you'd get to bed at a decent time, you wouldn't be yawning at ten-thirty in the morning." Shana stared straight ahead, but she smiled.

"I'm a night owl." Martie covered another yawn.

"That's redundant. All owls are nocturnal."

"Yes, Miss Science Teacher." Martie stuck her tongue out.

"I saw that."

"I meant for you to." Martie laughed. "So. Ethan Allen, huh? We have come up in the world, haven't we?"

"I wanted to go there when Elliot and I bought our furniture, but he wanted something old, so we compromised and did it his way. We went to an estate auction." She shrugged. "The set was nice." She chewed at her lower lip. "I'm ready for something new. He's not part of this. He won't be part of my life anymore." She blinked. "This time I please myself."

An hour later, Shana had picked out a mahogany four-poster king-size bed. She looked at the price tags on the matching chest, dresser and nightstands, swallowed hard, then bought those, as well.

After she convinced the salesman that if she couldn't have it delivered by tomorrow she'd go somewhere else, she had a written promise of a delivery time for tomorrow evening.

Grasping the sales slip as if a tight grip would keep her from changing her mind, Shana walked to the car with Martie.

"I think I lost my mind when I lost Elliot," she said as she got in.

"You didn't lose Elliot. You kicked him to the curb." Martie clicked her seat belt closed.

"Whatever. I think what was left of my common sense went with him. I guess this shopping trip means that I'll be doing the summer sports program after all. The money can pay for this impulse buying. Besides, I won't be able to afford a vacation after this, anyway."

"What about the found money from the bank accounts?"

"I figured I'd better hold on to at least half of it. I don't know if I'll have to give it to Elliot."

"They were joint accounts, weren't they?"

"Yes, but I still don't know the legal aspects. This is all new to me. I thought I'd better play it safe until the attorney tells me differently." She sighed. "I am still trying to deal with that lying, lowlife, cheating, soon-too-be-ex husband."

"Time heals all wounds. Better still, it also wounds all heels." Martie grinned. "As for your furniture, buying it was a good decision. Your mind is as intact as it ever was. You need the furniture and it will last longer than any vacation memories would have."

"It had better." Shana closed her eyes and leaned her head back against the seat. *I already have vacation memories that I want gone. All of them star Elliot.* "I still can't believe I spent so much money."

"You're like that shampoo—you're worth it. Now let's go get some lunch. My treat since you're destitute."

Shana started the car and headed for the mall a block away.

"It's a good thing you're buying. I'll be eating yogurt or peanut butter and jelly sandwiches for dinner for the rest of the year."

"It won't be that bad. You'll just squirrel less away into your savings account."

Shana pulled into a parking space. "I'm still not sure

I did the right thing in buying that furniture." She shook her head. "I have only my income, now." She frowned. "Maybe I should go back and tell them I changed my mind and get something cheaper somewhere else."

"No, you shouldn't. You made the right decision. You can handle the payments. And don't forget—we get a raise in September." Martie patted her hand. "It will be all right."

By the time she and Martie got back to her house, Shana had decided that buying the furniture was a good decision after all.

She pulled over to the curb and looked at the driveway. Elliot's things were gone. Even the bed. *That's a good thing. Right?*

"You okay?" Martie took her attention. Shana was grateful.

"Sure. Want to come in?"

"No, thanks. I have a ton of stuff to do." She got out. "See you on Monday."

"Okay." Shana watched Martie drive off, but she didn't move. She sat in her car staring at the driveway for a while. It looked wider. And lonely. She shook her head and drove past the empty spots and into the garage.

Once there, she turned off the motor, closed her eyes and leaned her head back. Elliot was gone and so was his stuff. Would he share the bed with Ingrid or did he have somebody else already? She frowned. *Why am I thinking about it when I don't care?*

* * *

Shana tried to sleep late the next morning, but her thoughts prodded her awake.

After breakfast she got her bedroom ready for her new furniture. Hers. Only hers. She would no longer give up her room because of Elliot.

She rearranged the wall-to-wall closet and shifted some of her things to the other side. *I once complained about needing more space.* She sighed. *Now I have it all.*

By the time the furniture arrived during the late afternoon, she had cleaned out the closets in the guest bedrooms, too, just for something to do. She'd found a few more things of Elliot's. She'd started to throw them out, but bagged them. She wouldn't stoop to his level.

She spent the evening making her new furniture hers. She even watched television from her bed, looking at the TV set that was a bonus for buying the furniture. Elliot hadn't liked the idea of a television in the bedroom. She didn't care anymore what Elliot liked or didn't like.

When she turned off the light, she tried to ignore how big the king-size bed was when she was sleeping alone.

Monday morning Shana woke up earlier than usual. She took several deep breaths trying to make her body release the anxiety that had spent the night with her. It didn't work. *I hope Elliot doesn't try to hang on just as determinedly.*

She felt more apprehensive than she had on her first day as a track coach. Today she had to face the school staff and the parents who brought their kids to school just as she had that day. Today she would see other questions on the faces of the adults; a downside of how easy it was to get the news. She thought of the kids. They were the least of her worries.

At the time when she would usually be sitting at her desk drinking her second cup of Earl Grey tea and scanning the newspaper, she was backing her car out of the garage.

She got to the middle of the driveway, frowned and stopped. The car felt funny. She got out and looked.

"Great. Just what I need. A flat tire." She grimaced as she looked closer. "Two flat tires?" Her frown deepened. "How did I do that? I must have run over something. Probably something from Elliot's junk."

She got the can of pressurized air from the trunk. Elliot didn't like using it. He said it would ruin the tires but she had bought it anyway. She had used it once and her tires had been fine afterward. Elliot didn't know everything. He didn't even know as much as he thought he did. And he didn't live here anymore.

I hope there's enough in one can to inflate both tires.

She looked down the rest of the driveway. Then she slowly walked to the street, examining carefully to make sure nothing was there to do further damage.

Maybe we dropped a couple of screws or something when Martie and I moved the furniture, she thought.

Just as slowly, she walked back to her car. Nothing.

She wished she had picked up whatever it was with her hand instead of her tires. She let out a deep breath. She wished a lot of things were true that weren't.

She put air in both tires until the can was empty. The tires were soft, but they would get her to school without damaging the rims. She hoped. *I've already got a full portion of damage in my life. I don't need any more.*

When she parked in the staff parking lot, the tires were nearly flat again. *I guess that stuff isn't as good as I thought.* She sighed and leaned against the fender.

If I thought it would be fun, I'd try to guess who will ask the dumbest or rudest questions today. She frowned. *A little fun would be welcome about now.* She shook her head. *I can't count on fun to see me through today.*

She took a deep breath and let it out slowly. Then she walked around the corner to the school entrance and stopped. A news van was parked in front of the Floyds' house across the street. Shana recognized the television reporter standing there. The woman ran toward Shana, seeming to ignore the cold wind causing leftover leaves to dance along the street. Shana set her jaw. *A shark wouldn't mind a possible distraction when it was on the blood scent, either.*

"Mrs. Garner." The woman waved her microphone at Shana before she stepped onto the sidewalk. "May I ask a few questions?"

"No." Shana didn't pause as she continued toward the front of the school. The woman followed a few feet behind.

"Did you suspect your husband of having an affair? Do you believe Ms. Alderdice? How do you feel about the affair? What do you intend to do now?"

The questions flung at Shana bounced off her back, but more kept coming. The woman didn't let Shana widen the distance between them. This reporter was one of those people who didn't understand any part of the word *no*.

Shana wished that the parking lot were closer to the school entrance.

Finally she reached the front of the building. When she walked up the steps, the reporter stayed on the sidewalk.

It was early, but there were enough girls jumping double Dutch rope to make Shana feel as if she were walking a gauntlet.

She sighed and shook her head. *No. Facing the kids was nothing compared to the reporter who had just bombarded her. The kids had sympathy on their faces.*

"Hi, Mrs. Garner." Julie Arden's usually loud voice was just a whisper this morning. If voices could tiptoe, that would describe how she sounded. The rope stopped turning.

"Hi, Mrs. Garner," Julie's shadow, Abby, echoed her friend's greeting. She pushed her glasses up higher on her nose. "I hope you're feeling better." Shana shrugged. Abby was young. She didn't know it would take longer to get over what was ailing Shana than it took to get over the flu. It takes more than a few days healing time to get over a cheating husband.

"I am, thank you." Shana moved to the next group. *Anyone who thinks that all kids watch is music videos and all they listen to is music, is out of touch.*

She took a deep breath and walked into the building that was quiet in its waiting.

"Hi, girlfriend." Paula came from behind her desk in the office and hugged Shana. Shana stood within the comforting shelter for a minute. Then she stood back. The softness on Paula's face made tears gather in Shana's eyes. "How you feeling?" Paula asked. They both knew she wasn't talking about the flu, either.

"I've felt better more times than I can count. I even felt better than this when I went home sick." *Was that only a few days ago?*

"Was that parasite with the microphone still across the street?"

"She was there until she crossed over to this side. She's probably still there."

"Cora told her not to come on school property."

"The reporter didn't." Shana sighed. "We can't do anything about words crossing boundaries."

"Unfortunately." Paula touched Shana's arm. "How's the flu?"

"I think it got scared of this mess and ran away."

"It's got to get better."

"Can't get any worse." Shana tried to smile at her.

"Let me know if I can do anything." Paula pulled a covered plate from the top of the cabinet behind her. "I mean anything else besides giving you this piece of my chocolate cake that you love." Her eyes widened after she said *love*. "I mean…"

"Paula, the word *love* is okay. Besides, chocolate cake is a safe love." Shana smiled. "Let me get to my room before—"

"Before it gets busy in here," Paula finished for her in a soft voice.

"Oh." Shana turned back. "I have to call the automobile club. They will probably send my regular mechanic since he's assigned to this area. I had two flats this morning." She used the phone on the desk.

"Two?"

"Yeah. I guess one wasn't enough." She gave the information over the phone.

"It's got to get better from here," Paula repeated after Shana hung up. "You've already used up your allotment of bad luck for the year."

"I hope you're right." She handed her the car keys. "Will you give these to the mechanic when he comes?"

"Sure thing."

Shana made it to the gym without running into anyone else.

She looked through the messages she had picked up from her mailbox in the office and put one aside. Mrs. Simms had left a note asking her to stop in before she left today. She wanted to discuss a new after-school and summer program. Shana thought about her new furniture. If this program meant extra money, *no* was not an option.

The special-ed teacher whose room was down the

hall and the librarian each peeked in on their way past. They smiled and spoke, but both danced around the news. Shana understood. It must be worse than seeing somebody after a death in the family. Death of a person was a common occurrence. How do you approach the subject of a cheating husband and a dead marriage that made the local news programs?

Shana had just taken out the equipment for her first class when Daisy, another teacher, came in, pulled the student desk from the corner and plopped down on it.

"What are you going to do? I know you must be devastated. I mean, to catch your husband like that. And in your own bed. Are you going to keep it? The bed, I mean, of course. Didn't you suspect anything?" She shifted position and tried to flick her hair but it wasn't long enough. "They say the wife always knows. Is that true?" She crossed her legs and then crossed her arms. "I know I would know immediately if my husband were cheating on me." She sniffed. "If I were married." She sat up straighter. "I'd fix him so he'd never cheat on me again." She finally stopped talking and stared at Shana, waiting for a response.

"*If* you ever have a husband." Shana fixed her with a stare. "I have to get ready for my class." She pulled a bag of balls from the closest and wrapped both hands around the top.

Daisy, the shark, had smelled blood. She barely spoke whenever she passed Shana in the hall or saw her in the office, yet she had come all the way down to the basement instead of going to her room on the second floor. She always managed to appear when something bad happened to someone.

Shana and Martie had joked that maybe she was a voodoo woman and caused the terrible things to happen in the first place. Martie had said they should find a way to get into her house and look for her black-magic stash. It had been funny at the time. Shana shook her head and got out the pump. There was nothing humorous about it now. Daisy was just one of those people who fed off the misery of others.

"I guess you don't want to talk about it," Daisy continued her one-sided conversation. "It must be so humiliating." She smiled and shrugged. "I mean, the whole world now knows that you can't hold your man."

Shana let out a deep breath and turned to face Daisy. *Exactly how much damage could a bag of volleyballs do to an empty head? I guess it depends on how hard you swing it.*

Standing before Shana was living proof that some people *did* need a brick wall to fall on them before they got the message.

"Daisy." Shana kept her voice low and her hands to herself. "I want to make sure you understand me, so listen carefully. If you were the only other person in the world and I was bursting to tell the most amazing secret ever held, I would explode before I told you anything."

Daisy straightened. She let out a sharp breath. "I was just trying to give you support."

"I'd rather collapse."

"Well." She shoved her feet to the floor and stood. "That's the last time I try to give you sympathy."

"Promise?"

Daisy glared, grunted and left the gym. Shana turned her back. The only way she knew Daisy had left was the slamming of the door.

Martie rushed in. "I'm running late as usual, but I had to give you this hug to help you make it through the morning." She hugged her, then stepped back. Then she hugged her again. "You need two. I saw the barracuda leave. I was hoping I would be here to help you fend off her feeding frenzy. I'm sorry I was late."

"You and I decided that she's a shark, remember? And I withstood the shark attack without getting hurt." She smiled at Martie. "And without hurting her, too. That was definitely a possibility."

Shana hadn't expected to be able to so soon, but she laughed with Martie.

"Come up to my room for lunch. I brought you something good."

"What?"

"It's a secret." Martie waved. "See ya."

Shana watched her friend go. It didn't show, but she was taking some of Shana's burden with her.

Shana met her first class—fourth grade—in the yard and she was glad for something to occupy her mind.

Chapter 7

From time to time one of the kids in her first class looked at Shana as if they were trying to find the right words to say, but they kept the conversation to the kickball game they were playing.

At the end of the class, Nora, one of the quieter kids, came to her. She touched Shana's arm with one finger as if she was afraid she would hurt her.

"My mom and dad got a divorce last year." Her voice was barely above a whisper. She patted Shana's arm. "It will be all right." She nodded.

Shana smiled at her. *Out of the mouths of babes.* "Thank you, Nora." She watched the class leave. It *would* be all right.

In each of her other classes, at least one kid came to her, either before or after the class, and told about a divorce in the family, usually between the parents. Shana shook her head. Even to a child, it was logical for a divorce to follow cheating.

Her morning classes ended and Shana got her lunch from the refrigerator in the staff lunchroom and went to Martie's science lab on the first floor. At least twice a week they ate lunch together. If Monday had not been one of their regular days, Shana would have suggested changing their pattern for this week. She had survived the morning without too many hurting questions— except for those from Daisy, who didn't count—but she wasn't up to facing any more from the staff. Tomorrow's weekly meeting would be early enough.

I wonder who's the opening story on the noon news today, Shana thought as she walked up the stairs. *I don't wish anyone ill, but I hope Elliot is old news since he dragged me into it.*

She shook her head. *Elliot could have the spotlight all by himself, or with his latest hoochie-mama of choice.* Shana didn't care as long as her name wasn't in it. She didn't intend to be linked to Elliot much longer, anyway.

When she met with the lawyer this afternoon she'd have an idea of how much longer it would be before she could put her fiasco of a marriage behind her. She swallowed hard and pushed open the fire door at the top of the stairs.

"You made it through this morning and I don't see

any scars." Martie smiled as Shana walked into her room. She got a long sheet of blue construction paper and put it on the table. "As you can see, you're the first to use this beautiful place mat." Her smile widened. "But then, you deserve it."

"I'm the *only* one who will use it." Shana sat down. "You know that no matter how careful we are, we always spill something. Then we turn the paper over to get a second use from it. These are the ultimate in throw-aways." She frowned. "Some marriages are throw-aways, too." She shook her head slightly and took containers from her lunch bag.

"Bad marriages aren't worth saving." Martie stared at Shana. "Only you can make the decision about yours."

"I already made that decision. Some things aren't made to be shared. Husbands are at the top of the list, right above toothbrushes." She looked up from the table. "I'm definitely changing the subject. Okay?"

"Works for me."

"You're a teacher. Do you think my salad and yogurt will subtract calories from Paula's delicious chocolate cake?" Shana unwrapped the cake and sniffed deeply.

"Paula's cake is good, and I told her so," Martie said. "But, child, you haven't forgotten my cake, have you?" Martie set a plastic container in front of Shana. "We both know that my cake doesn't need embellishment, but since this is for you, I went all out and put it in my good plasticware. You don't have to swear to return it, even." She removed the top and held the container up.

"Here you have the epitome of chocolate cake. A slice of quintessential chocolate perfection. Chocolate cake for which *ultimate* and every other word used to describe something almost too delicious is used." She laughed. "I told Paula that, too, but of course she didn't agree. She couldn't without being kicked out of her family. She uses her grandmom's recipe." Martie took out her sandwich. "I gave her a slice of my cake and promised not to tell her grandmom."

"I'm glad you're modest about your cake. You wouldn't want to break your arm patting yourself on the back. You need it for your teaching."

"If you don't toot your own horn, nobody will know you have one." Shana laughed with her.

As they ate, they talked about Shana's new furniture.

"Now that you see how good that set looks in your bedroom, aren't you glad you bought it?"

"Yes, but now my drapes look shabby. Then I'll have to get a new bedspread to match." She frowned. "But I'd need that anyway since I dumped the old one with Elliot." She shook her head. "I'm still having a hard time believing he did that to me. I don't understand how I could not know about it." She stared at Martie. "I'm supposed to be intelligent. There must have been clues. How could I not know? How come I didn't see any signs?"

"Because you weren't looking for any. You trusted him."

"I was *supposed* to be able to trust my husband."

"That's true. But he was supposed to be faithful."

"Yeah." Shana put her trash in the wastebasket. "*Supposed to be* is the operative phrase here."

"Are you still worried about the cost of the furniture and how you're going to pay for it?"

"I got a note from Cora about a possible new after-school program. I don't know what it is, but I have to say yes. I need the money."

"I don't think you'll be as bad off financially as you think, but I can understand you being cautious." Martie squeezed Shana's shoulder. "Whatever the program is, you can handle it. Nothing can be as hard as what you went through." She shook her head. "Uh-uh. I mean as what you're *still* going through." They walked to the door. "See you after school. I'm coming over to see how the furniture looks in its new environment."

"Make it this evening. This afternoon I begin the-dumping-of-Elliot process with the lawyer."

Shana went back to her classroom. Martie was right. After the Elliot fiasco, Shana could handle anything.

Her afternoon classes seemed to go faster than the morning ones had, but only because she had gotten through them. She put away the equipment and went to the office.

"How'd it go?" Paula asked.

"Better than I expected."

"Good. Go on in. Cora is waiting for you. Wait a minute," she said. "Here." She handed over her car keys. "The guy from the automobile club said for you to call him."

"Did he fix the tires?"

"He said he did."

"Then why do I have to call him?"

Paula shrugged. "He didn't say." The phone rang and she answered it.

Shana shook her head. *One thing at a time.* Her car was working. What the guy had to say couldn't be too important.

She crossed her fingers and walked around Paula's desk and into Cora Simms's office. *Please let the program be something I won't mind doing.*

"I hope your first day back wasn't too hard." Cora smiled at Shana. "If I could have, I would have made that reporter move ten blocks away. Have a seat."

Shana sat in the chair beside the desk. "Thanks for that with the reporter. I made it through all right, but I'm relieved that this day is over."

"Here's something that might help take your mind off what's going on." Cora handed Shana a blue folder. "A former student wants to fund our after-school track program as well as a summer athletic camp. What do you think about the idea? I know you haven't read the details yet, but would you be interested in such a program if the proposal looks okay?"

"I just went out and bought an entire expensive set of bedroom furniture. Now I have to get new bedding to go with it. And drapes to go with that. Then I have the divorce lawyer's fees." She held up the folder. "If this program is legal and meets your approval, it will look okay. I'm interested."

Cora laughed. "I think you'd take this program even if you hadn't gone shopping and dumping. I'm excited because it will put our upper-level phys-ed program above the self-contained middle schools in the district." She nodded and pointed to the file. "Jot down any questions that come up as you read over the proposal. Kyle Rayburn will meet with you after school on Friday, if that's okay. He's out of town and won't be back until late Thursday. He's anxious to get something started this school year, but, as of now, he intends to fund it for as many years as we want it."

"Kyle Rayburn. Rayburn." Shana frowned. Then she shrugged. The name sounded familiar. Maybe she taught his sister or brother. "Friday is fine. I'll read this over tonight, but I know I'll do it. I need the money and we need the program."

"It's a long-term commitment on his part. We don't get many of those. Let me know tomorrow morning if you still think it looks good after you look at it closely."

"I tell you, it will look good. It has to." Shana walked to the door.

"Shana." Cora's voice was softer. "It will get better. Today was the hardest."

Shana sighed. Then she smiled back at the older woman who was her friend as well as her principal.

"I hope you're right."

She left the office with the papers clutched in her hand as if they would disappear if she didn't keep a tight grip.

She still held them tightly when she got to the parking lot. She stared at her car, gasped and rushed the last few feet to it.

"My car." She didn't look at the tires. She forgot the papers in her hand and reached out to her car. The folder fell and papers fluttered to the ground, but Shana didn't notice. Her gaze was fixed on the long, angry gash ripped along the entire passenger side of her car. The bare metal winked at her as the weak sunlight skipped through the leaves of the large maple tree at the curb.

Maybe it's not as bad as it looks, Shana thought. *Maybe the contrast with the dark blue paint makes the scratch stand out.*

She ran her hand along the groove. She shook her head. It was as bad as it looked. *Who would do this? Would Daisy go this far?* Her *car was gone. Did she do this because of what I said to her? Or did one of the kids transfer anger at divorced parents to me? Or maybe it happened while the mechanic had it. Maybe that's why he left the message for me to call him.*

She picked up the papers that had scattered across the nearly empty parking lot and stuffed them back into the folder. Then she got into the car.

She used her cell phone to call the mechanic. She told him about the scratch.

"It was never out of my sight, Mrs. Garner. I drove

it inside and did the tires right away. Then I brought it back. I swear it was in perfect condition when I parked it. I would tell you and make arrangements for us to fix it if anything happened while your car was in our care."

Shana sighed. "I believe you, Stan."

"I asked you to call so I could tell you about your tires. I had to replace them. Somebody slashed them and I couldn't repair them. Maybe the same person scratched your car."

"Slashed my tires?"

"Yes. Both of them. I went ahead and replaced them."

"Thanks." Shana felt numb. "I'll—I'll stop by and let you put them on my credit card."

"No rush, Mrs. Garner. I know you're good for it."

"Thanks, but I'll be by today. Maybe you can take a look at the gash?"

"Sure. No problem."

Shana broke the connection and let out a deep breath. Another unplanned dip into her funds. She straightened.

I can handle this. After the other stuff that life has thrown at me lately, this is nothing. The other stuff that happened was changing her life.

She took a deep breath, started her car and left the lot.

This is just about things, she thought as she drove to the mechanic's shop. *Only things.* She glared. *But Elliot better not be responsible.*

Chapter 8

The next day, Shana parked in the lot as usual and walked around the corner to the school. This time, even though the reporter approached her from the other end of the block, Shana was ready.

The Floyds must have complained about the use of the sidewalk outside their home because the reporter had moved down the street. Shana hadn't seen the Floyds since their last child had left Murdock School, but she'd make it a point to thank them.

She took a deep breath and walked toward the steps. The questions flung at her by the reporter were louder today because of the distance, but they were the same ones as yesterday.

"Why don't you leave our teacher alone?" Julie shouted from her usual place by the brick wall in front of the school.

"Yeah, she didn't do anything to you," Abby added from beside Julie.

"How would you like it if somebody got all up in your business?" Tasha walked over to the reporter standing in the street on the other side. Once there, she placed her five-foot-seven-inches well within the woman's personal space.

"I'm just doing my job." The reporter's response was weaker than her questions had been. She backed up a few steps.

"Then you need to find you another job." Julie left the wall, put her hands on her hips and walked to the curb.

"Thanks, girls," Shana said quickly and moved toward the kids. "It's okay. Tasha, please come here." Shana wrapped an arm around each of the girls and walked them back to the school. "Don't pay her any attention. If we ignore her, maybe she'll get tired and go away."

The reporter backed up a few feet more toward the news van. She kept the microphone to her chest and her mouth shut.

Shana smiled and went up the steps. Her kids took up for her. After her future WNBA star, Tasha, had got up in the woman's face, maybe the woman got the message and wouldn't come back.

I hate to do it, but I'll have to give them a short

lesson on free speech. Shana's smile widened. *Maybe I'll throw in a lesson on self-control, but Tasha already demonstrated that. There was a time when she would have snatched the woman's microphone away and hit her with it.*

"Kids," she muttered to herself as she went inside. "You got to love them."

Shana got through the morning fine. It was as if the weight of her situation were gradually lifting. By lunchtime she was feeling closer to normal than she had since the mess had begun.

"Okay," Shana said once she and Martie were seated at the table in her room. "Here's the short version of the proposal Mrs. Simms gave me. A former Murdock student wants to fund a track program."

"You already have a track program. What's to fund? The kids run."

"Spoken like an unenlightened but nice person. We don't have any funding at all except for the one day a week in the spring when the after-school programs kick in for a few hours. This new program will put us way ahead of the other schools. He's also talking about supplying shoes and uniforms and transportation to a real field so they don't have to run around the yard or in the gym. He's even coming out to help with the coaching."

"Who is this angel of the track team?"

"Kyle Rayburn." Shana looked at the top sheet in her file folder. "It says here that he used to play for the—"

"Houston Rockets before he came to the Sixers six years ago." Martie jumped up. "He was a point guard. He was a star until he blew out his knee in the last play-off game season before last." She grinned at Shana. "Only in basketball could somebody as tall as that be considered short." Her grin widened. "In fact, I'll bet *nothing* about his fine body is small." She shook her head. "Girl, have you been living in a vacuum for the past six years?" Martie paced across the front of the room. "As crazy as this city is close to, during and right after the basketball season, how could you not recognize the name?" Martie stared at Shana as if she had grown a second set of eyes.

"I told you. I've heard of him…." She shrugged. "Sort of." She took a bite of salad. "You know football is my sport, not basketball. Basketball is too complicated. It's supposed to be a no-contact sport, yet somebody is always getting bloodied up or sliding across the floor and I don't mean on their feet."

"Who's talking about basketball?" Martie shook her head. "Who's talking about sports? I'm talking about a brother who makes the fabulous brother on the latest romance book you're reading look like a refugee from an ugly camp. The man is way past fine." Martie put her empty lunch bag on her desk. "When he walks, even those baggy shorts advertise every muscle in his legs and his backside and…" She fanned herself with the bag. "My, my, my." She frowned. "I wonder whose bright idea it was to change from the tight shorts they used to wear." She shook her head. "Anyway, I digress. I'm borrowing my brother's tape of one of the championship games that Kyle played in." She smiled. "The one where they show a lot of close-ups of Mr. Fine-as-Wine."

"You don't drink wine. And he probably knows he's fine, too. He's probably one of those men who thinks he has to have every woman he meets. You know how men are. Besides, he probably let his body go when his career ended, but he's too conceited to realize it."

"We're not a bit biased, are we?"

Shana sighed. "Anyway, I don't want to see the tape. I'm doing this because I need the money—but more importantly, because the kids need the program. I don't care if he's as ugly as a pig wallowing in a muddy sty, as long as he funds our program." She headed for the wastebasket beside the door.

"I'm bringing the tape over to your house on Saturday anyway. You have to see for yourself what I'm talking about. I'm telling you, words cannot describe his degree of fineness." She followed Shana to the door. "Just do me a favor—after you get your furniture paid for, can I take your place in the program? I can go back to school and get the credits I need to become a coach. Do you think he'll wait for me?"

"Get your napkin and use it, girlfriend. When your

next class comes in, you don't want to explain to the kids why you're drooling. They're too young to understand."

Martie laughed and Shana did, too, but a sigh made her laughter disappear as soon as she left Martie.

Why did the new program have to hinge on a conceited ex-jock?

Shana's words to the girls about the reporter losing interest proved right. On Wednesday, the embezzlement of funds by the director of a local charity had pushed Elliot's story farther down the news chain and Shana felt more of her tension fade.

By Thursday evening's news, it was as if Elliot had been forgotten; or his scandal had never happened. *Now I have to do as the media has—I have to move on.*

Shana got ready for bed. Tomorrow she had something else to be concerned about. She had to meet with a conceited jock. She sighed. *I just have to remember that, no matter how obnoxious he is, the kids need this program.*

The world was still dark when Kyle awoke. Midnight had come and gone when he'd got to bed, but years of habit had him awake before daybreak. He stretched. Usually his thoughts of what-might-have-been-if-only rushed at him before he got out of bed.

Today they must have decided to sleep in. Or maybe they'd finally decided to go away for good.

He got out of bed, pulled on exercise clothes and went to the gym he had built in his house back in the day. Back when he was… He shook his head. Old habits died hard. Two seasons had come and gone without him, but still he did his daily workout as if he expected to drive down the floor and hit a three-pointer again.

He stared at the treadmill for a long time before he got on it. His left knee protested the stretch the warm-up put on it, as it always did. He ignored it, as he always did.

Soon he was warmed up and running in the zone as if he could outrun his part in the Lakers game two seasons ago. As if he could leave that last play behind. Or maybe find a time warp and go back and change the past. He found a breathing rhythm and synchronized it to his pace. *Only on television and in the movies, Kyle.*

When every muscle in his lower body was screaming, he pushed it for another fifteen minutes. If this had been training camp, the coach wouldn't have let him quit.

Finally he stopped the treadmill and bent over. His chest heaved in a search for air. When he found enough so he could move, he went to a weight machine. If he'd still been playing basketball, he'd have had another workout this afternoon. He was glad he had something planned to fill in that time. Maybe, just maybe, this time he had found something to take his mind off where it had wanted to stay for the past two years.

As he went through his reps, he thought about his appointment later today. In spite of the heavy weights he was lifting and the number of repetitions, a smile crept over his face.

It had been a while since he had looked forward to

anything. He should have thought of this before his old high-school coach had called and asked him to fund a sports program there.

Kyle's smile widened. It had been his own idea to sponsor a program for junior high kids at the K–8 feeder school, too, and to give time as well as money. Even though his old elementary school included seventh and eighth graders, it still wasn't funded like the junior highs were. School funds had always been stretched too thin. Now they were thinner than ever. *If not mandated by the state, phys ed and sports probably would have disappeared from public schools a long time ago,* he thought as he placed the free weights back on the rack and stood.

I may be selfish, but getting involved with a school program will benefit me, too. A frown creased his forehead. He had been hoping for a male teacher, but that wasn't the case. Folks didn't name their sons *Shana*. *I hope she isn't a groupie type. I had more than enough contact with that kind of woman when I was playing. That part I don't miss at all.* His frown deepened.

He had been married to one. As if that wasn't enough, he had been stupid enough to get engaged to another just like the first. He shook his head. *I can't condemn all women because of Sara and Rita. Those two would have been the same whether they were groupies or corporate executives. People are what they are inside. The outside is just a facade.* His jaw tightened as he sat on the weight bench.

Sara and Rita had the same problem: they wanted

more than one player at a time. To Sara, a wedding ring was just another piece of jewelry. He shook his head again. *She wasn't worth thinking about. She was her current husband's problem now and good luck to him.*

He rested a minute, then did another set of triceps and biceps exercises.

His ex-girlfriend, Rita, could have been Sara's sister; they were so much alike. This time he had found out *before* he got married what kind of woman she was, but that hadn't made it much easier for him to end things. After he'd broken off with her, she'd called every evening for too long. He'd thought she had finally let go when a month went by without a call. Then, late one night a week ago, the phone had been ringing when he'd turned off the shower.

"Where were you?" The shrill voice skipped pre-liminaries. "Do you know what time it is?"

Kyle tightened the towel around his waist.

"What do you want, Rita?" He wasn't going to tell her that he had been home. It wasn't any of her business anymore.

"I want *you,* sugar." She had found a fake Southern accent somewhere and decided to try it out on him. She should have saved it.

"We've been over this ground before. Too many times."

"I know, but you can't still be mad at me. I—I know that I made a mistake. I explained that to you. That Jim took advantage of me. He knew you were on the road at the time and I was lonely. You've got to give me another chance."

"What about the other men? Were you lonely then, too?"

"I—they…"

"It doesn't matter, Rita. Really, it doesn't matter." He let out a hard breath. "I'm just not interested in you anymore. I can't make it any plainer than that."

"I thought that after I gave you enough time you'd find some sense." Rita's accent was gone and her words had edges as sharp as broken glass. "You'll be sorry. Humiliating me like that by dumping me. Do you know that everybody's laughing at me? They say I can't hold a man. I was good for you. I was good *to* you. It's your fault, anyway. If you hadn't been so hung up on your game, if you had spent more time with me, taking care of business…"

He had hung up. When the phone had rung again, he had let it tire itself out.

He sighed and returned to the present. The only purpose either woman served now was to remind him of how poor his judgment was when it came to women.

Showered and dressed, he headed for his car dealership on the Main Line. He couldn't drive all of the luxury cars, but he could sure enjoy looking at them. He enjoyed selling them, too. Usually he went to the Cherry Hill franchise on Thursdays, but today he changed his schedule because of his appointment at the Murdock School.

He sighed as he maneuvered through heavy traffic. *How could I have been stupid enough to think that selling cars would make up for not being involved with sports?*

He parked in his spot beside a white Rolls and went inside. He had just gotten to the showroom, but already he was looking forward to the time when he would leave today.

Yeah, getting involved in sports again, even on a junior high level, was going to be good for him.

Chapter 9

Kyle parked on the street past the parking lot. Excitement flared up in him, but was quickly replaced by apprehension.

Don't expect too much. If miracles did happen, you'd be looking ahead to the next training camp instead of trying to keep your mind off basketball altogether.

In spite of his lecture to himself, excitement slipped back and rode with him as he went toward the building.

He walked around to the front. The sound of a piano drifted from the auditorium. The music teacher still hadn't gotten a real music room. Kyle smiled. If he tried just a little harder, he could remember the words to the song the kids were singing. He opened the heavy entrance door, stepped inside and closed his eyes.

The smell of floor wax, pine cleaner, chalk and school greeted him. *Maybe they aren't the things we want to,* he thought, *but some things do stay the same.* He let out a deep breath and went up the steps and into the office.

"I'm Kyle Rayburn. I'm supposed to meet the phys-ed teacher, Mrs. Garner." He held out his hand.

"Yes, you are and yes, you are." Paula's stare lasted until Cora came in and introduced herself to him. She tapped Paula's shoulder gently as she passed her, then invited Kyle into her office.

"Was that who I think it was?" Jan, the art teacher, stood beside the mailboxes and, mouth open, stared at Cora's door.

"If you think that was one fine brother, then yes."

"Is it too late to become a coach?" Jan sighed. "Better still, maybe I could get him to pose for me. He could be my incentive to dig out my oil paints and get back to work." She sighed again. "I don't know if I could do him justice, but I'd enjoy trying." She shrugged. "I just have to think of an excuse that Bob would accept." She frowned, left the office, then came back. She shrugged, smiled sheepishly, hung up her keys, then left again.

Paula stared at the papers on her desk as if waiting for them to remind her of what she was supposed to do with them. She frowned, then picked up the house phone and gave the message to Shana.

"Cora said for you to go right in," she said when Shana came into the office a few minutes later. Paula let out a heavy breath and walked over to the counter. She leaned close to Shana. "He's here and finer in person than I thought was possible," she whispered. "As they say, 'He's larger than life.' And he smiled at me." She grinned and shook her head. "He should be against the law."

"Yeah, right." Shana sighed.

Maybe Paula's mind had run off with Martie's. May as well get this over with. Let him know right from the start that it's all about business. My experience with Elliot has inoculated me and I am now immune to guys with good looks and inflated egos. She clenched her teeth. *Been there, done that, don't intend to go there again.*

She walked into Cora's office and stopped just inside the door as if a fence were blocking her way.

"Come on in, Shana. This is Kyle Rayburn."

"Hello."

Kyle held out his hand, but the smile he'd been wearing when she'd entered the office was gone. *Cheerleader and groupie type combined,* he thought. *Probably thinks she's all that and that every brother should think so, too. I wonder if the fact that she's married will mean more to her than it did to Sara? I doubt it.* He withdrew his hand immediately.

"I thought you two would like to work out the details of the program. You can use my office." Cora stood. "I have to go make sure everything is okay outside. Then I have to take something over to the district office." She looked at Kyle. "Thank you again, Kyle, for your most generous offer." Then she looked at Shana. "I'll check with you on

Monday morning to see how things went." She smiled at both of them, but neither gave an answering smile.

After Cora left, Shana breathed in deeply and took a file and notebook from her canvas bag.

You could manage without the extra money, but the kids need this program, she reminded herself. She focused on the plans.

Shana asked questions as Kyle explained his ideas in detail. Several times, she made suggestions and he readily accepted them. They would do track basics on Mondays in the schoolyard or in the gym. Kyle had already arranged to use a nearby track that had been unused since a university built a new one closer to its campus. It wasn't near enough to walk, so he would contract for a bus to take them on Wednesdays.

"I'd like to provide track shoes for the kids involved."

"I know they'll be excited about that."

The discussion moved to the summer program and the sports camp, and they made tentative plans for that.

Finally the discussion was over. Shana checked her notes to make sure all of her questions had been answered. The only ones left unanswered were the ones she hadn't asked: How could she make the time with him go faster? How long before the novelty wore off for him and how would she console the kids when he decided to move on?

She tucked her notes into her bag and glanced at the clock on the wall. She was surprised to see that an hour and a half had gone by.

"I'll see you after school on Monday, Ms. Garner."
Kyle stood and held out his hand. He tried not to notice
how small her hand was in his. Nor how her eyes were
such a warm brown even though her expression didn't
match them. Sara's brown eyes had been warm at first,
too. So had Rita's.

He was glad Shana hadn't smiled at him. He wasn't
going to pretend to be happy about working with her. If
she kept it to business, they could make this program
work. For the kids' sake, he hoped they could.

"It's *Mrs.* Garner, but I guess you may as well call
me Shana since we'll be working together." She still
didn't smile and what warmth had been in her eyes had
cooled. "I told the kids about the program. Now I'll
share the details with them. I have some of the permission slips already. I'll have the rest of the slips by
Monday. Most of them came in the day after I handed
them out. We'll have about forty kids to begin with, but
some will probably drop out."

"That's fine. We can handle as many as want to come.
I don't want anybody who's interested to be left out."

"Okay."

Shana led the way from the office. She couldn't
help but walk with him after they left the building;
they were going in the same direction. When he
walked past the parking lot to get to his car, Shana felt
some of her tension ease away, but a good portion
decided to stay.

More than two months until the end of school. She'd

worry about the summer sports camp after she got through the rest of the school year. She frowned.

Mr. Ex-jock had better keep things between us on a business basis and save his charm for some woman too stupid to know any better. She sighed. *Why couldn't he be one of those ex-athletes who forgot about working out after their career ended?*

Kyle went back to the showroom. *Was her cold attitude a front? How long before she came on to him? She had already put things on a first-name basis.* He shrugged. If he were lucky, she wouldn't make a move on him at all. He frowned.

He hadn't been lucky when he'd still been playing. He'd tried to keep to himself, but he'd had to go out sometimes and, when he had, at least one groupie had always managed to find him. It didn't matter if he'd been at the grocery store or at a concert; before he left, some woman would try to slip him her phone number. He glared.

If I'd been working a low-paying nine-to-five, they wouldn't have even seen me.

Shana was married. He had never fooled around with married women, although that hadn't stopped some of them from coming on to him. She'd been quick to let him know that she was married. He frowned. Why had her eyes gotten cold when she'd told him that? He shook his head. *It doesn't matter. None of my business. My involvement here is to provide a sports program for the kids. Besides, I'm not in the spotlight anymore. Even if I still traveled with the team, the groupies would probably leave me alone.*

He'd barely pulled into the showroom lot when Kareem, his manager, met him.

"I was just planning to call you." He took a deep breath and let it out slowly. Then he did it again. "Alvin was getting a Rolls from the end of the lot and he noticed that somebody…" He swallowed hard and took a deep breath. Then he started again. "Kyle, somebody splashed yellow paint all over the far side of a black Rolls. A Rolls-Royce." He shook his head. "I don't know when it happened, but I was back there two days ago and it wasn't there then. Whoever did it dropped the paint can right beside the car. We didn't touch a thing." He took several more deep breaths. "Do you want me to call the police?"

"I'll handle it." Kyle frowned as he went into his office. *We never had a problem with vandals before.*

He called and a squad car pulled up as soon as he left the office.

"I know you can't do anything about this," he told the two officers as he walked them to the back of the lot, "but I want you to be aware of it in case this is the start of a series of vandalism acts. As you can see, they left the empty can." He tore his gaze from the spot on the car. "Have any of the other dealers had a similar problem?"

The officer shook his head. "Nobody else reported a

problem." He touched the splash gently. "It's dry. I figured it would be." The other officer used his pen to pick up the can and put it into a large clear plastic bag. "We'll have this checked for prints, but only a fool would leave any." He grunted. "It'd take a fool, anyway, to do something like this to such a work of art." He stared at the car for a minute. "What's the expense of fixing this? The cost will decide how we classify the crime." Kyle told him and the officer whistled. "Wow. That much?"

"You don't know how many coats of paint and finish will have to be applied after we remove the spot and get down to the bare body. We can't paint over it or the surface will be uneven. People pay too much for a car like this to put up with a flaw in the paint or anywhere else."

"We'll include this in our report, Mr. Rayburn. From time to time some kids decide to have what they call fun, but it's been a long time since we've had anything like this happen." He looked at the car again and shook his head. "Who would consider this fun? It's a shame to do that to such a beautiful set of wheels."

They left and Kyle looked at the splash once more. The paint marred the front and back doors and both fenders. *If they were trying for maximum damage, they achieved their goal.* He shook his head and went back to his office to call the security company.

How had they missed a bunch of kids doing this when he was paying for a security officer to be assigned while the office was closed? Somebody had better have some answers. They weren't the only security company available.

"So you survived your meeting with Mr. Perfect," Martie said when she called Shana that evening. "How was he?" She laughed. "I mean, how did it go?"

"I know what you meant." Shana switched the phone to her other ear. "It went okay." She took a sip of tea.

"Okay? It went okay? Just okay? You were alone with Kyle Rayburn for hours and all you can say is 'it went okay'?"

Shana held the phone away from her ear for a few seconds. Then she pulled it close again.

"Girl, you need to learn to speak up. I don't think they heard you in Chester. Anyway, it wasn't hours. It was an hour and a half."

"Sorry about that, but you know how I get." She laughed. "So tell me, did he look as good in person? Paula said he did, but she wouldn't let me peek in to see for myself. She acted like she was guarding some kind of treasure." Martie's sigh floated through the phone line. "I guess she was. If Kyle Rayburn isn't a treasure, I don't know what one looks like. Did he tell you to call him *Kyle?*" The name dragged out and floated on another sigh. "And getting back to the beginning, an hour and a half is plenty of time to take care of business. Hey. He's coming on Monday, right? If I behave, can I come meet him? Why don't I come help you with the kids? I ran track in high school with you. I remember a little. I remember enough to help. I could be your assistant and maybe you'll get sick and I'll have to take over." She stopped long enough to catch another breath. "Not bad sick," she hurriedly added, "just sick enough so you can't do the after-school program. You could still do your regular coaching. You know I'm not wishing you ill or anything, girlfriend. I haven't forgotten how you suffered with the flu just a little while ago. I brought you chicken soup that I made with my own two hands, remember? Hey—" her voice climbed a few more decibels "—I got it. You have to take care of a sick grandmother after school. She has somebody during the school day, but after school…"

"Martie. Stop it." Shana laughed and decided to stop the runaway train of thought before it got any further out of control. "Kyle Rayburn is just a man." She paused. "And to tell you the truth, he was kind of dull."

"That's okay. I can deal with dull if that's what it looks like."

"Looks aren't everything. I can tell you that from my own experience. Elliot is good-looking. For verification, ask Ingrid and whoever else has been stupid to fall for his line."

"We're not talking about Elliot. We're talking about someone way, way finer. And he has to be nicer."

"I have to agree with that last part, at least until I find out differently. It would be hard for him not to be nicer than Elliot."

"Speaking of Mr. Sleaze," Martie continued, "have you heard from Elliot? Do you think he got the letter from your attorney yet?"

"Oh, yeah. Mrs. Damon got the return receipt, but she hasn't heard from him. I hope Elliot just signs the papers and sends them back, but I have a feeling that he's like fried onions—sure to draw your attention again."

"He hasn't been in the news lately, so maybe he and Ingrid made up."

"Maybe." Shana sighed. "I don't care as long as he stays out of my life." She let out a heavy breath. "I'm sorry I ever let him in. I gotta go. I have to finish my plans for next week. Did you do yours?"

"Turned them in this afternoon."

"Sometimes I can't stand you."

"Love you, too. Bye."

Shana hung up the phone and sat at the kitchen table. She took out the permission slips the kids had handed in. They would all train together, but they needed to be grouped into practice teams for the relay races and for different heats.

When a strong face floated up in her mind, she made her thoughts switch to Elliot. That was enough to keep Kyle away. She sighed.

Ten weeks until the end of the school year. Take away a week for Easter vacation. That leaves nine weeks. Minus the last two weeks of school. We won't meet in June. Too much will already be going on with trying to wrap up the school year. That leaves seven weeks. Two meetings a week—that means I have to get through fourteen times of seeing him.

She sighed again. She was not going to think about the two weeks of camp they had planned.

Why does it have to be an overnight camp? Because too much time would be wasted traveling if it wasn't, she answered herself. She shook her head slowly. *They say it's bad enough to ask yourself questions, but when you start answering them, it's time to really watch out.*

She tightened her jaw. *Fourteen times to see the jock. Too many days. I'll keep reminding myself that I'm doing this for the kids.* She put away the papers. *Next year a coach from another school can do this.*

She went into the kitchen and pulled a frozen dinner from the freezer.

I have it all worked out for next year, but first I have to get through the rest of this year.

Chapter 10

Shana pulled into her driveway late Friday and stopped. She took a deep breath. She had just jogged off the stress from the school day by circling the art museum. She looked at the familiar car blocking the garage and shook her head. *I just might have to go run again in a little while. New stress coming up.* She held her head high and got out of her car.

"It's about time you got home. Where have you been? What did you do to the door locks?"

Shana stared at Elliot as he came from the side porch. She could have pointed out that the last time she'd seen him she had gotten home too early, but she wasn't going there. That was old and tired and she wasn't going to revive it.

"What do you want?"

"This is ridiculous. Let's go inside so we can talk. I don't need the neighbors getting in our business."

"The whole world would be in your business if the press had sent your story out. You and I have no business except the papers that my lawyer sent. Why didn't you sign them and send them back?"

"Let's go inside."

"I don't think so." She stared at him and shook her head slightly. How could she have once thought that he was so great?

"I miss you." Elliot took a step toward her. Shana didn't step back, as she was tempted to do.

"You'll get over it. Get out of my driveway."

Elliot's stare threw heat at her like a sudden burst of flames from a just-fed fire. She flinched. She had never seen that look before. She was glad she hadn't let him go inside the house.

"I'm not through talking."

"I'm through listening." Shana walked to her car making her feet move at a casual pace, not letting herself turn around to face him.

"You come back here." He grabbed her arm.

She turned to face him. The heat in his eyes had grown. She jerked away and stepped back. Her heart-beat raced as if she had just run fifteen miles.

"Don't you ever put your hands on me again. Now move your car so I can get into my garage." She was proud that her words didn't shake as she let them go.

Elliot stood as if he had taken root in the driveway.

"Elliot, you don't want me to call the police. You don't want any more publicity." When he didn't move, she added, "Or do you?"

Mrs. Sterling, the next-door neighbor, chose that time to walk her dog, Friskie. *Bless her,* Shana thought.

"Hi, there, Shana."

Friskie pulled on the leash, but the neighbor of ten years didn't move. She looked from Shana to Elliot then back to Shana. "I'll be back in a few minutes. Maybe we can have a cup of tea?"

"That sounds great."

Mrs. Sterling let the terrier pull her down the street, but she glanced back several times. Shana looked at Elliot. Her stare met his and held. Finally he got into his car.

"Enjoy your new tires," he said. He gunned the motor, shot out of the driveway and used the street like an empty highway.

Shana jumped into her car and sped into the detached garage. That was an Elliot she had never seen before.

She let herself into the house, glad that she had changed the locks. The alarm hadn't gone off and the signal light was still green and steady, but she checked the downstairs windows anyway to make sure they were still intact.

Satisfied that everything was as it should be, she put the kettle on. *Mrs. Sterling can have as many cups of tea as she wants and if I don't have the kind she likes,*

I'll go to the store and get it. Anger spiked in Shana. *That no-good slashed my tires.*

She took out a package of the white-chocolate macadamia-nut cookies she ate on special occasions, set them on a plate and waited for Mrs. Sterling. This was just such a time if there ever was one.

By the time Mrs. Sterling came over, Shana had calmed down.

"More tea?" she asked holding the white ceramic teapot.

"No, thank you, baby." The woman smiled. "I really didn't want the first. I just wanted you to know I was coming back real soon." She shook her head. "Not all snakes stay in the grass and crawl on their bellies."

"You're right about that." Shana smiled. "Thanks."

"I know from experience that things might feel hard now, but you can adjust. You're still young. I was fifty-two when I got rid of my second husband." She shook her head again. "I don't know why men can't be satis-fied with what they have." She stood. "Some men, that is. There are some men who are good and loyal. It just wasn't my good fortune to meet one of them." She patted Shana's hand and stood. "It will get better."

"Thanks again." Shana walked her to the door.

"If you ever need a shoulder to cry on or the voice of experience, just give me a holler. Remember, 'This too shall pass.'" Mrs. Sterling hugged her and left.

I'm lucky to have her for a neighbor, Shana thought as she shut the door. She went into the living room and opened the ads she had saved from the Sunday newspaper. She still had drapes and a bedspread to buy. Might as well go after school on Tuesday.

I know Martie will be glad to go on this second field trip with me. I'll tell her tomorrow when she brings that tape over. She shook her head. *Why she insists that I watch that game, I don't know. I told her it's not about looks.* Shana smiled. *Sometimes it's as hard to get through to my friend as it is to get through to some of the kids.*

The rest of Shana's day was uneventful and she was grateful. She hoped Saturday would be the same.

"So. Was I right or was I correct?" Martie removed the tape of the basketball game they had just watched. She tucked the case into her bag, then she sat back beside Shana and waited for her to answer.

"I guess so."

"You guess so? What's there to guess about? When was the last time you had your eyes checked? I know you saw Mr. Adonis in person, but I also know he was dressed in long pants and a long-sleeve shirt. Right?"

"He didn't take off his coat."

"You didn't get to see his arms? You couldn't check out those biceps and triceps that make him look like he could lift a truck?"

"No. Sorry."

"You'd really be sorry if you knew what you missed." Martie closed her eyes. "I miss those old uniforms they used to wear, the ones that really showed off a body."

Martie looked up at the ceiling. "Whoever invented whatever stretchy fabric they use, wherever you are, I thank you deeper than from the bottom of my heart." She frowned. "And whoever decided to get rid of them—have you lost your mind?"

Shana shook her head and laughed. "I never said he wasn't good-looking. And buff. I just know from experience not to count looks for anything."

"Girlfriend, I hope you get over your hurt. You can't let it ruin the rest of your life." She stood. "Okay. Showing that tape is my good deed for the day. Now, you do something for me. You sure you don't want to go to the mall with me now? You can get your shopping over with today."

"I would rather have root canal without the anesthetic than go to the mall on a Saturday afternoon."

"Don't be wishy-washy about it. Why don't you express your true feelings?" Martie laughed. "I'll be on my way. I'm sure there's at least one bargain waiting for me to discover. Maybe a new pair of shoes."

"Any more shoes and you'll have to build an addition onto your house."

"To paraphrase somebody—'One can never be too rich or own too many pairs of shoes.'" She chuckled and went to the door. "See you on Monday. If I'm lucky, I'll be wearing something new."

Monday morning, which usually dragged past, flew as if Tuesday were chasing it. In a hurry to get there,

Shana knew that, when her last class ended, the rest of the day would squat in place and make Tuesday wait.

As the last gym class left the yard, the kids for the track program rushed to their usual positions as if there were a prize for the first in place.

They never rush to get to my class, she thought, and they move even slower going to their other classes. She shrugged. *I'd probably act the same way if I were them.*

"Hi," Kyle called to Shana as soon as he saw her. "I intended to get here early, but something on Lincoln Drive had traffic stopped both ways for about half an hour before they finally detoured us off," he explained before he reached her.

"It doesn't matter."

"Yes, it does. I'll leave earlier the next time and listen to the traffic report so I can get here on time."

"Hi, Kyle." Tyrone, built for running, sped over from the fence. "I was wondering if you were gonna show up."

"I keep my word."

A circle started to form around Kyle as he tried to get to Shana. The circle moved as he did. By the time he reached the center of the yard, every kid was bunched around him. If he hadn't been so tall, he would never have been seen.

Shana stayed off to the side and watched the group approach her.

Kyle stopped when he reached the shade cast by the side of the school building. The kids moved as if tied to him by a string. Their questions flew faster than he could answer them, but they didn't seem to mind not getting replies. Kyle didn't seem to mind, either. Shana tried not to admire his patience with them. After ten minutes, she blew her whistle. The last question was never finished.

"Okay, kids. Enough. Give Mr. Rayburn some space." The kids moved back a bit and the circle opened up just a little. "I know you know him already, but I'm going to introduce our guest. Then we'll explain the program."

"Can't we ask questions?"

Shana looked at Kyle and raised her eyebrows. He nodded.

"You mean more questions. You may, as long as you wait for the answers."

"Hey, Kyle," Carl called out as soon as Kyle had been introduced.

"It's Mr. Kyle," Shana corrected.

"Hey, Mr. Kyle." Carl didn't miss a beat. "How come you don't got your rings on?"

"I don't wear them."

"Aw, man. Why not? I really wanted to see what a championship ring looks like." Tyrone, who was usually bored with everything, stuck his hands in his pockets.

"Are you really coming back on Wednesday? Can you bring your rings then? Why you doing track instead of basketball?"

Joel, taller than Shana, but with a face like an eight-year-old, stared at Kyle.

"He thinks he's gonna play pro," Tyrone said. "He thinks he's gonna earn a ring just like yours one day."

"Maybe he will." Kyle looked at Joel. "If you work hard in high school, maybe you can get an athletic scholarship. You have to keep your grades up, too, though. Colleges look for players that can make good grades as well as play ball."

"I get good grades."

"You got a C in English last report," Carl offered.

"I'm bringing it up this report period." Joel glared at him. "Why don't you mind your own business, anyway?"

"You think you're something."

"I *am* something." Joel stood straighter and, although he was slow to do it, Carl tilted his head back so he could look up into Joel's face.

"I can beat you any time."

"I just know you two are talking about winning a race, so on Wednesday you two will run the first heat." Shana stepped between the two who always argued about something. They didn't know it, but they were going to be on the same four-by-four relay team. She'd even make them take turns handing off the baton to each other.

"I'd sure like to see those rings," Tyrone continued pulling attention away from the other two kids. "I wish you wore them."

"Yeah," Carl and Joel agreed.

Kyle looked at Shana. Then he looked at the kids who had closed the circle around him again. He hesitated, then shrugged.

"I don't wear them, but I have one with me." He pulled a small case from his pocket. He unwrapped the tissue paper as the kids squeezed around him. "Can I try one on, huh? Can I?" Joel leaned closer. His face almost touched the ring.

"Mr. Kyle doesn't want your grubby finger anywhere near his ring," Carl said.

"It ain't your ring."

"It ain't yours, neither."

"If you guys want to try it on, you got to cut that out." Kyle's words sliced through the fussing.

The argument stopped immediately. The kids stood in a line that would make the teachers of the younger grades envious. The noises of kids playing two streets away drifted into the yard.

Kyle moved slowly down the line making sure that each child got a chance to try on the ring before he moved on.

Shana was again surprised at his patience. He let each child decide when to remove the ring. Then she shrugged. *Why not? He's only ego-tripping.*

She wondered how long it would be before he got bored with the kids and decided to just send his money to work so he could move on to something else. *Two, three weeks tops.*

Yasmeen, at the end of the line, tried on the ring and held it out. She had to use her other hand to keep the ring from turning down on her slender finger, but she held it up so the sunlight glinted off it. Finally she slid it off, smiled and gave it back to Kyle.

"I never answered Joel's question about why track," Kyle said as he slipped the ring back into his pocket. "It's true that I played pro basketball, but I ran track first in school, so I know a little about it. In fact, it was my track coach in college who suggested I might want to try basketball, too, because of my speed. So I did both. As for why track here at Murdock, a track program is easier than running a basketball program and more kids can be involved."

Shana looked at her watch and moved to the group. "That's our time for today, but before you go, I want to share with you what we'll be doing on Wednesday. First of all, there will be a bus outside the upper yard. You have to come out right away so we don't waste time. When we get to the track, we'll start by running basic laps. For those of you new to track, we'll try to find out your best event." She smiled. "You guys want to win at the Penn Relays next year, don't you?"

The cheers kept any other sounds from entering the yard.

"Okay, then. That's it." The kids started to leave. "One more thing." They turned back. "Anybody who doesn't keep a C in all subjects, doesn't run. You run into a problem in any subject, you let me know right away. Understood? We'll get you some help." Grumbles and moans drifted from the kids. "And I don't need to tell you that, as usual, discipline problems can get you out of the program, do I?" She looked around the circle of faces and paused when she got to Joel and Carl. They nodded and looked away. Shana watched as the yard emptied.

"I'm sorry that I distracted the kids." Kyle shrugged. "I wouldn't have bothered with the ring, but I figured the kids would have kept on about it. I carry one so I can show it and we can get past that. I won't bring it again." Kyle pinned her with a stare. The sun grew hotter. Shana tore her gaze away.

"No problem. You earned it. You have a right to show it off."

"It's not about showing off. If that was my goal, I'd just make the circuit of all of the schools so I could get my ego stroked by more kids."

Shana felt her face redden. "We'll get a good practice in Wednesday." She moved from the yard, but he walked alongside her.

"Okay. I'll see you then."

"Sure." She continued to the parking lot and never looked back.

"I'll be early." He called after her.

"Not too early. We're talking about after school let's out."

"Right."

He was talking to her back. He watched her walk to the parking lot as if somebody were grading her on her posture.

What did I do? Kyle stared at her back.

She had been cold. The inside of his freezer was

warmer. Even her eyes had frozen him out. He hadn't wanted her to come on to him, but this chill was even worse. He frowned. Why had she given him that treatment and why did he care?

By the time he reached his car franchise, he still hadn't gotten any answers.

Chapter 11

"Okay." Martie had called as soon as Shana had walked into the house. "Tell me about practice," she said over the phone. "Did he wear those tight shorts?"

"*No* and there's nothing to tell. He came late." She ignored the reason for his lateness even though she believed it. "He saw and he conquered the kids."

"But not you."

"Of course not me."

"How could you resist that crooked smile?"

"I didn't see any smile."

"He always smiles. Every time somebody interviews him before or after a game, he smiles. Not during a game, though. Whenever you see a shot of him during a game, he's strictly business. What did you do to him that he didn't smile?"

"I didn't do anything to him and this is strictly business. We don't need to be smiling."

"You going to let Elliot control the rest of your life?"

"I'm not going to discuss Elliot."

"Good for you. It's about time you moved on. Don't let your mind bring him up, either. Hey. Maybe I'll come to practice on Wednesday to see for myself this new, nonsmiling Kyle Rayburn."

"You can't. On Wednesday we're going over to the field to practice."

"Then next Monday I'm coming."

"Why are we always talking about me? Why are you trying to set me up?"

"We're always talking about you because I don't have anything close to a life. And I'm always trying to set you up because I don't have a life and no prospects in sight." Martie's sigh drifted through the phone. "I need to meet somebody too old to be mistaken for my son. I'm tired of this drought."

"Come to the yard on Monday and meet Mr. Personality. You're welcome to him."

"If this was in your power to give, I'd take you up on that offer. As it is, I'm on my own. See you at lunch tomorrow."

Shana decided to keep her mind off the entire Kyle Rayburn thing. She was sure that if she gave him enough time, he'd show how much he was stuck on himself. All it would take was a little time.

Tuesday came and went and the Wednesday school day whooshed past just like Monday's had. *It was true that time sped by when you weren't looking.* Before Shana knew it, Wednesday after-school time was staring at her.

She changed into a sweat suit, closed up the gym at the last possible minute and went to the yard. *The only way to get through this was to start it.*

The bus was waiting at the corner and a group of kids of all sizes stood in a bunch on the sidewalk beside it. A few adults were on the fringe.

Kyle, his shoulders stretching a T-shirt to the maximum, stood in the middle. Even if he had not towered over them all, she would have known he was the reason. Only he could attract so much attention from so many age groups.

She sighed and cut across the yard faster than she wanted to go, which wasn't hard since she didn't want to go at all.

After today it will be two days down and way too many left to go.

Her gaze was drawn to Kyle as if he held some magical attraction for her. As she walked toward him, she tried to concentrate on other things: the way the warm breeze hinted at the month to come even though time held on to the end of April.

Shana pulled her gaze from Kyle and glanced at the

trees outside the fence, noticing how tiny tips of leaves were peeking out.

Her gaze crept back to Kyle. She dragged it away again and to the house across the upper yard, and wondered when the Bennett family would start setting out spring plants.

Yet again her gaze stole back to Kyle. This time it caught on his and stayed as she closed the gap between them. Even from a distance, she could see the intensity in his stance, how he looked as if he were waiting for her and not just because of the kids' sports program. Was he stuck on what was happening between them, too? Her breath tried to catch in her throat, but she shoved it out. *Nothing is happening between us and nothing will.* She continued to focus on him.

Why didn't he have on a jacket? His T-shirt molded to every muscle in his upper arms and chest. She could use him as an illustration for the health unit on anatomy. *Do they make custom-made T-shirts?* She swallowed hard.

This whole thing is for the kids. That's all it is. Keep it to that and you can't get hurt.

She forced her gaze in the direction of the kids, but she didn't see them. Her mind was busy keeping Kyle's image in front for her. She blinked and looked across the street, trying her best to find something to shake him from her mind, but his image clung as if glued in place. Finally, another thought squeezed in and reality surfaced to drag her back.

Elliot is just a professor and he's *a babe magnet. Kyle*

has to have more women that he can keep track of. I won't be another conquest for him. I'm not falling into that trap again. A teacher would only serve to add variety to his life.

She tried to hang on to that thought. Maybe it would keep her from doing something stupid. She took a deep breath and hoped the group would keep her mind anchored in a safe place. Then she made the mistake of looking at Kyle again and all of her self-admonitions fled.

The kids saw her coming and crowded around before she reached Kyle.

"Mrs. Garner, I want to sit next to Mr. Kyle." Joel peeled away from the group. "I called it, but Carl, said he was gonna get there first." He glared back at Carl who moved closer to Kyle. The other kids stood quietly. They may as well have not been there for all the attention they got from Shana. She still wasn't seeing what was before her eyes. Her ears weren't working too well, either. She was a few feet away, but her stare insisted on remaining on Kyle.

Shorts. I know it's warm today, but why did he have to wear shorts? She couldn't stop staring. His thighs did to the shorts what his arms did to his shirt. She forced her gaze lower and was sorry right away. *Wow. Why couldn't he have spindly legs like some of the other players in the videotape Martie showed me?*

She blinked and tried to change what she saw even though the common sense she had left told her it wouldn't work.

"Mrs. Garner?" Karen came over to her. "I didn't know you could call a seat in school. Since Joel and Carl are fighting over the seat, I think I should be allowed to have it."

"What?"

Karen, bless her heart, had succeeded in pulling Shana's gaze from Kyle.

"I said I should get the seat next to Mr. Kyle since Joel and Carl are fighting. That's what my parents do at home when we kids argue over something. Neither one gets it and if somebody else wants it, they get it." Karen put her hand on her hip.

"You ain't at home and your parents ain't in charge here. Mrs. Garner is." Carl stared at Karen. "Why should you sit next to him? You don't know nothing about basketball. I think a boy should sit next to Mr. Kyle."

"It should be me," Tyrone said as he joined the other kids grouped around Shana. "I wasn't arguing and I wanna talk sports with him."

"So do I." Young voices joined together as if somebody had rehearsed the line with them.

Shana looked at Carl. "I hope those *ain'ts* and double negatives don't show up when you're in class, or your academics will be in serious trouble and then your sports participation will be, too." She was grateful for the distraction, but didn't show it.

"Aw, Mrs. Garner. I know how to talk in class."

"Standard English isn't just for academic classes."

"I know, I know." Carl took a step closer to her.

"Please, please may I sit next to Kyle?" He held up his hands, locked together, in front of him.

"I can say *please,* too, and I *still* called it first." Joel moved beside Carl.

"It's *Mr.* Kyle and no one will sit beside him." Shana glared at Kyle as if the argument were his fault. Then she looked at the kids. "Now, do you kids want to go to the field to practice or do you want to stand around here arguing?"

"I'm not arguing. I want to go. Why don't we leave them here?" Julie's voice came from the back of the group. "I want to win at the Penn Relays next year. Every time I talk to my cousin, Sarafina, she reminds me that her team beat ours last year. I want payback."

"We're not leaving anybody." Shana stared at the faces surrounding her. "We will get on the bus and fill it from the back as we usually do."

She called out names and checked them off as the kids boarded.

"Glen." She looked at the tall boy still standing in front of her. "Your doctor's note is still on file from September, but I don't have your permission slip for this program."

"I kept forgetting to bring it in. That's why I wasn't here on Monday. I have it right here." He held out a crumpled paper. When she didn't take it, he smoothed it out as well as he could. "You know I wouldn't miss this. I love track. Track is my life."

"But not last Monday." Shana looked at the paper and shook her head. Glen tried to smooth it out even more.

"I thought I had it with me then, but when I looked, I couldn't find it. I ran home after school. I was afraid my little sister had used it to practice writing her letters. I tore up the house looking for it." He grinned sheepishly and shrugged. "It was jammed in the bottom of my book bag. By the time I found it, it was too late." He looked at the paper again. "I'm sorry it looks like this. I've been carrying it in my hand all day because I was afraid I would lose it again. It's such a little piece of paper."

"It was a whole sheet when I gave it to you."

"I know, but I thought it was taking up too much space." He shrugged again. "I guess I shouldn't have cut it off, huh?" His eyes widened. "I can still go, can't I? You can still see my dad's signature, can't you? You're not going to make me miss today, are you?"

"Get on the bus, Glen." Shana shook her head again.

"Wait a minute." Martie ran across the yard as if she were trying out for the track team. If she were eligible, she would have made it.

"We have to go," Shana said when Martie reached them.

"I know, but I have to ask you a question." She turned to Kyle with wide eyes. "Oh. Hi, Kyle Rayburn." Not even a first-grader would have believed her surprise act. "My name is Martie Drayson." She stuck out a hand. "I'm Shana's best friend."

"Pleased to meet you, Martie Drayson, Shana's best friend." Kyle held her hand for a few seconds.

"Martie, we have to go."

"I know. I just want to ask you one question." She turned her wide eyes on Shana. "Did you get your divorce papers from Elliot yet?"

Shana glared. Martie, her soon to be ex-friend, knew that if Shana had gotten the papers, she would have called her.

"No. Goodbye."

Shana stared at the bus for a few seconds, trying to think up the ultimate payback for Martie. Then she let the rest of the kids board.

When the last kid was on the bus, Shana followed Kyle up the steps. The only seat left was the one behind the driver. She stared at it. *Why didn't I plan on Glen showing up today? I know how he feels about track. If not that, if I hadn't been too lazy to assign seats, I still would have avoided this situation.*

"Is something wrong, Ms. Garner?" Julie asked.

"No."

"When we go to shop class at Waring School, the bus driver won't go until everybody is sitting down." Julie's not-so-subtle reminder didn't add an extra seat.

"Do you want the window or the aisle seat?" Kyle's deep voice cut across Julie's. He was right behind Shana.

She forced her gaze up to his face. His eyes had a sparkle she hadn't seen before. His face was on the edge of a smile. Would it be the crooked smile Martie had mentioned? If she didn't know better, she would swear that he had put Glen up to coming today. And what had inspired Martie's act?

Shana looked at the kids. All were staring at her, waiting for her to sit. She took a deep breath. Too bad one of her choices wasn't *neither of the above.*

"I'll take the window seat. You need the leg room."

She slid into the seat. If not for the side of the bus, she would have slid right out and into the street. That possibility didn't sound too bad right about now. She would not look at Kyle, not even when he eased into the seat beside her. Not even when he shifted his leg and his thigh brushed against hers. Definitely not even when heat radiated from his leg to hers and spread through her body. She felt as if her sweatpants weren't even there.

The bus moved. The field was only a few miles away, but today that was too far. Any distance that wasn't walking distance was too far.

If they could have walked there, she could have kept as much space as she needed between her and Kyle. She sighed. That much space didn't exist.

Kyle shifted his leg again and Shana automatically tried to jerk away.

If we wanted a fire, we wouldn't need two sticks to start it. I could touch whatever we wanted to burn to my right leg and it would flare up immediately.

"Sorry." He shifted his position again. "It's this knee."

"That's okay," she lied.

She tried to ignore the heat that his leg continued to generate. It was like trying to ignore standing too close to a burning fireplace. How many more weeks of this?

No matter how she figured it, the answer was always the same. Too many.

To take her mind off Kyle, she thought of Elliot. He had been able to generate a lot of heat in her, too, at first, and look what had happened.

She hadn't heard from him since that day at her house. She shivered in spite of the heat. Today she'd call her attorney and see if the papers had come back from him. The sooner he was out of her life, the better she'd feel. At least about that.

"How do you want to do this?" Kyle was standing and looking down at her. The bus had stopped.

"Huh?" She looked up at him. Unwelcome images sprang up in her mind. She frowned them away. "Sorry. My mind was somewhere else." She stood and directed the kids to line up inside the fence enclosing the field.

"We'll start with a couple of laps to warm up." The regular kids began jogging around the smooth track.

"All the way around? We have to go all the way around?" Wade's eyes widened as he looked from her to the track and back. He had trouble running around the gym during class. He needed this.

"That's what a lap is." She smiled at him. "You can do it. It won't be easy at first, but you can build yourself up to it."

"You mean we have to go around more than one time? In a row? Without resting in between?" He frowned. "The track looks bigger up close. You really mean we have to go around more than one time in a row?"

"Yes, but I believe in you." She patted his shoulder. "You can make at least one lap. When you feel that you can't run anymore, you can walk the rest of the way. Okay? I'll run, too."

"I told you it wasn't easy." Tyrone stood beside him. "After a few times, though, you won't have no trouble. Come on, man. Just pace yourself. I'll run with you."

"Yeah. You're only a little bigger than me, and I can do it." Joel said as he stood at Wade's other side. "I couldn't at first, though. That first time, man, I thought I would die. I couldn't breathe and my legs were killing me. My whole body felt like somebody wrapped a fist around it and was squeezing." He shook his head. "But I kept with it and it got easier. Come on. Me and Tyrone will go with you."

Shana smiled as she watched the three boys walk toward the track, then break into a slow jog. For all their toughness, Tyrone and Joel were good kids.

"You coming?" Kyle looked back at her. She nodded. This was one way to put distance between them. His bad knee should make it easy for her.

She started her jog. After once around the track, she quit trying to move away from him. For somebody with a bad knee, he was doing more than pretty well.

She pulled her large sweatshirt out from her arms. If her sweatpants hadn't been two sizes too large, they would be plastered to her legs. What was she trying to prove? That she didn't have enough sense to dress for the weather?

"Please, can I quit now?" Wade called when they got close to him. He was at his first quarter point but they were in their second lap. "I'm so warmed up my legs feel like they're on fire." He bent over gasping as if there were a shortage of air.

"Finish this one lap at a walk. You can go as slowly as you want." She jogged in place. "You might even decide to walk a little more when you get back to the beginning." Shana understood about legs on fire. She had experienced it when she'd been just sitting on the bus with Kyle's leg touching hers.

In spite of the sweat covering her body inside her baggy clothes, she stepped up her pace. Kyle kept up with her.

She was glad Carl jogged the last lap with them. She shifted so that he was in the middle. She glanced at Kyle, who smiled at her maneuver. She lifted her chin and finished her run, ending in front of the kids.

"This is the way it will go every Wednesday." Shana looked at the kids sprawled on the grass. Wade was stretched out on his back, gasping for air.

"Every Wednesday?" he managed to say. "You mean we have to do this every Wednesday?"

"Hey, homey. Me and some of the boys run after school every day," Carl said. "Why don't you come with us? You can walk," he added when Wade's eyes widened.

"Ask me again after my lungs can find enough air." Wade stretched his arms out to his sides.

"Man, you need to stop letting your mom pick you up after school," Joel said. "You can get a little walk in then."

"Little walk?" Wade sat up. "I live eight blocks away."

"So what? I live a block past your house." Karen stared at him. "Tell your mom you're walking home with us tomorrow."

"Maybe." Wade rubbed the front of his thighs. "I just wanted to meet Mr. Kyle. That's the only reason I came. I'm not into fitness."

"Duh. Tell us something we don't know." Joel stared at Wade. "Tomorrow you walk home with us. We promise to let you take it slow."

"Any more questions?" Shana smiled and looked around at the kids. Peer pressure could be a positive thing.

"Ain't you hot in them sweats?" Shana stared at Tyrone who quickly corrected himself. "I mean, aren't you hot in those sweats?"

"I am a little warm." Sweat was dripping from every inch of her body. *A pool must be collecting at my feet.* She felt as if fire were coming from her head. *Sweat clothes are properly named.*

Kyle cleared his throat. She refused to look at him. He did it again. She glared at him.

"Why didn't you wear those shorts that you usually wear when the weather is nice?" Karen asked. "You'd have been a lot cooler."

"I never saw you sweat so much, Mrs. Garner," Julie added.

"You kids can get on the bus." *Out of the mouths of babes.*

"You always tell us to dress for the weather," Tyrone

said, not letting it go. He stopped in front of her. "You look like it's wintertime."

"Get on the bus, Tyrone. We have to get back."

"Same seats?"

Shana took a deep breath. "Yes, same seats."

A couple of the kids grumbled. Shana felt like joining them, but there wasn't enough time for her to assign seats.

She slid into her seat. She could understand why it felt hotter. But smaller? She turned toward the window as Kyle slid in beside her.

"What—"

"I don't want to hear it." She lowered her voice, but she didn't move her head closer to his. "I don't want to hear your opinion of how I'm dressed."

"Hey, I try not to judge others. If you want to sweat yourself into dehydration, that's none of my business. You're a coach, so I know you know about dehydration, proper attire and such, so I'm sure you know what you're doing better than I do."

It was hard, but Shana continued to stare out of the window. She tried not to see his reflection looking at her. When she didn't comment, he continued.

"I just want to know what you think of the way things went today."

"Oh." Shana resisted the urge to pull her shirt away from her body and let cool air in. "I thought it went well. The new kids were the ones who had trouble today. My gym classes do some running, but not in every class. The kids from the track team run regularly. I've marked the upper yard off so we know how many times around equals a lap. When the weather is bad, we run in the gym. We also run wind sprints." She finally looked at him. "The new kids only came because of you." She shook her head. Her voice got lower. "Poor Wade." She shook her head again.

Kyle shrugged. "Maybe he and the others will stay with it. This is something they can continue for the rest of their lives."

"That's true." Shana nodded. "Last year a team from the local senior citizens' center swept all of their events at the Senior Olympics in Harrisburg. They came to the school last September and talked to the kids and showed them their medals." She smiled. "Our track team doubled after that and most of the kids stayed."

"When did you start running?"

"Junior high." She stared out the window as if looking back to that time. "When I was in the middle of seventh grade my mom and I moved and I had to go to a new school."

"Rough."

"Yeah."

She stared at her hands gripped together in her lap. A school full of kids around her age and she hadn't known even one. No one had bothered her. They'd just acted as if she weren't there. Some of the kids in her classes had spoken to her, but that had been it. She had never felt so alone. She blinked and the old pain eased.

"My gym teacher had us running laps in the gym. After a few classes he suggested that I try out for the track team. I did and I made it. We were city champs that year." She smiled. And she had made friends. One of them was Martie. "I continued running in high school and then college." She looked at him. Instead of glaring, she smiled. "How about you?"

"Huh?" A crease showed in his forehead.

"How did you get started?"

"How did I get started in what?"

"In sports." She frowned at him.

"Oh. My mom signed me up for basketball at the local gym when I was ten."

"And you loved it."

He shook his head. "Uh-uh. I hated it. None of my friends played. Oh, they'd shoot hoops on the playground, but nothing organized. They were too cool for that." He let out a hard breath. "In fact, they laughed and teased me every chance they got. They even came to a couple of games just to tease me." He shook his head again. "But Mom was serious. She said I wasn't going to spend my time hanging out on the corner or in front of the television or letting 'junk that passes for music' fill my head. After I saw that she wasn't going to let me quit, I got into it." He laughed. "It was a long time, though, before I let her know that I no longer considered playing basketball to be punishment."

"How did you get from basketball to track?"

"Coach Montague made us run laps as part of our

warm-up and training. I found out that I liked that part as much as the game itself. When it was time for me to go to seventh grade, he introduced me to the coach at Greely Middle School. Coach Montague knew I was interested in computers and Greely was a computer magnet school so I got double benefits. I was on the track team. Then I played basketball at Central High, but I continued with track."

"Hey, Mr. Kyle. Did you get letters in both?" Joel leaned close to them from the seat behind.

Shana looked around. All of the kids whom she could see were looking at them. Only the sounds of the motor and the wheels disturbed the air.

"Yes, I did." Kyle stared at Joel. "I also made the honor roll every report period. My mom had added a rule. Her 'no hanging on the corner' was joined by, 'no honor roll, no sports.'"

"Man, that's cold." Tyrone sat back.

"No, it's right. There are more jobs out there for somebody with a head full of learning than for a basketball player."

"Yeah, but the big money is in basketball and other pro sports. See what I'm saying?"

The bus stopped, but nobody moved to get off.

"I see, but you have to look at the whole picture." Kyle stood and moved to the aisle. "Count the number of pro ball players in any sport. Then look at the number of kids playing high-school sports across the country. There's no way they can all end up with athletic scholarships. Now look at the number of college teams. Even if those kids were all great players in college, there aren't enough spots for them to play professional ball." He let his gaze slowly touch each kid. "How many of you shoot hoops after school?" The air was full of hands.

He nodded. "Okay. How many of you spend as much time hitting the books as you do shooting hoops?" The air was empty. He shook his head. "How many of you want to get a job making good money?" Again hands filled the air. "Which do you think gives you the best chance?"

He didn't wait for an answer. He stepped aside so Shana could get out. The kids stayed in their seats as if they were going somewhere else. She had to prompt them to leave. Anyone who wasn't looking would never have known that a busload of kids was unloading.

Kyle stood with Shana until the last kid left the schoolyard and headed for home.

"Thank you for that." Her gaze followed Joel down the street. He walked as if in a daze. "They needed to hear that from somebody besides a school coach. They need to hear it from somebody who's been there."

"How about coming for a cup of coffee?"

"No, thank you."

"I just want to discuss the program."

"No."

"Why not?"

"I don't think it's a good idea."

"Why not? Because you're all sweaty?" The look of innocence on his face was spoiled by the glint in his

eyes. "I never saw you sweat so much, Mrs. Garner."
Kyle's voice tried to duplicate Julie's as he repeated her
words, but it broke into a laugh at the end.

Shana glared, but finally a laugh broke through and
spread across her face.

"Hey. I didn't know you could do that."

"What?"

"Laugh." His voice got lower. "Or even smile. I
thought it had been my bad luck to meet the one person
in the world who couldn't smile."

"See you Monday."

"Since you have a thing against coffee, I guess that
will be it. Bright and early." Kyle held out his hand.
Shana stared at it before she put her own in it. The heat
was back and this time she couldn't blame it on running
around the track. It was coming from his hand to her
hand and flooding through her body.

She made the mistake of looking at his face. Her
gaze got tangled with his and she almost forgot to
breathe. Kyle's hand was still closed around hers and
Shana forgot to remove it. She forgot everything—
everything except Kyle. He leaned closer. So did she.
Slowly they closed the space.

"Hi, Mrs. Garner." The Massey twins called from
their porch across the street. Shana quickly pulled her
head back and her hand away as she tried to douse her
internal fire. She backed up a step, but she couldn't
pretend that it helped.

"Bye." She mumbled.

She refused to look at him again before she turned away. She stared at the ground as she went to the parking lot. She was glad Kyle wasn't parked there, too. She frowned. What was wrong with her? She was still frowning as she got into her car.

"How stupid can you get?" she asked herself on the drive home. "You haven't even gotten rid of one heart-breaker and here you are considering…" She shook her head. "Uh-uh. Oh, no. I am not considering anything with Kyle Rayburn. Nothing except running the best track program that I can for the kids."

She parked in the garage and turned off the motor, but she didn't get out.

He had been about to kiss her. And she had leaned toward him, ready for it.

Now she closed her eyes and leaned her head against the seat. She was not ready for this. She would never be ready to let somebody else pull an Elliot on her.

She swallowed hard and walked to the house. When she reached the door, she fumbled with the key for too long before she looked at it.

"More proof of your stupidity," she muttered as she switched keys.

The steel, garage door key would never do the job the brass door key was made for. She shook her head and separated the right key from the bunch.

As she entered her house, she was still trying to push Kyle from her thoughts.

Chapter 12

Maybe this sports program wasn't such a good idea after all, Kyle thought as he reached City Avenue. His conscience accused him of being selfish, but he ignored it. *I just wanted to give something back. I had no intention of letting a woman complicate my plans.*

He had never been accused of being dumb. Why had he started acting like it now? Hadn't he learned anything from Sara and Rita? He sighed and shook his head. Evidently he wasn't as immune to women who looked like groupie types as he thought he was. He frowned. This one didn't fit the role. She looked it, but she didn't act it. Far from it. She acted as if he had done something wrong to her. Maybe that was it. Maybe it was because of her aloofness that she was occupying his mind. His thoughts drifted further to Shana Garner.

Shana was dedicated to the kids. She loved working with them. She couldn't fake that. And they loved her, too. That was obvious. He closed his eyes for a second and her beautiful face and full, kissable mouth floated into view. He let it stay. She *was* beautiful. No arguing that point.

Today she had used a blue clip to hold her thick hair back. The first time he'd seen her, the clip had been red. He frowned.

The mood I was in when I met her, how did I notice that? I thought I was busy thinking I could group her with Sara and Rita. His thoughts went again to her hair. Sara and Rita faded to nothing.

Did she ever wear it down? Did she ever let it fall free to frame her enticing face so it could draw attention to her warm eyes, melted-chocolate eyes?

Maybe she let it down for a man who was special to her. Maybe her husband? Kyle frowned at the stab of jealousy that spiked in him. *You've got no right to be jealous. She doesn't belong to you. She's married. Besides, from her actions, it's obvious that you are not even way down on her list of favorite people.* His mind ignored the logical and went back to her face.

Did her eyes warm even more and give a special promise to the man privileged to get close to her? Kyle felt his pants tighten. Just the memory of her face had this effect on him. He frowned. *Good thing you're not in front of the kids. They're old enough to understand what's going on.* He was uncomfortable, but he let his mind stay on Shana.

Who had she let brush her hair back? What man got to use his hands to frame her face? Who had she allowed to touch her lips with his? To sample her sweetness? Whose tongue had she allowed to dance with hers? Who had she allowed to touch her? Who had she shared her body with? Her husband, of course. Maybe some other man? Marriage didn't mean anything to some people. Was she one of those? He frowned as he turned the corner.

She was getting a divorce. Why had that news immediately made him almost float above the street when Martie had mentioned it? He had no intention of getting involved with Shana. This was the business of giving a program to the kids. What difference would her marital status make? The logical answer should have been none, but he wasn't being logical right now. Was the divorce the reason why she never smiled? At least not until today.

Kyle had felt as if somebody had suddenly thrown August temperatures at him when her face had lit up for him. When her full lips had parted in a wide smile—again just for him—his thoughts had gotten so jumbled that he'd forgotten where he was. He shook his head. He had even forgotten *who* he was. He glanced out the side window, shook his head and grinned.

No big deal. I can turn at the next corner. The way my mind is functioning, I'm grateful that I'm only one block past my turn. He slipped the control to air-conditioning. The outside temperature had nothing to do with it.

Right now he felt as if he were the one in a sweat suit and that the car heater was performing its job with a vengeance. It was a good thing he hadn't showered yet. If so, he'd have to step right back in for another. A frigid one. He smiled as he remembered her in that ridiculous suit.

Did she really think that by covering it, she could keep somebody from remembering how her body looked in clothes that fit? He recalled how she'd looked when he'd first met her. He chuckled. If she was trying to hide from him, now, she must feel the attraction, too.

He was still smiling when the driver behind reminded him that the light had changed. He released a hard breath and drove through the intersection. Then the smile crept back and settled in place.

She had smiled at him, and at that moment, everybody else had disappeared. A busload of kids—gone, just like that. He wanted to do whatever it took to put her smile back and keep it there.

She was getting a divorce. That fact sang through his mind. Her marriage wasn't in the way of them... He frowned.

No. No way. Get far away from the end of that thought. Not now. Not ever. Keep it business. How many lessons will it take? You still have scars from those last two. His frown deepened.

Maybe she and her friend, Martie, had set the whole scene up in order to let him know that she was free? He shook his head. No way. Not the way she had reacted.

If she was that good an actress, she wouldn't be a gym teacher. She'd be waiting for the Oscars so she could accept hers. No, she had been irked by her friend's tactics. Evidently Martie liked to play matchmaker. Maybe he'd have reason to thank her in the future, if his future included Shana.

Get off that track before you get run over again, he told himself. *Most men would learn their lesson after being hit once. You had two lessons. You never had the reputation for being dense, before. Why start now?* He finally turned onto the street that led to the franchise. His mind went back to Shana.

Who had chased away her smiles? Who had hurt her so much that she had built a brick wall around her so no one could get close? It wasn't him. She had been wary the first time he had met her. He frowned. But then, he hadn't been any friendlier to her, either.

Relationship baggage is like the smell of fried fish— it hangs around long after the cause is gone.

He looked out the window, blinked, then shook his head. *You've lost it, Kyle. That woman is so firmly embedded in your head that you can't think straight.*

He went to the end of the block and turned around. This time he paid attention so he didn't drive past the franchise entrance. His frown stayed as he parked and went inside the building.

One part of him was already looking forward to the end of the program for the year, but another part was anxious for Monday to come.

He hoped the car business would be busy tonight. He didn't want time to consider which part he wanted to win.

As Shana cooked her dinner, her mind went back to the track session, or rather, to Kyle. The image of a strong face with intense eyes kept nudging her. She tried to ignore it. Only a fool repeats a mistake.

She tuned the radio to the oldies station and hoped this wasn't the day for Motown love songs.

Little Richard and Wilson Pickett took turns with the music her grandmom had played when Shana was growing up. The Geator was cooking as usual. Jerry Blavat knew his music and its history. And he definitely knew what to play.

Shana danced as she put the mixed vegetables beside the baked chicken on her plate. They didn't write music like that anymore. She blinked. *A lot of things are different from the way they used to be.* She felt her joy slipping away.

When the Shirelles started singing about love and tomorrow, Shana switched to the television. She ate her dinner to a rerun of a rerun of an old detective show. It wasn't good, but it served a purpose. It kept her mind from her situation and she knew how the show was going to turn out.

"After the first two meetings, how are things going?" Cora was in the office when Shana signed in the next morning.

"Okay." Shana shrugged. "The kids are really excited. It's a great chance for them. This is the first time I've seen a couple of the kids interested in anything."

"I'm glad to hear it. If we don't get them involved at this level, it won't happen in high school."

Shana agreed, then went to the gym. This was a good time to start taking inventory of the equipment. It wasn't due until the end of the year, but why not get an early start?

She dragged a box out of the storage room. The fact that she didn't want to think about the next meeting with Kyle didn't have anything to do with anything.

She was glad that her first class was third-graders. They weren't involved with Kyle's program. She frowned. *You're not supposed to think about him.*

"Hey, Mrs. Garner?" Dave asked before the class even got into the gym. "Was Kyle Rayburn really here twice? I wanted to come see for myself, but Mrs. Dalton told us to stay away from the upper yard."

So much for third-graders not being interested. I should have known that the future jocks would ask about him.

Shana sighed. "Yes, he was here." She looked around at the sad faces as *aw, man* rippled through the class; boys and girls were disappointed. "Maybe he'll come for an assembly so everybody can see him," slipped out of her mouth before she could stop it.

The cheers from the class told her that they thought it was a great idea, but if voices could kick, that's what her inner voice would have been doing to her right now.

Hands waved in her face. "I don't know when. Mr. Rayburn is a busy man and I haven't even talked to him about this yet." The hands dropped and the faces drooped. She took a deep breath. "I'll talk to him as soon as I can, but I can't promise anything. I told you that Mr. Rayburn is a busy man. He has a business to run and he already spends time here on Mondays and Wednesdays. We can't take up too much of his time. Don't get your hopes up."

"But you're gonna try, right?"

"Yes, Anton, I'll try."

"All right."

Everybody cheered as if Kyle were standing in front of them. She may as well have kept her words of caution to herself. The kids looked like sunflowers that had suddenly found their namesake. Bright eyes and wide grins were all around her.

"Okay. Let's get to the game."

She formed the kids into two teams for a game of relay basketball. The smiles stayed on all of the faces no matter which team was ahead.

Her other classes were repeats of the first. She hadn't known that the third- and fourth-graders were so interested in basketball. The girls had as many questions as the boys. By the end of the day, she was sick of hearing Kyle Rayburn's name.

When she got home, she cleaned out the hall closet. Then she did the linen closet. She looked at her bedroom closet. She couldn't pretend that it needed cleaning after only a few weeks. She gave up and went to the phone.

Maybe he wouldn't be in. She dialed and waited. *Why am I such a pushover for kids' sad faces?*

"I'd like to leave a message for Mr. Rayburn," she said when the receptionist answered.

"Please hold while I connect you."

"No, don't bother I can just leave a—"

"Kyle Rayburn here."

Why wasn't his voice squeaky like that burly boxer's? She sighed.

"This is Shana Garner from Murdock School."

"I recognize your voice. What can I do for you? You aren't calling to cancel next Monday, are you?"

"No. I couldn't do that to the kids." She hesitated. "Actually I'm calling to see if you'd be willing to speak to the other kids in assemblies. The younger kids wanted to meet you, but they aren't allowed in the yard during track practice." She rushed on. "If you can't, it's okay. I know you're busy. I told them that you have a business to run and you're already committed to spend a lot of time here. If it's…"

"When do you want me? I mean, when do you want me to come?"

"Whatever is best for you." *Best for* me *is never.* She shook her head. *This was for the kids. Besides, Cora could handle the assembly.*

"Can I let you know when I see you? I have to check my schedule."

"Sure. And as I said, if it's not convenient for you to

do this, I'll explain to the kids. Children can be very understanding."

"I'll let you know when I'm available to speak with the kids when I see you," he repeated. Then his voice softened. "Are you one of those people who can't take *yes* for an answer?" Was that a smile in his voice? Was he wearing the crooked grin? Shana dragged her attention back to the question when she realized that he was waiting for an answer.

"Of course not. I just…" She frowned. "I'll—we'll see you next Monday."

"Bright and early this time."

"Not too early."

"Yes, ma'am."

I will not let him get closer to me than business length, she promised herself as she hung up. She forced herself to keep that in mind while she fixed dinner.

Wide shoulders, tall and with the perfect degree of hardness to his muscles as defined by his shirt intruded into her thoughts. *No. Cut it out.* She frowned.

Kyle would not disturb her. Business. That was all. There would never be more than business between them, and the business was only for the sake of the kids. She set her plate on the table and stared at it.

Please don't let him show that smile to me on Monday. She sighed. *Or ever.*

Chapter 13

Shana stared at the phone and sighed. For once, Kyle was not the reason for her sigh. She tightened her jaw and called Mrs. Damon, her lawyer, even though she knew it was a waste of time and energy.

"You haven't gotten the papers back from Elliot, right?"

Shana sighed after the woman's answer. She wasn't surprised. The surprise would have been if he had returned the papers.

"No. I don't know how to reach him." She nodded even though her lawyer couldn't see it. "I'll ask around." She shook her head. "If I find out where he is, I'll call him myself." She nodded. "Yes, I know, but I don't see how it would make things worse than they are if I did." She hung up and started for the kitchen, but the doorbell rang.

"You must be having a big party." A young man grinned at her and shifted five pizza boxes to his other arm.

"What?"

"Where do you want these, lady? The other five are in the car." He switched arms. "I got here in fifteen minutes even though the others are still in the car, so it counts as being on time." He shifted the boxes again. "Where can I put them?"

"I didn't order any pizzas." Shana frowned. "You must have the wrong address."

He looked at the slip of paper taped to the top box. Then he looked at the brass number beside the front door. "I got the right address. See?" He pointed to the paper and looked at her. "Are you Shana Gardner?"

"Garner."

"Close enough. You called in an order for ten pizzas. Four plain and the other six with different toppings."

"I didn't order any pizzas."

"Maybe somebody else did. You got any teenagers living here?" He peeped around her and into the house. "They're always hungry."

"No teenagers. No one here ordered pizzas," she repeated.

"Well—well—what do I do with these?" He didn't pretend to smile anymore.

"Look, I'm sorry, but you'll have to take them back."

"Take them back? All ten of them?" He shifted them yet again.

"I'm afraid so. I don't eat pizza. Sorry." Shana watched him trudge down the steps, shifting boxes as he went. She eased the door shut after he got into his car. Then she went back to the phone.

Elliot had better be where she could reach him and he'd better explain about ten pizzas appearing at her door.

An hour later, Shana was still trying to locate Elliot. She had called everybody she thought he might have been in contact with, including the university. She knew he hadn't vanished. Problems didn't do that. She shook her head and frowned. She had one last call she could make. She didn't want to do it, but she was desperate. She took a deep breath and made the call.

"I'm sorry to bother you, Mother Garner, but I need to locate Elliot."

"Why?"

"Ma'am?"

"Why are you looking for Elliot?"

"I want to ask him again to sign the—the divorce papers." She wasn't going to mention the pizzas. If Elliot would just sign the papers, she'd forget about the pizzas.

"He's not staying here, Shana, but I might be able to reach him. If so, I'll talk to him."

"Thank you. Uh, Mother Garner…?" Shana searched for the right words for this woman who had been her friend as well as her mother-in-law. "I'm sorry if I caused you any pain."

"Shana, honey, Elliot is my son and I love him, but that doesn't mean that I condone everything he does. He was wrong and just plain dumb. He threw away the best thing that ever happened to him. You." She sighed. "If I had been in your place, I would have put his behind out of my house, too, and I told him so." For a few seconds, silence was the only thing using the telephone. "I'll see what I can do. You stay in touch, you hear?"

"Yes, ma'am. Thank you." Shana's whisper pushed the silence out of the way.

She eased the phone back in place, but she didn't move from the chair. How could such a nice woman have a sleazebag for a son?

Hope hitched a ride with Shana and stayed for the rest of the evening. Maybe Mother Garner would succeed.

By nightfall Shana had convinced herself that Elliot would send the signed papers back and would soon be out of her life for good. She had also convinced herself that the almost-kiss with Kyle had never happened.

On Thursday, Shana's conviction was still at work. She convinced herself that she'd get a call from the lawyer after she got home from school saying that the papers were in hand.

Friday she tried hoping all over again, but by night-fall her hope supply was low. She had to do something, but she wasn't sure what. She just knew that waiting and wondering was grating on her nerves.

She went to her computer and located a site that she hoped would be helpful in case Elliot proved as elusive to her as he was available to other women. She found an option, but it was expensive. She decided to wait a while longer.

"I'm coming to get you," Martie said on Saturday afternoon when Shana told her that she couldn't leave the house in case the lawyer called. Martie's voice said, *Don't try to argue your way out of this.* "We have to get you out of the house. Don't you know that a watched phone is like a watched pot? It won't do its thing if you're watching. Get dressed. A run around the art museum will take your mind off everything else except trying to finish the eight miles."

"Martie…"

"I'll be there in twenty minutes. If you're ready on time, I might treat you to a cheesesteak for lunch."

"That way we can undo the benefit of the run."

"I was going to get one, anyway. Now I can preburn some of those calories and trust my still revved-up metabolism to take care of the rest."

"Don't you wish it were that easy?"

"Yep." Martie laughed. "See you in twenty. Don't be late or I'll have to leave you after we finish, and a good cheesesteak is better when it's eaten with company. That way somebody can witness the juices oozing onto the paper wrapping." She laughed again.

"Make it fifteen minutes. My mouth is watering already. Bye."

Shana laughed as she hung up. Martie was right about not sitting around waiting. It wouldn't make the phone ring and the idea of a cheesesteak did sound delicious. She'd count fat grams next week.

She was sitting on the porch swing when Martie drove up. "So? How did Wednesday go?" Martie asked as Shana got into the car.

"I'm proud of you for waiting this long to ask. In fact, I'm more than proud. I'm downright shocked."

"Are you calling me nosy? Never mind." She held up a hand. "I'm not letting you change from such an interesting subject to an insulting one." She grinned as she turned down Lincoln Drive. "Speaking of interesting subjects, how *did* Wednesday go?" She parked on Kelly Drive and they left the car and warmed up.

"It went well."

"You didn't pass out and Kyle didn't have to save you?" Martie asked as she stretched.

"Why should I have passed out?" Shana moved into the same stretch. Then she started a slow jog toward the museum.

"Because you were dressed for a January run and we had June temperatures." Martie glanced at Shana. "Actually, you don't even wear sweats when we run in the winter." She moved past a runner coming from the other direction and looked at Shana again. "Girl, what got into you? Were your shorts all in the cleaners?"

"You know I don't dry-clean my shorts. I—I just didn't want to wear something too revealing."

Martie laughed. "If that's the case, then you succeeded. My ample self would have been swimming in that suit. Where did you get it, anyway?"

"It was one of my mom's that I hung on to."

"Hanging on to it is one thing. Trying to wear it is another." They rounded Boathouse Row. "You don't *own* any revealing shorts. In fact, I don't think you own anything revealing. You dress more conservatively than my grandmom."

"Thank you for your fashion statement."

Shana tried to act indignant, but she couldn't pull it off. Martie was right. Was the way she dressed one of the reasons why Elliot…? She shook her head. *Uh-uh. Oh no. The breakup is not my fault.*

They put the conversation on hold and concentrated on making it around the path and back to the car.

"Today it felt as if somebody added a couple of miles to the circuit during the night," Martie managed to get out when they slowed to a walk.

"Be's that way sometimes," Shana said. She bent over hoping that would make breathing easier.

"I need to do this more often. At least you get some running in at practice. I don't even have to chase after the kids." Martie held a deep breath before releasing it slowly. "Whose dumb idea was this anyway?"

"Well. There are only two of us and it wasn't me."

"Come on. If we can make it to the car, I can sit

down." Martie walked slowly to the car. A grinning Shana followed. "We doggone sure earned those cheesesteaks today," she said as she drove toward Lincoln Drive. "At least I did. I think you're faking breathing hard so I won't feel so bad." She glanced at Shana, who laughed at her.

When they got back to Shana's house, she couldn't resist checking the answering machine. She also couldn't resist being disappointed that there were no messages.

Shana spent Sunday checking the phone every so often to make sure it was still working. Finally she quit and went to bed. The papers would come when the papers came.

After her last class on Monday, Shana changed her clothes. The wide legs of her khaki shorts skimmed her knees and she had enough room to tuck a sweatshirt into the waistband if she hadn't worn a belt and if she had been foolish enough to wear a sweatshirt again. She had to admit that the shorts were better suited to the weather.

She refused to look in the mirror. She took a deep breath and went into the yard to meet the kids. And Kyle.

"Hi." Kyle's voice was too soft for a man his size. It wrapped around her like a warm blanket and tried to settle around her body. She tried to shake it off. Ignore the effect.

"Hi." Her glance skittered off him and onto the kids. "Hi, kids. Sit along the fence so we can go over some things." She took a quick count. Everybody was there.

She smiled at Wade and nodded. Then she gave an overview of what they could expect in the eight sessions remaining.

"Any questions?"

"What about the sports camp?" Joel shifted forward. "Are we still gonna have a sports camp like the pros?"

"We'll have a camp." Finally she had to look at Kyle. "We still have to work out the details, but we will have a camp."

Kyle showed his athletic ease as he stood and walked over to her. Shana felt her gaze drawn to his as if it were a fish and he had hooked it. She had forgotten how tall he was. She felt like a kid standing next to him. She shook her head slightly. Not like a kid. Kids didn't have feelings like those rushing through her. She could swear the heat from him was reaching her.

Her gaze went up for days before it reached his face and settled on his generous mouth; the mouth that had almost touched hers.

Danger flashed through her mind and she pulled her gaze down. It got caught on his shoulders that stretched the T-shirt. She sighed. *Didn't he have any loose-fitting shirts?* He lifted a clipboard and his arms showed which muscles performed that task.

"All right!"

"Way to go!"

Yelling and clapping flew from the kids. Each one wore a grin. Their faces looked as if somebody had stamped the same smile on each one. Shana blinked. *What did I miss?*

"Do you want me to get the sizes now or wait until we get back?"

"Now. Please, Mrs. Garner, let's do it now so we don't forget," Joel begged. The others echoed his words.

"My own track shoes. I can't believe it. I'm gonna have my own track shoes. Maybe that will help me get around the track better," Wade said. Nobody disagreed.

"Maybe we should do this now. That way we can get on with practice," Shana said.

"May I have the class list?" Kyle held out his hand. "The kids can just write their sizes next to their names. Okay?"

"Sure."

As she fumbled to remove a sheet of paper from her own clipboard, her mind struggled to make sense of the conversation that had just taken place. She frowned. *Sizes. Track shoes.*

She handed a list to Kyle and he tucked it under the clip on his board. *Track shoes. That's right. He's going to buy track shoes for the kids.* She smiled. *Of course.*

Excitement buzzed among the kids like a swarm of yellow jackets around an open can of soda. It wasn't long before Kyle had the paper back in his hand. It was as if the kids were afraid he would change his mind before they finished.

"Okay," Shana said. "Let's go over a few basics for when we practice here. What I say will be new for some of you and a review for the others. We'll warm up by jogging around the yard five times." She looked at

Wade. "It's a small yard. As usual, go at your own pace. Then we'll have a few of you run a couple of heats." She glanced at her watch. "After that, I'll ask some of you to demonstrate stretching and loosening-up exercises, which can also serve as a cooldown. Questions?" The kids stood ready. Even Wade was in position. "No? Let's go for it, then."

She watched and made notes as they circled the yard. Wade must have been practicing with Tyrone and the others. After one lap, he slowed to a walk, but he wasn't struggling and gasping as he had the first day. He completed the run with Tyrone and Carl beside him. Shana smiled. They had taken an extra lap.

She had the kids follow one who volunteered to lead the exercises. Then she explained the different races. "After we find out which is the best race for you, we'll divide you into groups according to that. On Wednesday we'll go through the mechanics, but I won't time you. We haven't had enough practice for that yet. Some of you won't be at that point until camp."

"But we can run and try out our new shoes on Wednesday, right?"

"Yes, Joel, we can. You need them for practice even if you aren't competing."

"Can those of us who have been practicing since March run some heats on Wednesday?" Tyrone asked Shana the question, but he looked at Carl.

"Yeah. I want to show him what I can do."

"You mean you want to watch me smoke you."

"All right, you two. That's enough. We'll see about running heats on Wednesday." She looked at her watch. "Okay. That's it for the day. See you all out here on Wednesday."

"Let's go for a cup of coffee." Kyle pulled her attention from the kids leaving the yard.

"I don't think so."

"We have to work out the details for camp." His gaze was steady.

Her mind scrambled to find an excuse. Any excuse. The excuse bin was empty.

"Whatever you decide is okay."

"Uh-uh." He shook his head. "It's your program, you have to help plan it." He smiled. "Besides, I might decide to have them run a marathon through the mountains. How would you like to explain that to the parents?"

"Okay." She sighed. He was right. The program was her responsibility.

"Try not to sound so happy. I might think that you're looking forward to being with me." He laughed. "Where do you want to go?"

"There's an old-fashion diner on Germantown Avenue."

"Come on. We can ride together and I'll bring you back for your car."

"I'd just have to backtrack. I'll drive." No way was she going to sit next to him if she didn't have to.

"I'll follow you."

"Okay." Shana turned away.

"Hey, Mrs. Garner." Kyle's voice made her turn to face him. "I'm glad you decided to dress for the weather today." His gaze traveled over her body before it settled back on her face. "That sweat suit was definitely not you." His laughter covered the short distance between them.

Shana glared then turned away. "Follow me." She headed for the sidewalk.

"Any time. Any place." His words made her stumble. She resisted the urge to pull out her calendar and count the sessions remaining. Counting wouldn't change the numbers.

"I didn't know places like this still existed," Kyle said fifteen minutes later when they were standing outside the diner. He touched the chrome siding as they walked up the steps. "Did it really used to be a trolley car?"

"That's what they say. The owner had it moved here a few years ago." She stopped just inside the door. No room left at the counter. She looked at the booths. Why couldn't they have at least one table? A big one?"

"Is something wrong?" Kyle's warm breath fanned across her neck.

"No." She stared at each booth. One must be a little larger than the others.

"Where do you want to sit?"

"Wherever." She led the way to a booth near the middle of the row and slid in. Kyle slid in across from her. Their knees touched and she shifted. What was worse—across from him or beside him? *Beside him,* she thought as she remembered the bus ride with him. *Definitely beside him.* At least this way she only had to deal with a knee rather than the side of his leg. How long would it take to plan a program?

The waiter offered her a menu, but she refused. "Just a cup of tea, please." She set her notebook on the table. The sooner they did this, the sooner she could leave him.

"Coffee for me, please." Kyle spoke to the waiter but he stared at Shana.

"This shouldn't take long." She picked up her pen. "All we have to do is plan one week. Then we can repeat the schedule the next week." She scribbled on the paper. "In fact, we don't even have to plan the whole week. Only two days. After the first day, the schedule can be the same."

"Why don't we just plan one hour and repeat it every hour every day until the kids go to bed? That way we can be out of here before your tea and my coffee are cool enough to drink."

Shana stopped writing and looked at him. She felt color flood her face. "I'm sorry." She shook her head.

"I'm sorry, too," he said. "I'm sorry this is such an ordeal for you." He frowned, but his gaze remained on her. "Maybe after we get the program going, the other gym teacher can take over." He shifted his gaze to the window. "You can still be involved in the planning, if you want. We can work over the phone. You won't even have to meet with me."

"I'm truly sorry," she said again. "I'm going through

a rough time and I'm taking it out on you." She took in a deep breath and let it out slowly. "What did you have in mind?"

Kyle turned his gaze back to her. He stared for a minute, then he nodded. He put a folder on the table and opened it. "I thought the second and third weeks in July would be best. That way the Fourth of July won't interfere. I have a cook and a helper lined up." He took out a notebook. "Do you think we need additional staff? We can hire a couple of college kids if you think we need them."

"I have thirty-three kids in each class every forty-five minutes every day. I think we can handle one set of forty kids all day."

"They are pretty evenly divided. Eighteen girls and twenty-two boys." He shrugged. "I guess I didn't expect so many girls."

"After Marion Jones and the other women athletes at the Olympics, we had a surge of interest all over the city. Probably all over the country." She smiled. "One of the reasons I stayed involved in sports and became a phys-ed major is because of Jackie Joyner-Kersee." She nodded. "She was some athlete." She nodded. "She and Flo-Jo. Every year I play the tape of the Olympic track events for my teams."

The waiter brought their beverages. Shana stirred hers to cool it off, but stopped when Kyle stared at her. She shrugged and picked up her pen.

They charted a program and planned each day. They

planned special programs for the evenings. Campfires complete with s'mores and singing were planned along with nights of skits and talent shows.

"When do you want to go look at the camp?"

Shana forgot to close her notebook. She dropped her pen and it rolled across the floor.

"The Poconos?"

"That's where the camp is."

"With you?"

"I can give you directions if you want to go up there alone." His jaw tightened.

She shook her head slowly. "It's your idea. And you know where it is. It doesn't make sense for me to go alone."

"There's that happiness bubbling up in you and escaping." She didn't have a comment. "When do you want to go?"

She wished she had a full schedule. "I don't care."

"Spring break is week after next, right?"

"Right."

"Do you want to go during that week, or do you have vacation plans?"

"No plans. Any day that week will be okay."

"Shall we say Tuesday? Weekends are always busy for me."

"Fine." She didn't want to, but she imagined many reasons for his "*bus*yness" on weekends. All of them involved beautiful women.

It's none of my business. Nothing in his personal life

concerns me. She frowned. *Then why does this feel like jealousy?*

"Is something wrong?"

"No." *Nothing that a huge dose of common sense couldn't cure.*

He stared at her. Then he closed his book. "I guess that's it." He stood. "I hope it wasn't too painful for you."

"I…" She stood and gathered her things.

"I'll see you on Wednesday."

Shana watched him walk away. He never looked back and she didn't blame him.

I've got to get it together. I'm blaming him and he hasn't done anything to me. He doesn't deserve to be caught up in Elliot's fallout. As she left, she resolved to remember that.

Kyle drove out of the parking lot. *I had been worried about her coming on to me.* He let out a sharp laugh. *She's avoiding me as if I'm bad news.* He frowned. *I could take payback if I deserved it.* He shook his head. *Her husband must be a real piece of work to damage her like this.*

He drove to the franchise wishing he had met Shana in her prehusband days.

When Shana got home, the light on the answering machine was blinking. She pushed the play button, but didn't get her hopes up. As she listened, her thoughts left the diner and centered on the message.

"I don't know what you did, but we got the papers from Elliot in this morning's mail. By the middle of June it will all be over. He also sent a bunch of pizza coupons with instructions to forward them to you. What's that all about?"

Shana's anger reared up but she tamped it down. "Elliot's got a warped sense of humor. Actually, it's not a sense of humor at all. Just a warped mind. You can throw them away. I don't eat pizza and he knows it."

Just the word *pizza* brought her anger back up again. *He has a lot of nerve. He couldn't be any more wrong, yet* he's *picking at* me. She nodded. *I've got to get rid of him ASAP.*

"Shana? Are you still there?"

"Oh. Sorry. Yes I'm here. I had an idea and I've been searching the Internet. I wasn't sure about doing this, but I want Elliot out of my life faster than it would take to go the usual route. I want him out like yesterday." She took a deep breath. "What do you think about a divorce granted in Guam?"

"Guam?"

"I read that there's a United States court there and a divorce through it would be legal. Do you know if that's true?"

"It's true. But it's really expensive."

"Fourteen hundred dollars for a divorce in four to six weeks. Five hundred more if I want it in two."

"What's the rush?"

"I don't want to be tied to him any longer than necessary. I'd make it retroactive, if I could. Also, I don't want to take a chance that he'd try to undo this just for spite."

"Well, if you really want to go that route, you can do it without me. Just follow the directions on the Web site."

"But you've been working on this."

"I'll bill you for the hours so far. It will save you a few bucks you would have spent on me if you continue by yourself, although, if you're talking nineteen hundred, the money factor must not be so important."

"There was enough money in the joint account to cover it."

Mrs. Damon laughed. "So he gets to help pay whether he wants to or not, huh?"

"I earned it."

"That you did. Let me know when you get the final papers from Guam. Also let me know if you hit a snag."

"I will. Thanks for everything."

After she hung up, Shana danced around the kitchen. Then she went to the computer and put her plans in operation. When she logged off, she circled a date two weeks from then. Then she called Martie with the news.

"I know it's a school night," was Martie's response, "but this calls for dinner out. Do you want to go to the diner?"

"No," Shana answered quickly. "Let's go somewhere else." Already the diner held memories of Kyle. "I heard that Roberta's on Germantown Avenue has good soul food. Let's give her a try."

She hung up and went outside to wait for Martie.

What is going on between me and Kyle? Why is he having this effect on me? I'm not healed from Elliot's wounds yet, but here I am thinking thoughts that I have no business thinking about Kyle. She leaned against the porch column. *I've never been a masochist before. Why did I turn into one now?*

Chapter 14

When Shana got to the yard on Wednesday, all of the members of the track team were standing along the outside of the fence as if waiting for her to start the event of the year and she was late.

"Hi, Mrs. Garner." They sounded as if they had rehearsed speaking in unison.

Their gazes followed her until she got close. Her gaze, however, was on the man standing a little apart from them. She watched as he came closer to meet her.

"Good afternoon, Mrs. Garner."

Kyle's greeting draped over her. She couldn't put the blame on him. His greeting was innocent. No hidden meanings lurked behind it. Anything else she heard was in her mind, probably brought on by the smile he finally showed her. Martie was right about that smile. It was magical. It could make everything else disappear. Was he thinking of their almost-kiss? She pulled her thoughts back.

"Good afternoon." It was a struggle, but she managed to avoid eye contact with him.

Thankfully Joel grabbed her attention. "Mr. Kyle brought our shoes. See?" Joel pointed to the boxes stacked beside the bus. "Can we put them on now?"

"Let's wait until we get to the track." Shana smiled at the kids. Forty faces looked at her as if she had just canceled the coming vacation.

"They won't disappear, kids." None of them gave any indication that they believed her.

"I'll give you your shoes and you can hold them until we get to the field," Kyle said as he looked at Shana. "We won't have space otherwise."

"That's fine with me," Shana said. "You bought them, why don't you do the honors?"

"I'll help." Carl moved forward.

"No, I can do it better." Joel and Carl nudged each other.

"Do you guys need to go back to kindergarten and learn how to behave?" Shana's tone made both boys take a step back. They stared at the ground. "Suppose both of you wait like everybody else?" They moved back to the fence and Shana turned to Kyle. "Why don't we have everybody get on the bus as you give them their shoes?"

"Sounds like a plan."

He read the name on the top box and handed it to Andrea, who wrapped both arms around it. She thanked him and rushed onto the bus as if afraid he would change his mind and take it back. Kyle picked up the next box.

Soon the pile was gone. Shana got on the bus and again was sorry that an even number of kids had signed up.

Because of what she had told them before, they left the front seat empty again. They were probably in the same seats as before, too. There was no way she could change seats without giving a reason, and not wanting to sit beside Kyle because she felt attracted to him was not something she wanted to share. Not even with Kyle.

She took a deep breath and sat. She moved over against the window as if she could squeeze a few more inches from it. She knew that was impossible, but when Kyle sat next to her, she tried harder.

"Can we at least look at our shoes?" Carl asked.

"Yeah. Please, can we?" Joel added.

History had been made. For once Joel and Carl were in agreement.

"I guess that would be okay."

Shana didn't correct their *can* to *may*. She doubted if they would have heard her. Obviously she wasn't the only one preoccupied. She had barely finished giving permission when the scrape of box tops mixed with the buzz of voices.

"Look at mine," Julie whispered as if she were afraid of breaking a spell.

"They look really fast." Wade held up a shoe.

"They can be if you make them," Carl pointed out.

"I wish the bus could go faster."

"I wish the field was right next to the school."

"Me, too," somebody added.

Me, too, Shana's mind agreed as Kyle's leg brushed against hers yet again.

When the bus stopped, she thought of reminding the kids to take their time getting off, but she changed her mind. It would be a waste of breath. They were too busy focusing on their shoes to hear anything.

"Very good, kids," Shana said as they got off the bus. She had noticed how well they controlled the urge to push past and be first off. "Okay, let's go to the benches."

She had barely finished her sentence when they rushed to find places on the benches along their side of the track. She shook her head and smiled as every one of them abandoned their old shoes and thrust their feet into the new ones.

"How do they look, Mrs. Garner?" Joel held up his foot.

"Look at mine, too." Wade held up his.

Shana looked at the kids sitting along the benches. They looked like the Miss America contestants in the "Show Me Your Shoes" part of the pageant parade.

"I'll bet these help me run faster," Tyrone said. "I'll probably set a world's record." He laughed and the others laughed with him.

"I just hope they make it easier for me to get around the track." Wade looked at his shoes again. "Uh-uh. I *know* they will." His grin didn't leave any space on his face. "Track shoes. My very own track shoes." He nodded. "Maybe this track stuff ain't…" He glanced at Shana. "I mean, *isn't* so bad after all.

"Awesome," Andrea said.

"We got shoe bags and everything." Julie held up the blue bag that had been tucked on top of the shoes.

"Way better than a plastic grocery bag," Karen said. "I won't have to try to hide this."

"Let's warm up so we can see about setting a new record," Tyrone said.

Some of the kids began to jog in place. Others paced in front of the benches while they stared down at their shoes. Some just jiggled from one foot to the other.

"Okay. Take your laps, but don't forget to…" They were gone before Shana finished talking. She blew her whistle and they stopped. She motioned for them to come back.

Tyrone had made it halfway around and Carl wasn't far behind. Joel had to be close enough for Carl to feel his breath. Shana smiled. *Too bad this wasn't a meet. They'd win with no problem…unless the other team had new shoes, too.* She forced her smile away. "What do we always do first when we hit the track?"

"Warm-up laps," they muttered. When she looked at Tyrone, he shrugged. Carl nudged him. Tyrone shook him off.

"That didn't look like a warm-up lap to me. That

looked like a going-for-the-gold lap. Let's try it again." She smiled. "Later we'll let you see what your shoes can do."

She watched them jog around the track. Wade ran halfway before he slowed to a walk. A new first for him. This was the first time he had shown any excitement about running.

"It's a good thing this isn't basketball." Kyle chuckled. "If it were, the kids would be flying from one end of the court to the other, hanging from the basket and swearing it was because they had on the right shoes."

Shana laughed with Kyle as they waited for the kids to finish laps.

"You know, Mrs. Garner, Michael Jordan wore a new pair of shoes for each game," Tyrone said as he jogged in place in front of her. "I can understand why. I feel like my feet barely touched the track." Shana and Kyle laughed again. Tyrone stared at them. "What's funny?" He frowned. Shana and Kyle looked at each other and laughed harder. "What's up?" Tyrone's frown deepened.

"Nothing." Shana wiped her eyes. "We were talking about basketball, too."

"Can we run some heats?" Joel ran up to them.

"Maybe." She watched as the last kids joined them. "Who's been running on days when we don't practice?"

Most hands went up. "Does sometimes count?" Norman asked from near the back of the bunch.

"Norman, you know how many practices we get in before we run a heat. Did you run enough?"

"I better just watch this time." Norman looked as if he had lost a race.

Shana looked at the faces. She didn't need words to tell her who met the requirements and who didn't. She stared at them a bit longer. "I guess it won't hurt you to run a little. Just don't go all out and only run one lap." They groaned. "Okay, two if you think you're ready for it."

The overcast day could have used the brightness on the kids' faces as a substitute for the missing sunshine.

Shana smiled at them. "You new kids will go first." She let her gaze rest on Wade before she moved on. "If anybody wants to just watch, that's okay, too. You already did your warm-up. You can learn by watching, too."

"I want to try," Wade said.

"Good for you. If you have to, slow down and walk the rest of the way. Listen to your body and set your own pace." She looked at the kids. "Okay, anybody who wants to try to run a lap, line up." About a dozen kids lined up.

Shana had Abby and Carl remind them of the proper starting position by demonstrating. When she was satisfied that everybody was in position, she blew her whistle. The kids took off strong. Even Wade managed a little speed at the beginning.

"You've got some good potential for your team out there." Kyle's words reminded Shana of his presence. She smiled. It was a good sign that she had forgotten, even for a little while, that he was there.

"That's true. Besides that, they're all getting exercise.

Some of these kids never move from in front of the television once they get home from school except to get something to eat." She nodded toward the track. "Look at Wade. He ran more than halfway before he slowed to a walk." She made a mistake and looked at Kyle and her next sentence got lost.

His smile reached her and caused heat to flow through her body. Had she been able to think, she would have been glad she hadn't worn a sweat suit today because she would look as if her own personal rainstorm had occurred. If her mind had been functioning properly, she would have pulled out Elliot's image as an example of what happened when she got involved. If her body hadn't known how to breathe without instructions from her, she would have been dead.

"What do you want me to do?"

"Huh?"

"When they get back. What do you want me to do?"

Shana felt her face flush. *I will not even think of the thought that brings to mind.* She blinked and took a step back. *He's got me asking "Elliot who?"*

Her mind shuffled thoughts until it found one that made sense and wasn't suggestive. *Wow. When had her thoughts of Kyle changed from keeping him away to* maybe? She frowned. *I can't go any further with Kyle. Regardless of our relationship, I'm still married to that sleazebag, Elliot.*

"Shana?"

"Oh." *Girl, get a hold of yourself.* "Uh, let's let them

watch the others run their heats. After that, we can break them up and work on passing the baton."

"Okay. I'll get the batons and blocks from the bus."

Shana watched him go.

"What—do—we—do—now?" Joel gulped air between each word as he walked slowly back and forth.

"Mr. Kyle will work with you."

"Can we sit down?" His chest still heaved. "Please? It's a long way around the track when you're going all out."

She smiled at him. "You can sit, at least until Mr. Kyle needs for you to stand." She looked at the kids who hadn't run.

"Okay, kids." She pointed to the fence. "Those who practiced enough and want to run a heat may line up over there." She got as far as *line up* before the kids were in place and waiting. *Too bad this wasn't a meet.* She shook her head. "Way too many for one heat. We'll have to run three."

She divided them, making sure that Carl, Tyrone and Joel were each in a different group. Tyrone started to say something, but Shana's stare made him change his mind. He shrugged and went over to his group.

After Kyle placed the blocks on the track, the first heat took off. The other kids cheered for favorites. By the third heat, none of them had lost their enthusiasm. Finally the last ones were back.

"Okay. We have a little time left. There's more to track than running. We'll practice a little on passing the baton during a relay race. That's very important and it's not as easy as it looks. The U.S. lost gold during a couple of the Olympics because of bobbled passes." She regrouped the kids.

Two of the kids walked through the passing process. Then Kyle worked with one group while Shana worked with the other.

"How come it's so hard giving a stupid stick to someone?" Abby picked up the dropped baton for the third time.

"It doesn't look this hard on television." Norman stopped his baton from rolling across the hard surface.

"The baton is small and short, both of you are running. The front runner can't look back and you only have a short distance to complete the hand-off. All of those factors enter into it. You'll get it. Others have. It just takes practice."

"Hey, Mrs. Garner? Why do I have to run on the team with Tyrone? I wanted to smoke him."

"You mean you wanted to watch me smoke you."

"That's why I have you two on the same relay team. When we're against another team, we don't need to be fighting among ourselves." Both boys shrugged and stared at the ground.

"Who's going to run against Houston School?" Abby asked.

"The regular team. Houston has a few more kids than we do, but their gym teacher and I agreed that everyone who's ready should run. The rest of you can watch."

"I might have fussed about just watching before, but

after going around the track today, I know I'm not ready." Greg, one of the new kids, shook his head.

"Yeah, new shoes don't take the place of training, man," Joel added.

Kyle chuckled, but said nothing.

"You got that right," Carl agreed.

"Okay, kids," Shana said. "It's time to go. Good practice, everybody. Let's load up."

Little talking showed itself on the ride back. The kids were worn out. Shana missed the distraction. She sighed.

Who am I kidding? Nothing could distract me from being aware of Kyle sitting close enough for his body heat to reach me and make my body kindle a fire of its own. She frowned. *Would it be so wrong to let something develop between us?* Her frown deepened. *Yes, it would. No matter how much I wish it wasn't true, I'm still married.*

When they reached the school, she was still mulling over the situation.

The bus wheels had barely stopped rolling when she stood. She got off the bus and Kyle, then the kids, followed.

As they left the bus, each child thanked Kyle again as if a parent were standing beside them prompting the words from them.

The last one headed for home and Kyle pulled her attention to him. As if he needed words to do that.

"I'd suggest we go for a cup of coffee, but I'm sure you have plans." This time he was the one who walked away.

Shana stared as he left. No one had ever accused her

of having bad manners, but Kyle would have an easy time proving it.

She walked to her car determined to improve her behavior toward him. It wasn't his fault that she felt an attraction. He didn't even know about it. He probably thought she was just a foul-tempered woman. She couldn't blame him. That's the face she showed him.

Kyle wouldn't have reached his car much faster if he had been running. He wished he had parked another three blocks away. At least. Three *miles* would have been better.

He got in his car, put the key in the ignition, but didn't turn it. He needed some time to get it together so he wouldn't use the streets as a raceway.

She was in the process of getting a divorce, but that didn't matter. She wasn't interested in him. How could he be attracted to someone like that when it was obvious that she couldn't stand him? The answer came as an image of wide eyes and silky milk-chocolate skin that made his hands ache to touch her. The few times she had smiled at him, his mind had stumbled off the track. His temper eased.

He didn't want to, but he thought of how her smile made him aware of his own body. Exercise had nothing to do with the way it had swelled at that sight. His imagination took over. She would fit perfectly in his arms. Their other body parts would fit together just as well. He released a hard breath.

If he could only find a way around the barbed wire she had placed between them, he could prove it. He could make her happy again, make her get over whatever had made her block him. She was attracted to him. He could tell by her reactions to his touch, just to his presence. Why couldn't she give him a chance?

He leaned his head back. *Was it worth the effort?* The *oh, yeah* came as soon as the question ended. *How long did it take to get a divorce anyway?*

Chapter 15

Shana had just finished dinner when the phone rang. She looked at the clock on the mantel. Seven o'clock. *The magic hour for making me an offer I can't refuse. What incentive will this company offer me? How come so many companies are exempt from the Do Not Call list?* She sighed and picked up the phone.

"Hi. Is this a bad time?"

Kyle's voice wiped away the relaxing effects of the run around the art museum and the hot shower. Tension filled her. A telemarketer didn't seem like a bad thing right now.

"Oh. Hi. No." *Is there such a thing as a good time where Kyle is concerned?* She frowned. *Or am I afraid of experiencing "a good time" with him?* Her eyes widened. *Where did that come from?*

Her question went unanswered, but that didn't stop an image forming of Kyle holding her; touching her; making her ask herself, as she had been doing a lot lately, "Elliot who?"

Kyle's image grew stronger. In her mind, Kyle kissed her, finally. Then she'd feel his hard chest beneath her hands while his hands…

"I can call later, if that's what you want."

"Huh?"

"I can call back tomorrow."

"No. this is fine. I was thinking about—about something else. What's on your mind?" *I know it's not the same thing that's on mine.*

"I'm sorry to disturb you. I guess we should have done this after practice, but I didn't think of it. We never set up the time for me to come talk to the rest of the students and I thought I'd better do that before my schedule gets full and clashes with yours."

It wasn't a "clash" that she was afraid of. *A "clash" I could handle. This other—this is something more dangerous. I could get hurt.*

She hesitated. She didn't have to handle this part. She could let somebody else handle the assemblies. She shook her head. *I can't do that. This was my idea. It wouldn't be fair to Kyle for me to hand him off to somebody else. He's going out of his way for the kids.*

"I don't anticipate a problem. Cora is open to scheduling two special assemblies back to back and we can do that on any day except a Tuesday."

"Wednesday after spring vacation, then? I have to come for track anyway so we could do it before then."

Words refused to come to her.

When had the word *it* taken on a suggestive meaning and why did her mind choose this time to zero in on that meaning? She frowned. *Probably my mind went there because he said* we. *Of course, there were lots of activities that we could participate in. Why did my thoughts go to that specific activity?*

Again the image of Kyle touching her body in sensitive places and stroking and making her heat up and ache for more until he finally…

"Shana? Are you still with me?"

Oh, yeah, you'd better believe it. Another second and you would hear how much I'm with you. She went to the door and opened it. Maybe a breeze would come in and bring reality with it. At the least, maybe it would cool her down. She cleared her throat.

"Yes. I'm here. I think…" She released a long slow breath. "Let's make it the week after that, but still before track. By waiting a week we'll give the kids a chance to settle down from vacation before they get revved up again. We usually have the lower grades' assemblies at twelve forty-five and the upper grades' at one forty-five. Is that okay?"

"Sure."

"Do you need any help with planning? The assemblies last for forty-five minutes." *Why did I do that? Please let him say no.*

"I don't think so. I've met with school groups before. They usually have more questions than we'll have time for."

Good. I won't have to pay for my stupidity. At least not this time. I won't have to meet with him on this. She shook her head. *Maybe I can find a way to develop some mind control before we meet again. What in the world is going on with me?*

His words were innocent, but the voice itself made her go places she had no business going. She sighed.

No, it was even more so. Without him to look at, his voice took over in the attraction department. The word charisma *is too weak.* Sexy *is much better.* She frowned. *Cut it out,* she told her raging hormones. And people thought teenagers had cornered that market.

How would he act if he knew what she was thinking? She forced her attention back to what he was saying and tried to block out his image, which fixed itself in front of her mind.

"I was wondering…" He hesitated. "Should I bring photos for the kids for the assemblies?"

"I'm sure they would appreciate them."

"Okay." He paused again. "Shana?"

"Yes?"

"See you for track on Wednesday."

"Okay."

The connection was broken at his end, but still he filled her thoughts.

What words would he use in that sexy voice if we were close? Really close? What would he say if I were in his arms and his hands were learning my body? What secrets would his body share with mine as he set me on fire?

She tried to hang up the phone, but missed the cradle. She didn't know why it was necessary to recharge the phone in the conventional way, anyway. Kyle had just made enough electricity flow through her so that she could charge the phone just by touching the contacts. She sighed and tried again. She got it right the second time and went back to the living room, trying to avoid images that put her together with Kyle and the words *touch* and *contact*.

She turned on the television, but the Kyle in her mind was stronger than any character on any program.

After the eleven o'clock news, she turned off the television. It was a good thing she wouldn't be tested on what she had watched. *Watched* was the wrong word. The word *seen* was even worse. She had sat in front of the television, but the only thing she had seen or watched was Kyle in her mind. Kyle doing marvelous things with her, to her, and she doing wonderful things back.

She went to bed. She refused to count the number of track sessions left. It would only overwhelm her. How was she going to keep this surprising attraction from showing when she was with him?

She fell asleep with the image of her "with him" glued in her mind. It was not an unpleasant thing.

* * *

You blew it, Kyle. Why didn't you jump on her offer to help you plan your presentation? He frowned. *Because my brain refuses to function properly when she's around. Because it was so unexpected. She's been avoiding my company as if I have some deadly disease and there's no cure.* He frowned again at the phone. *She's not interested, man. She can't make that any clearer. She practically grits her teeth when she has to be around you.*

He stared at the phone awhile longer then went to his workout room. Maybe he could find a way to get rid of his frustration. Or at least figure out why he was more attracted to her than he had been to a woman in a long, long time.

Wednesday passed without anything unusual; Shana still tried to fight the attraction to Kyle; fought to keep him from realizing that she had done an about-face. She was relieved when the bus got back to the school. The kids left and she turned to go home.

"See you Tuesday." Kyle's words stopped her escape.

"Tuesday?" Shana turned back toward him. "School is closed for vacation next week. The assembly is the week after next and on Wednesday."

"We're visiting the camp on Tuesday. Remember?"

"I forgot." *How could I forget?*

"Maybe we should meet on Monday to go over our plans."

"That won't be necessary." The situation was bad enough already.

"Okay, then." He hesitated. "See you on Tuesday. What time is good for you?"

How could she tell him that there wasn't any such time? At least two hours shut up in a close space with Kyle and with no way to put distance between them. Then the reprieve of motel rooms separating them for the night followed by another two hours ride back home. Four-plus hours with him one-on-one. And all the time she had to keep acting indifferently toward him.

"I get up early so it doesn't matter. You say when."

"How about nine? I'll pick you up."

She shook away the image of a different kind of picking up. The kind where he held her close enough for her to notice if his chest was as hard as it looked in his shirt, the kind of picking up where they wouldn't go anywhere except upstairs to… She stared at the ground so he couldn't see the heat filling her face.

"Okay. Bye." She walked away promising to have a good talk with herself as soon as she got to her car.

"Wait." Kyle closed the space between them.

She sighed before she turned around. She'd almost made it. Hopefully her face was looking normal again.

"What is it?"

"Where do you live?"

"Why do you need to know that?"

It was Kyle's turn to frown. "So I can pick you up on Tuesday."

"Maybe I should meet you here."

"Why would you want to do that? You live over near the diner and Route 309 is near there. We'd just have to backtrack." He stared at her. "I promise not to come in. I'll wait in the car and use my cell phone to call you when I get there."

Heat flooded her face. This time it had nothing to do with Kyle being close.

"That's not necessary. I'm sorry. Again." She said softly. Then she told him her address. "I'll see you Tuesday morning."

When she got home, she decided to go for a run in the neighborhood. Wednesday wasn't her usual running day, but she needed it to clear her head. She had to find a way to control her reaction to Kyle, and all of her efforts had failed so far.

An hour later she was back home, tired, but relaxed. Kyle Rayburn was just a man. True, he was better than average in the looks department, and the physique department, and the smile department and... Her mind returned to the physique-department part. The man could sure fill out a T-shirt and shorts. It was enough to make a woman wish he would...

Shana shook her head and went to take a shower. Maybe that would wash away the layer of foolishness. And forgetfulness.

Elliot was all of those things too, and look what happened to my relationship with him. She shook her head. She had to find a way to make herself remember that Kyle was capable of breaking her heart just as Elliot had done. She had to make herself see *heartbreaker* stamped all over him whenever she looked at him.

On Thursday and Friday, it took all of Shana's energy and concentration to keep the kids' minds on what they were doing. Both days crept past for her as if she were afraid to face an empty school next week. Thankfully, Kyle stayed off her mind. At least most of the time.

The kids spent time talking about what they were going to do with a whole week off, instead of concentrating on the work that should have had their attention. They played as if they had forgotten the rules and were using equipment for the first time. Kids who spent after school shooting hoops suddenly forgot how to make a basket. Some of the girls whispered about their Easter dresses rather than outscoring the other team. Shana was glad she didn't have academics to teach. Sports were bad enough with kids forgetting rules they had known for years.

If somebody were taking a poll about what the kids were planning to do with their time, sleeping late would be all by itself in the number-one spot.

Many kids talked also about family vacations. That would have had second place. So many were going to Disney World that Shana was glad she didn't have such plans; the place was sure to be mobbed. She refused to think about her old plans for the week, plans made before she'd discovered Elliot's infidelity.

Finally three o'clock Friday came. Shana had barely said goodbye to her last class before they left as if being freed after a long term in prison. Shana smiled as she put away the equipment. She remembered that feeling, and it hadn't been so long ago. She swallowed hard and the smile left.

If she and Elliot had still been together, she'd have felt the same way right now. They would have been taking off for one of the islands in the morning as they always did during Easter break. They had talked about going to Barbados this time. She blinked hard. Her vacation plans had disappeared with him. *You're better off without him,* she reminded herself and she believed it.

She sat at the desk in her office long after the last footsteps disappeared from the hall. Then she left for home. The kids weren't the only ones unfocused, and the vacation wasn't the only reason she was having trouble.

No matter how many times she checked the calendar, Tuesday was right around the corner and getting closer with each minute.

Why couldn't I find an alternative for visiting the camp with him? Why couldn't he go alone? Why couldn't the camp be five minutes away instead of two hours?

She pushed aside the picture of what had been her vacation plans as she changed into her running clothes. Maybe a run would make her forget her vacation that had vanished.

She thought about Tuesday morning. Maybe the run could hold off that trip, too. She started her warm-up.

Maybe the Poconos would get a foot of snow over-night. Then the trip would be off. Never mind the fact that it was April and snow this late was extremely rare even for the Poconos. Still, she wished on. If it were a heavy snow, she would have more time to prepare.

She picked up her pace and headed toward the art museum. *Yeah. Right. As if that much time existed.*

before the future would be a burden above everything. Then and July woke he on. Her to find, the man
lived however, and now of the tale. We were still was
when he did because that, she wished on, if it mark it
for was not he would have been what it meant.

She smiled as her only life, it kept to seem, tried a
moment. But now to do it that only have noticed.

Chapter 16

Shana woke up earlier on Tuesday morning than she
would have if she had had to go to school. The sun was
just showing itself through thickening clouds, but it was
obvious that a snowfall was not going to save her. The
most they would get would be a drizzle. How fitting:
gray weather to match her gray mood.

She folded her arms behind her head and did something she had been doing a lot of lately; she thought over
her situation with Kyle.

*I'm in deep trouble and getting in deeper. I can't
deny my feelings anymore. I am so attracted to him that
it scares me. I don't want to make another mistake.
Mistakes like that hurt too much, so I pushed him away*

so I can be safe. She frowned. *Is that what I want for the rest of my life—to be alone and safe?* That idea didn't appeal to her.

She got out of bed and got ready. Soon, mind churning as it tried to reason things out, she put the kettle on and made her tea.

Maybe I'm stressing over this for nothing, she thought. *Except for a couple of times when he joked, he's never acted any way but professionally toward me. I'm sure he has a woman, maybe more than one. To him I'm just the junior high coach who comes with the program he's funding.*

As she drank her tea, she tried to decide if she wanted that to be true.

At eight fifty-nine Kyle rang her doorbell. She took a deep breath, opened the door and let him in. At the sight of him, her caution hid and boldness appeared in its place. Evidently her heart had overruled her head.

"Would you like a cup of coffee?"

"If it's not too much trouble."

"No trouble." Frowning, she led him into the kitchen.

If I hadn't opened my big mouth, we could be on the road right now. Two minutes saved here, two minutes there—they add up. She smothered her sigh. *This is worse than a teenager trying out the boy-girl thing.* A frown flitted across her face, then her features relaxed. *For once, I'm gonna just ride with the tide.* She gave her attention back to Kyle.

"Let me guess. Your favorite color is blue." Kyle smiled and Shana had trouble processing his words.

"Huh? Oh, yeah." She looked around with new eyes. The pale blue walls and darker blue accents around the kitchen left little space for other colors. She smiled as she put on the kettle. "For as long as I can remember."

"Did you use blue throughout the house?" He sat at the table.

"Pretty much so. At least I do now." She frowned.

Elliot didn't like blue. He said it was too feminine, so she had compromised in the bedroom. She had used his colors. Green and brown. *Brown. Like the dirtbag that he is. Don't think of him. Think of this instead— today the divorce is final. Elliot Garner is history.*

She smiled. *If I weren't going with Kyle today, Martie and I would be going out to celebrate.*

"What's with the smile after that deep frown?"

She hesitated. The kettle's whistle gave her time to think. Would he think she had hidden motives if she told him? No. He asked. I'll answer. "If we weren't going to visit the camp, Martie would be helping me celebrate." She filled a cup and set it in front of Kyle.

"Celebrate what?"

"My divorce is final today."

"Yeah?"

"Yeah."

"Good."

She almost got lost in his smile. Then she looked away. "Sorry I don't have anything sweet," she murmured.

Kyle stared at her for too long. Then he smiled. "Congratulate me." He took a sip.

"For what?" She looked at him and was snagged by the smile again. For once she didn't mind.

"For not touching that statement." His stare pinned her in place. She felt like a butterfly in an exhibit she'd once seen in a museum. None of them had been blushing, though. She waited.

"You have no idea how many possible responses raced through my mind at your words," Kyle continued. "*I* don't even know. They came too fast for me to count." He smiled again as her blush deepened. "And we were off to such a good start for all of—" he glanced at his watch "—five whole minutes." He shook his head. "I know. Hurry up so we can get this over with." He drained his cup and stood. "Ready when you are."

Shana closed her eyes for a few seconds as she set the cup in the sink.

After his comments, a different reason for not leaving crept out. *He must be joking. If we wait until I'm ready to leave, we'll never get to the camp. We'll go upstairs and... Stop it,* she ordered herself. *Maybe you better go back to thinking of Elliot. It's safer.* She sighed. *But not as much fun.*

She turned back to Kyle. The trip was going to take longer than she thought. A whole lot longer. She didn't want to think about how they had decided to stop at a motel for the night since it would be late when they finished checking out the camp. Yeah, it was going to be a very long trip.

Soon they were on Route 309 going the speed limit, but still moving too slowly for Shana, toward the Pennsylvania Turnpike.

"Do you mind?" Shana asked as she reached for the radio.

"Help yourself."

The new so-called oldies station eased a Nina Simone song into the air. Shana tried to ignore the words of "Fine and Mellow" followed by "My Baby Likes." It was hard trying to block the images that the words conjured up, but easier than ignoring the man sitting beside her, who was a prime example of fine even though he wasn't her baby. *Yet* crept into her mind and shocked her. The attraction she had been fighting tried to slip back into her. She sighed. Oh, yeah. It was going to be a very long trip.

"Do you have any brothers or sisters?" Kyle asked as they turned onto the Northeast Extension. He turned off the static that had replaced the music.

"No. There's just me." She glanced at him. "It runs in the family. Dad was an only child, too. Mom had a sister, but they never were close. She said Aunt Floretta got mad and cut off all ties. Mom tried to locate her, but couldn't." She blinked hard. "It's just me."

"It can be lonely out there."

"You get lonely?"

"Sure." He glanced at her. "Not what you expect, huh?"

"I figured you stars have all the company you want." She shrugged.

"There's company and then there's company. Sometimes being alone is better than the alternative."

"I never thought of that."

"Few people do, but after the game is over, the married guys go home to their families and the single guys…"

"The single guys go home with the pick of the groupies," Shana finished his sentence for him.

"That's what people assume, but it's not usually the case. I was going to say that the single guys are at loose ends. If it's a home game, they go home and might meet with friends. If it's not, they're at loose ends until time to leave for home." He switched lanes to get around a truck. "Even if a guy is into the groupie scene, he usually gets tired after a short while. I never got into it."

"I'm sorry." She resisted the urge to place a hand on his arm. "I insulted you. I hate when people use stereotypes about me and I'm doing the same with you."

"Don't get me wrong. Some of the guys are like that. Not as many as people think, though. It's a business. If you don't keep your head on straight and your body in condition, you won't last long. Groupies disappear when your career does. I've seen it happen."

"Oh."

The silence that eased in was more relaxed. After about ten minutes, Shana started talking again.

"Tell me about the camp. How did you find it?"

"A friend owns it. He was traded to Seattle and hasn't decided what to do with it."

"Why would he own a camp?"

"Several reasons. It's a business. He lends it to churches and other nonprofit groups for tax purposes. Now that he's no longer in the area, he's looking into the feasibility of donating it to a nonprofit group as a tax write-off." He glanced at her and smiled. "Meanwhile, the Sixers' loss is our program's gain, at least for this summer. If we want it for two weeks every year, he said he'll put it in the sales agreement."

She smiled back. Why did she like the sound of the *our* and *we*?

As they rode, they each talked about their camping experience. The conversation stopped long enough for Kyle to pay the toll, then it continued as they traveled country roads and crossed one-lane bridges.

"It's really off the beaten path, isn't it?" Shana looked at the thick stand of trees lining the road. Around one bend she gasped as she saw three deer grazing beside the road. They glanced at the car, then went back to grazing. As a steady rain began, the deer ambled gracefully back from the road until they were under the trees.

"This isn't anything. When we get to the camp, it will seem as if there are no roads, no towns, no other people for hundreds of miles of around." Kyle smiled at her, then gave his attention back to the twisting road.

Shana frowned. *This is a good thing, right? It feels so right. Me and Kyle, the only two people in the world.*

She struggled to pull her mind from the possibilities that that situation would present, but her mind decided to keep the image.

A modern Adam and Eve in our own Eden. No worries, no distractions except each other. She frowned. *Wow. These are the feelings I was trying to avoid. Where is my defense mechanism when I need it?* She glanced at him. *He's not Elliot. He's nothing like him. It's time to move on, time to take a chance again. I got my legal freedom today, but I have been emotionally free from Elliot for a long time.* At her decision to stop denying the attraction, a sense of peace draped over her.

I don't know how he feels about me. I don't know if he's been flirting because that's how he is, or if he means it. Is he interested in me in that way? He said he's not a player. I believe him. She smiled and nodded. *Yeah. I believe him.*

She held on to that as they moved down the road. She felt as if she had taken a turn of her own and was on her own road to her destiny.

"Almost there," Kyle said. Shana looked around. They were parked at the curb in front of an old-fashioned country store. "I have to go speak to Miss Corrine in the store," he continued. "I haven't seen her since last year when I was here with my friend. Come with me. We'll get some lunch to take with us."

The rain had increased to a steady downpour. Kyle grabbed the huge umbrella from the backseat and went to Shana's door.

Shana got out and looked at the store that was taking up a considerable amount of space on this side of the block. She glanced around. If this qualified as a block.

When had they left the road for this bit of civilization? Both sides of the short block were dotted with houses, but directly across the street from the store was a garden shop with flats of bedding plants along the curb. A gas station anchored the far end. Across from that, but back a bit, stood a small church with its simple steeple pointing the way to heaven.

Beyond the end of the strip, the road continued on its way, hemmed in only by wild bushes and trees. Shana smiled as the old term "peep and plumb" came to mind. *Less than one whole peep would take you plumb out of town,* if this were considered a town. The four streetlights on each side and the sidewalks that disappeared into the grass at both ends said it was. She followed Kyle into the store.

"Kyle Rayburn. As I live and breathe." The thin woman wearing an old-fashioned bib apron came from behind the counter, grinning as she approached them. "What brings you up to this neck of the woods this time of year?" She brushed the flour from her hands along the sides of her apron before she hugged him close and squeezed gently. Then she stepped back.

"Hey, Miss Corrine." Kyle kissed the side of her face. "I missed you too much to wait until summer."

"If I buy that, you'll try to sell me a gold mine up the road apiece." She swatted his arm and they both laughed. "Who's this pretty thing with you?" She turned to Shana and smiled.

Kyle drew Shana alongside him and introduced them.

"Is this like bringing your girl home to meet Mama?" Miss Corrine asked. Shana blushed and Kyle laughed.

"Look at what you did, Miss Corrine." Kyle put his arm around Shana's shoulders and her color deepened.

She kept her hand from touching her face to see if flames were about to appear.

"Shana is a coach at my old school."

He explained the sports program to the woman whose gaze never left Shana's face, although she nodded from time to time as he went on.

"She seems like a keeper to me and those don't come along very often," she said after Kyle had finished. She reached over and patted Shana's arm. "Glad to meet you." She pointed around the store. "What do you make of our version of a superstore?"

"I've never seen so much in a mom-and-pop store before." Shana glanced at the racks and bins of clothes at one side. Shelves of food staples took up much of the space on the other side.

She took a few steps away from the counter and noticed several large freezers at the back. "It looks like you anticipate any need somebody might have."

"We try. This store had been here since my grand-daddy opened when my mama was a little thing. We may not have the quantity of goods those big-name places have, but we rival them in variety." She laughed.

"We have to. When we get a good snowfall up here, folks depend on us for everything. The main road gets plowed, but that's a far ways off. Sometimes we're snowed in for weeks back up in here. Ofttimes somebody from way back in the woods comes in on a snowmobile for their supplies. At least once a winter we get folks who came up for the day, but got caught by a storm." She pointed to a rack of sweat suits. "That's the reason for the clothes. They might not be the latest fashion, but they're serviceable. I got to make sure I have what they need."

"I guess there's no danger of snow today." Shana smiled. She was glad the snowstorm she had wished for hadn't happened.

"It is a mite late for that kind of snowfall even up here." Miss Corrine glanced out the window. "Today it's all liquid that the Lord sends us." The three of them laughed.

"What did you bake today?" Kyle asked.

"I must have known you were coming. I got a cake with coconut frosting just waiting for me to cut the first slice."

"It's worth the trip for that." He glanced at Shana.

"I love anything coconut," she said.

"We'll take two slices of that," Kyle said. "We'd better get a couple of sandwiches, too. Got any corned beef?"

"You know we do."

"I'll have a sandwich…."

"Make it two, please," Shana added.

"Give us all the trimmings, too, please. We can take it with us and eat at the camp."

Soon they were back in the car with the lunch bag on the floor in the back.

They rode for a few minutes before Kyle glanced at her. "I'm glad about your divorce. Because of your marriage, I have been struggling against what seems to be developing between us."

"I don't know what to say."

"Saying nothing is okay. I'm not pushing anything. I just wanted you to be aware of it."

Shana was glad Kyle didn't expect a response. She wouldn't have known what to say.

They traveled twenty minutes more on roads that narrowed each time they turned off and through now heavy rains. Finally they drove onto a gravel road that was just about choked by the brush on either side.

Fifteen minutes more the road went across a narrow wooden bridge spanning a rushing, swollen creek.

After several more turns that took them up the twisting road climbing to the top of a hill, Kyle stopped in a large clearing and pointed at a cabin on the far edge. He turned to her.

"Honey, we're home." He grinned. "This is the main building—combination mess hall and meeting room." Shana stared out the car window at the rustic building whose weathered structure blended into the surroundings. "It looks better from the inside. Honest."

"I've been to camp before, not only as a camper, but as a counselor as well. I know not to judge the buildings by the way they look on the outside." She pointed to three buildings on the other side of the clearing. "Camper cabins?"

"Some of them. Each one holds twelve campers. More are on the other side of the mess hall. The ball field is a short walk behind those cabins across the way. One of the first things Clark did when he bought this place was have a track put around the ball field. Any needed repairs will be made before we come up here this summer."

He drove to the large building and parked in front. "Let's go inside. We'll check out the field later when we look at the cabins."

He grabbed the umbrella and lunch bag from the back. By the time he opened her door, she was ready. Both huddled under the umbrella and dashed for the porch through rains that were falling by the bucketful. They managed to avoid the puddles already formed along the gravel path to the steps.

"I guess a little dry is better than completely wet." Shana pulled her soaked pant legs away from her skin after she reached the porch.

"I should have checked the Weather Channel. I'm sorry." Kyle opened the door.

"I could have done the same," Shana said as she stepped inside. "Don't worry. I won't melt."

"I'm sorry, but I can't resist saying this—some melting is desirable." His stare was intense. It held hers for a long while until a gust of wind reminded them that the door was still open.

"I'm not touching that." Shana tried to tamp down the heat and hope building inside her.

"Okay. We'll change the subject." He chuckled. "This is where the indoor activities will take place. I thought we could get a feel for how best to use the space." He led her into the kitchen. "The camp has had well over a hundred fifty campers plus staff, so we'll have lots of room."

Shana walked around the kitchen, noting the four large steel sinks lining two walls. Two industrial-size dishwashers separated them into twos. Steel cabinets full of dishes hung open along the walls all around the room.

At the far end, two freezers as wide as she was tall stood propped open. She wrinkled her nose at the small heap of dried grass tucked into a corner of the bottom shelf.

"Looks like we found something's home."

"Well, the wild creatures were on the land first."

"True. I'm surprised there's only one nest."

Across from the freezers was a room large enough to be a bedroom, but the shelves made it obvious that it was the pantry. The shelves were empty, of course, but Shana could see that they would hold enough food to feed an army or a huge group of hungry teenagers for quite a while. Another nest was in the corner under the bottom shelf.

"We won't have to shop for food during camp because we don't have enough storage space, will we?" Kyle chuckled.

"Not hardly."

Shana looked at the center of the room. Twenty wide,

long tables, ten on each side, should have dominated the space, but the size of the room prevented that.

"Typical camp mess hall. I guess nobody has thought of a better design."

"Some things can't be improved upon."

Kyle's stare could have generated enough electricity to light at least this building. Shana knew he wasn't talking about any kitchen. Her stare was adding to the tension building in the air. Silently they went back to the main room.

"Wait here a minute," Kyle said as he went out the door.

"It will take longer than that for me to figure out what's going on between us," Shana muttered to herself. She sighed. *I think I already know. I just have to figure out what I'm going to do about it.*

Kyle came back carrying a huge tote bag from his trunk.

"What in the world…?"

"We'll eat soon, but first we have to get rid of some of the dirt."

He took out a rag and a bottle of cleaner and went to work on one of the tables. Shana watched for a couple of seconds. Then she took the cloth from him.

"Let me. You drove, I'll clean."

"Yes, ma'am."

Kyle leaned back against the next table. He tried not to notice the fit of her slacks as she bent to reach across the table. He tried to ignore the way her blouse slid back in place around her breasts. He couldn't ignore his own reaction to what he was seeing. *Think timetables, man. Multiply every large number by pi. Look some-where else, anywhere else.* He shook his head and continued to admire the view. It was worth the discomfort he was feeling. Maybe she wouldn't notice. If she did, maybe he could tell her the reason. What would she do? He had the keys to the car and it was too far for her to walk even if she could find her way. He grinned.

Soon they were seated across from each other. Kyle unpacked the larger bag that Miss Corrine had fixed.

Bags of chips came out first followed by the slices of cake. Shana's mouth watered at the sight of the moist coconut sprinkled over thick white icing. Next came four slices of bread and two overstuffed sandwiches.

"Extra bread?"

"It's a running joke. The first time I got one of Miss Corrine's sandwiches, I told her it looked as if there was enough meat for another one. She laughed and gave me two extra slices of bread."

"If we had even more bread, we could each make two more sandwiches." She grinned. "Does she stuff all of the sandwiches like this, or does she just like you?" Shana's grin widened.

"What can I say." Kyle shrugged. "Most people find me a likable guy." He stared at her and his hand hesitated over the bag. "Others make it harder for me to break through their barriers." He grinned. "I'm working on it, though. I never was a quitter." He took out a six-pack of bottled water and set it on the table. Containers of coleslaw and potato salad completed the lunch.

"Did Miss Corrine realize that there are only two of us?" Shana asked as she stared at the food.

"Miss Corrine is used to fixing for folks who do a lot of physical work."

"Oh."

Their stares clashed. Shana knew he was thinking of a particular kind of physical activity that wouldn't be considered work by those participating in it. She knew this because she was thinking of the same thing. Kyle shrugged his stare loose.

"Hungry campers and snow bunnies and such." His voice had dipped to a warm growl on the last two words and his stare was back.

He reached into the smaller bag and pulled out paper plates and packets of tableware, mustard and mayonnaise and pickle spears wrapped in waxed paper. Shana's mind swirled with what was going on between them.

After eating a half sandwich and some of the salads, she wrapped the rest of the sandwich.

"Enough."

"I agree." Kyle wrapped half of his, too, and stood. "The rain seems to have let up quite a bit. Let's go look at the cabins and maybe the field."

Shana was glad to go outside. Maybe out there she'd find space enough for her battling feelings to come to an agreement.

They walked to a campers' cabin through rain that was now little more than a drizzle.

Metal beds standing on end were leaning against the walls.

"As you can see, each cabin sleeps twelve comfortably. The bathroom is at the end." He walked toward it. "All of the cabins are set up the same way."

Eight shower stalls, eight toilet stalls and eight sinks equipped the room.

"It's not one-on-one, but the wait shouldn't be long."

"The sleeping area is roomy enough for the girls to coexist in peace." Shana laughed. "My girls like to look good, but they're not hung up on their looks. The bathroom space is fine."

"Let's go look at the field."

The rain had gotten tired. Only a heavy mist hung in the air as they passed the cabins, but the bushes lining the path were bent over as if they were tired, too. Gradually the path widened.

They turned the corner. A regulation track ringed the clearing that would be the ball field once it was mowed and lined. A chain-link fence set the boundaries. A basketball court complete with bleachers stood at the far end within a second fence.

Slowly Shana and Kyle followed the dark red track around the field. Several times Kyle stopped to examine a spot. Then he moved on. When they reached the gate again, he stopped.

"Not too bad. After a little patching here and there, it will be good to go." He turned to her. "Or should I say, 'Good for the kids to go.'"

Shana laughed and shook her head. "Seriously, the kids will be so excited about this. They'll have a real track and their time on it won't be limited." She smiled up at him. "Thank you. Even if we never win a meet, this means more to them than a win."

"You're welcome." A slight frown flitted across his face as he stared at her. "Quite welcome."

Slowly he bent his head toward her, giving her more than enough time to stop him. She could have moved aside. She could have said something. She could have put a hand on his chest to keep them apart.

She did none of these. She stood her ground, staring into his eyes before she shifted her gaze and her attention to his mouth. She watched as it slowly descended toward hers. Then she closed her eyes, but she didn't wait passively. She leaned forward a fraction, as if impatient, as if she had known all along that this was inevitable. As if to let him know it was about time.

First his breath warmed her. *Who knew how sexy coleslaw could smell?* She leaned even closer. He touched his lips to hers and time disappeared. He closed his arms around her and she eased closer still.

The kiss deepened and Shana learned the meaning of *melting in his arms.* Her arms closed around him, tightening as he brushed his hands down her back and settled at her waist. One hand stroked lower until her hips were pressed against the evidence of his reaction. An ache started where he pressed against her, trying to reach her through her clothes.

The kiss deepened as they explored each other's mouth, as their tongues tasted each other one lip at a time, then both lips, as they tried to make up for wasted time.

Gradually, less than a slim part of a fraction at a time, Kyle moved his mouth from hers. He pressed kisses along her jaw, along the side of her neck, stayed there as her pulse jumped, then moved back to her mouth.

He pressed what was a chaste kiss compared to the last one against her mouth. Then, still cradling her, he eased his mouth from hers. His gaze found hers again in the same look that had started this sharing. He touched his forehead to hers and rocked her slightly in his arms.

"Wow. I'm not going to question how we got here so fast." He placed a quick kiss on her forehead then pulled back. "Wow again. Worth the wait."

"Yeah. Wow," Shana said softly and touched his lips gently with her finger. She frowned slightly, then took a step away from him.

"You're going to say that you don't think this is a good idea, that it's a mistake."

"I'm sorry." She blinked hard, but the shine in her eyes showed that in a few seconds the tears would win. She shook her head and went on. "I *don't* think it's a good idea and I *do* think it's a mistake." She shook her head. "At least my *mind* thinks it's a mistake." She stared away, then back at him. "Evidently my body disagrees." She sighed. "I'm not ready for this. I wish I was, but I'm not."

She frowned as she backed up until she felt the fence pressing against her back. She tried to control the regret spilling from her, but she had no more control over it than she did over her body right now.

"Yeah. I wish so, too." The same regret showed in Kyle's eyes.

"Is there anything else we need to see before we go back home?" She stuffed her hands into her pockets and made them stay there instead of finding him.

"No. I think we've spent more than enough time here." He reached for her arm, but pulled back before he touched her.

Side by side they walked back toward the cabins. The path was narrow enough so that they had to walk closely, but still they managed to avoid touching.

As they reached the porch, the mist turned into a drizzle again and quickly increased to a heavy downpour. The gray atmosphere matched Shana's mood.

The only sound as they gathered their things and got into the car was the rain that had decided to come back stronger than before.

It picked up strength as Kyle drove down the hill. Shana didn't notice. She had her own storm doing its thing inside her.

Why can't I open myself to Kyle the way I want to? How long before I can move on? How much longer will I let Elliot control me? Please, let me put Elliot behind me.

Chapter 17

"We have a problem," Kyle said as he stopped the car. Shana looked out the windshield and frowned.

The wipers were frantically trying to keep the glass clear, but they were failing. Badly. The rains were much stronger than when she and Kyle had gotten in the car. She leaned forward and stared where the road and the bridge should be. A pond had developed. The water stretched from the creek and up the banks on both sides. The bridge was not in sight.

"Where's the bridge?"

"Under that water, I hope. I doubt if it was washed away. I guess the creek had more than it could handle, too." He didn't look at her, but Shana winced as his words hit the target. She knew she was the *too* that he meant.

"Now what do we do?" The pond held her stare. "We can't drive around it."

"No, we can't. The water is spread out a good hundred yards from where the bridge should be." He shook his head. "The only thing we can do is go back to camp and be glad that Miss Corrine packed so much food. We'll need it for breakfast."

"Breakfast?"

"We'll have to spend the night. Looks like you're stuck with me."

Shana kept quiet and watched as Kyle slowly backed up a few yards and began to turn the car around. When the left wheel tried to stick in the mud, Shana gripped the edge of her seat, but Kyle gently rocked the car out of the mud and back onto the road. Water ran down the road and to the creek as if it didn't want to miss what was going on down there. Shana switched her stare to the miniature creeks rushing past on either side of the road as if trying to join the large one at the bottom. She could feel that the car was riding through a third, strong rivulet.

Once the car was well established on solid enough ground, Shana had formed her jumbled words into questions.

"What if the water keeps rising? Will it reach the camp? The buildings? What will we do then? Shouldn't we call somebody?" Trying not to panic, she turned to face him.

"Okay. Let me try to sort things out." Despite the situation, he smiled at her quickly then gave his attention back to the road. "The camp sits up a hill. Remember? A steep hill." When she didn't answer, he glanced at her. "Remember?"

"Yes." She swallowed hard and nodded slightly.

"The creek won't reach it. The builders probably considered that when they built the camp that far up. The camp has never flooded. They've had waters much higher than this around here. A couple of hurricanes hit awhile back. The waters never even threatened the camp. Okay?"

"Okay." Her answer was weak. He reached over and squeezed her hands, but they stayed locked to each other.

"We're going to be all right. Creeks overflow their banks all the time. Then the rains stop and the streams go back where they belong." He squeezed her hand again. "Trust me on this. I won't let anything happen to you. Okay?"

"Okay." She let her hands loosen their grip on each other and held on to his.

"As far as calling somebody is concerned, there would be no need even if there was somebody to call. It's a rainstorm. That's all." He spoke quietly. "This is a natural phenomenon. We'll go back to the mess hall and wait it out. Even if the storm lets up this evening, it will be dark and I don't want to take a chance on these roads in the dark. We'll have to spend the night."

"You think the roads will be okay in the morning?"

"Yeah, I do."

"You'd say that even if you didn't believe it, wouldn't you?"

"Yeah, I would." A grin covered his face. "But I believe it." He parked the car in the same spot where it had been before, as close to the steps as he could get. "Let's get the things from the backseat and make a dash for it."

They ran to the porch, then Kyle dashed back to the car and opened the trunk. Shana went inside and had just taken off her jacket when he came back in.

"We'll need these." He set their overnight bags on the floor. Then he placed a bulging plastic trash bag on top of a table. "Blanket," he said when he noticed her puzzled look. He took off his jacket and hung it on the back of a chair.

"Blanket? You carry a blanket in your car?"

"I'm on the road a lot so I carry one in the winter. I just never took it out yet." She frowned at him. He stared back at her. "You look as if I planned this." A grim look settled over his face and he stared at her. "If I had that kind of power, I'd do more with it than bring on a storm." His stare intensified. "A whole lot more."

"I didn't mean…"

"Yeah, you did, but that's okay."

Kyle went to the fireplace and took the metal match case from the tall mantel. Shana stared at his back. *Be fair,* she told herself. She took a deep breath then walked over to him.

"I see that's still the practice." Her words were tentative.

"What's that?" Not looking at her, he bent and struck a match to the crumpled newspaper poking from a few places between the bottom layer of wood.

"Laying the fire for the next time and leaving the matches."

"Especially here in the mountains." After making sure the fire had caught, he straightened. "You never know when somebody will get stranded in the snow. If so, dry wood wouldn't be available." He glanced at her. "Works in rain, too."

"Yes." She stared at the fire a few seconds. Then she walked over to a window. "It's still coming down."

"I would say ignore it and maybe it will go away, but I don't believe that myself." Kyle stood beside her.

They watched the rain for a good while, as if hoping to catch it taking a rest. What they *did* see was night slowly creeping up on the storm darkness. Finally, as if on signal, they turned back to the room.

"Got any marshmallows?"

"What?" Shana frowned at him.

"We got a good fire going to waste."

"No." Shana shook her head and smiled for the first time since they had turned back. "Know any good campfire songs?"

"Is there such a thing?"

"Of course." Shana looked indignant. It would have worked if not for the smile. She held up her hand and began counting on her fingers. "There's 'B-I-N-G-O,' several songs about ducks, farm songs, 'A Hole in the

Sea…'" Her smile widened. "There used to be some good ghost stories out there, too."

"I'll bet you were something at camp." He smiled. "Or were you something else?" He laughed. After a second, Shana joined in.

"I was a model camper, junior counselor and then counselor. At least I was until that hayride incident." She sat down cross-legged in front of the fire.

"You know you can't leave it there." He sat beside her.

"It wasn't my fault. He started it."

"That's your story and you're sticking to it, huh? Who 'he'?"

"I don't even remember his name."

"But you do remember it was his fault."

"Oh, yeah. He heard the farmer say don't throw the hay. I heard it and he was right there across from me. Still, as soon as we got on the road good, he threw a handful right at me and it got stuck all in my hair." She looked wide-eyed at Kyle. "I couldn't let him get away with that."

"Of course not. You threw back."

"Yep. Caught him right in his face. The other kids laughed. Then he threw again and some of the others came to my defense. They knew he was wrong." She shook her head. "That poor farmer's hay was all over the road. If that was all he had to feed his cows or horses, they went hungry that evening."

"What was the punishment for campers who ignored directions?"

"Uh…" Shana hesitated. "I wasn't a camper." She mumbled, but Kyle heard her.

"You were a counselor?"

"Please. A counselor wouldn't do something like that." She looked at him. "I was a junior counselor."

"How old were you?"

"Old enough to know better."

"What was the punishment? You had to rake the hay from the road? No more hayrides?"

"I got chewed out by the camp director who had had a high opinion of me up to that point." She shook her head. "I was so humiliated even before he said a word. I betrayed a trust." She frowned. Then smiled. "Come to think of it, I don't remember any hayrides after that." She laughed. "Okay. Your turn. What did you do at camp?"

"When I was a teenager, a couple buddies sneaked down to the girls' cabins one night."

"Oh?"

"It's not what you think. There was this one girls' counselor always riding us, acting like we were going to attack her girls if we got close. We took her bed and carefully put it outside her cabin, right in the middle of the path."

"She never woke up?"

"She stirred, but never awoke." His grin widened. "It wasn't our fault that it started to rain later, really hard."

"What happened to you?"

"Nothing. They never found out who did it." He laughed. "The next morning she created a storm of her own, but she couldn't prove who did it. After breakfast the director chewed out everybody, but we could tell his heart wasn't in it. That woman was a pain and he knew it."

Shana glanced out the window. "You think it will stop soon?"

"Probably. I haven't heard about anybody building an ark. If somebody was, Action News would have alerted us." He stood.

"Let's get some pots and heat some water. I don't want to wash in cold."

Soon large pots of water were nestled at the edge of the hearth up against the hot embers. The only light in the room was that of the fire.

Under other circumstances this would be romantic, she thought as she wrapped her arms around her knees. *What if I hadn't said what I said after he kissed me? She* touched her lips lightly. *What if I had accepted what was developing between us? What if I had admitted the way I felt about him almost from the start?* She frowned. *What if I admit that I still feel that way?*

She thought about Elliot. For the first time no feelings rose inside her at the thought. Not hurt, not anger— nothing. She relaxed and smiled. He was gone for good.

She glanced at Kyle. He was staring into the fire as if watching a television show. She did the same, feeling a connection and, for the first time, not fighting it. The rain pattering on the roof provided the only audio.

"I'm hungry." Kyle stood and reached a hand to Shana. She hesitated, then took it.

"I wonder what's for dinner." she said.

"I think I know, but I don't want to spoil the surprise."

They laughed as they went to the table. Shana dug the forks from the bag of trash. She looked at them, shrugged and handed one to Kyle. "The plates are a lost cause." She pulled out the squashed plastic plates.

"We could divide the containers down the middle of the food and each eat from our own side." He stared at her. "Of course, after the kiss we shared, that would be silly wouldn't it?"

"Yes." Her answer was soft, but enough to redden her face.

She busied herself unpacking the bag of leftovers. She nodded and smiled. "We have as much salad left as we ate."

Neither had opened the bags of chips before, so they had those, too. Soon they were eating.

"I am grateful that Miss Corrine makes overstuffed sandwiches," Kyle said as he finished his. He opened a bag of chips. "Country air gives you an appetite. That, plus the fact that it's dinnertime."

"How long do you think we'll have to wait before we can leave?"

"No way to tell without checking."

"I wish we had a radio."

"You probably wish we had a boat so you wouldn't be stuck with me."

"No, I don't." Her words held no strength, only softness.

"You probably will after I tell you that we have only one blanket and that I'm not chivalrous enough to let you have it by yourself. Despite the fire, it's gonna get cold in here tonight. When we bring kids up here, we have them bring heavy jackets and that's in July and August. Sometimes they don't need them, but usually they do."

"Yeah. I know. It gets colder in the country and colder still in the mountains." She was still dealing with the one-blanket fact. As if on cue, a chill seemed to seep in from the outside. Kyle took another log from the firebox and placed it on the fire. Then he stared at her and shrugged.

"Nothing to it but to do it." He got the plastic bag. "Hold this." He handed her the blanket.

"What are you doing?" She watched Kyle use a plastic knife to slit the bag.

"It might provide some barrier to the cold that will seep from beneath the floor." He held up the piece of plastic. Shana couldn't ignore how small it was. *We have to share that?*

Kyle spread it a little way from the fire. "I guess we should put this under our shoulders. Maybe we can make pillows from the clothes in our overnight bags?"

"Good idea." Shana stood. She rubbed her arms against the chill then got her bag and one of the pots of hot water. She went to one of the bathrooms on the other side of the kitchen. *At least they put in indoor plumbing,* she thought.

"You have to share a bed with him," she told her image in the mirror over the sinks. She shook her head. *Not a bed. A piece of plastic and a blanket. A small piece of plastic and one blanket that's not even king-size.* She closed her eyes. *Please don't let it be only a twin.*

She changed her jeans, brushed her teeth and washed her face with her hands. Drying them on the sides of the pants she took off wouldn't make much difference. That worry was way down her list of concerns. She took a deep breath and went back to the room to face Kyle.

Kyle watched her leave the room. *How am I going to sleep with her when I know I can't "sleep" with her? How am I going to make my body behave when she'll be within holding distance? When all I'd have to do is draw her into my arms and make us both forget about the storm outside? We'd be so busy creating our own disturbance.* He shook his head and went to the boys' bathroom.

Could something pleasant be called a disturbance? He leaned against the sink. *Man, what am I going to do? How am I going to act casual when my mind will be imagining her in my arms, our lips touching, our mouths exploring each other? When I'll be thinking of touching her, awaking her body, learning what she likes, making her forget all about Elliot and what he did to her?*

Despite the discomfort caused by his tightening pants, he smiled. In spite of warning himself, he had let her get next to him and he wanted to get even closer. He wanted to get inside her and make love to her until she forgot all about her ex-husband. He exhaled sharply. Too bad she didn't want the same thing. He shook his head and pushed off from the sink. *It's going to be a long night.*

When he got back to the room, he saw Shana staring at the sheet of plastic.

"I didn't cut any off. I swear," Kyle said from behind her.

If he thought it would do any good, he'd wish for a piece of plastic large enough to cover the floor. He'd throw in a wish for another blanket, too. It was going to be an awfully long night. How could he sleep close to her and not reach for her? How was he going to keep his body under control? They stared at the plastic together.

"I guess the best way to do this is to have our feet closest to the fire. That way we get equal warmth and our hair isn't in danger from sparks."

Shana shook out the blanket. Then she shook it again.

"That won't make it grow. It's only moving the plastic around." He bent and straightened the plastic. "Which side do you want?" He stared at her.

"I—I don't care."

"I usually lie on my left side."

"Okay." She didn't want to picture him lying next to her on either side. As usual, her wants didn't make any difference to her mind.

Kyle put a couple more logs on the fire, then got on the plastic and slipped under the blanket. "You going to stand there all night?"

If it wasn't so cold I would. Shana sighed, then got under the blanket on the other side. She left as much space as she could to still tuck the blanket edge under her. It wasn't enough space to make a difference. *It's going to be an awfully long night,* she thought.

The rain slowed to a drop every now and then. The crackling of the fire added its sound as time barely moved. Shana felt as if the two of them were alone in a small world.

"Was it your husband?"

"Ex-husband," Shana corrected automatically. "What about him?"

"Was he the one who made you like this?"

"Like what?"

"Afraid to let yourself feel. Is it with everyone, or just men? Or maybe it's just me?"

Shana debated whether or not to answer. What business was it of his? Then she thought of how she had been sending mixed messages. He deserved to know the truth.

"I caught Elliot in our bed with his graduate assistant. I later found out she wasn't the first." She was surprised that for the first time the memory didn't hurt.

She told him about how she had met Elliot. She skimmed through their marriage and stopped with the news media opening up the situation to anyone who wanted to know about it.

"I saw the news. Do you still love him?"

"Of course not. How could I?" She sighed. "I'm not even sure I ever loved him."

"Love is not rational. I know. I've been there myself. Twice." Kyle told her about his failed marriage and then his engagement. "It makes you second-guess your own feelings and everybody else's motives. It's hard to trust somebody after being burned."

"I promised myself that I would not let him color the rest of my life." She shook her head. "It was a whole lot easier to promise that than do it." She shook her head again. "I thought I was okay." She glanced at him then back at the fire. "Then you came along and my insecurities flared up again." She thought of how Elliot had accused her of not being good enough in bed.

"We can't always make ourselves feel what we want to when we want to. If we could, broken hearts wouldn't exist."

"I guess."

I've put Elliot behind me. How much more time will it take before I can let somebody else get close? How long before I can move forward? I feel something for Kyle and I know he feels something for me. Why do I have this "frying pan into the fire" feeling? And, on the other hand, why do I feel as if I'm ignoring the knock of the best opportunity of my life?

Shana's face was cold. That was the only part exposed. The rest of her was huddled into a ball under the blanket on the hard bed. She frowned. Her back was warm, too warm. So was her middle.

Her eyes popped open. The bright embers, still the only light in the room, stared back at her. The rest of the cabin and the outside world were still full of predawn darkness. She shifted a little and an arm tightened around her waist.

She tried to ease away, but the arm drew her back. A chin brushed against the top of her head.

"Don't go," he mumbled as he brushed his fingers over her waist.

Kyle was generating enough fire to warm the rest of her, the entire room, even. The heat was selective, however. It only wanted to settle in certain parts of her. Parts that were hidden by her layers of clothes; but the heat found them anyway and was spreading itself to her less personal parts, too.

She closed her eyes. Kyle. She was nestled against Kyle. She stiffened, then relaxed. It felt good. It felt natural, as if she belonged here. *But I don't.* She opened her eyes again, eased away and stood.

Quickly she coaxed the fire a bit with the poker, then placed a small log on top. She leaned back on her heels and watched the flames lick at it before she placed a larger log to the back of the fire. Satisfied that it had caught, she turned. And stared right into Kyle's gaze.

"You'd make a competent pioneer woman. I'd say *wife,* but I don't want to scare you." He flicked her end of the blanket aside. "Come back to bed. It will be a while before the fire gets hot enough to warm us." He patted the place beside him. She stared at it. "You spent the night sleeping beside me, you should feel safe when we're wide awake."

His words should have been logical. They weren't,

but she was too cold to debate them. She scooted back under the blanket.

"Did you sleep well?"

"Yes."

"Were you warm enough?"

"Yes." Her voice was a mumble.

"Nothing like sharing body heat, is there?" She inched away from him. "Okay, okay. I promise to behave." His warm breath fanned against her neck. "It's gonna be the hardest promise I ever had to keep, but I think I can manage. At least I can if you settle down and quit brushing against me."

Shana stopped as if suddenly frozen. She did not want to think about the part of him that was pressing against her. It was like telling yourself not to think of a herd of elephants standing across from you in a small room. She eased onto her back and stared at the ceiling as if Michelangelo had chosen it for his second such work.

"Do you think the water has gone down?"

"Yeah."

"Enough for us to get out?"

"Probably so." He laughed.

"What?" She resisted the urge to face him.

"I was thinking of how you refused to go get a cup of coffee with me and now we're sleeping together. Let's hear it for the passing of time."

"We did not sleep together."

"I was sleeping like one of those logs. I was even having a very interesting dream until you moved. Strike that. Until you woke up. We slept together, all right." His voice lowered. "I woke up with you in my arms. I would say that would never have happened if you weren't asleep, but look at us now."

Shana moved the blanket, intending to get up, but the cold drove her back. Besides, he was right. "You know what I mean."

"Yeah, I know what you mean. If we had *slept together,* we wouldn't have gotten much sleep."

"I don't want to talk about it."

"We agree on that. My relationships to date might not show it, but I was never a masochist." He lifted her hand from between them and laced his fingers through hers. She stiffened, then relaxed. "What *do* you want to talk about?"

"Do you miss it?"

"What?"

"Basketball."

His hand tightened around hers for a second, then relaxed. "Playing basketball is like a bad habit. You can't keep it from your mind all the time."

"Maybe that's what a failed marriage is like—a bad habit."

"The marriage failed, but I don't feel as though I failed. I did what I was supposed to."

"I know what you mean. I did, too. Elliot didn't do what he was supposed to do." She sighed. "I swore I wouldn't let him occupy any more of my time, and here he is."

"Relegate him to the trash heap."

Shana laughed.

"What?"

"I did that the day I caught him." She told Kyle about that day.

"I'm scared of you. I didn't think to do anything like that. I was very civilized. I had her get her things." He turned to face Shana. "Did it feel good?"

"Oh, yeah. When Martie and I put the bedding on top of the pile, I felt as if I had been thoroughly cleansed." She smiled. "I know what they mean when they talk about wiping the slate clean."

"Then why drag him back every time somebody gets close?"

"Nobody got close, not until you." She hesitated. "You frighten me."

"I do?"

"No. That's not true. It's the way you make me feel that frightens me."

"I have to admit, you frightened me, too."

"I did?"

"I felt a strong pull from the time we were introduced and I was not ready. My engagement had been over for months, but I wasn't over it."

"Do you still love her?"

"As much as you still love Elliot."

Shana laughed. "That much, huh?"

"One failed marriage, one broken engagement—I was oh-for-two. My faith in my ability was really shaken." Kyle eased her back against him and she didn't resist.

It's truth time and about time, too, she thought as she drifted back to sleep.

Dawn slowly turned to strong daylight as the two slept into a new level of their relationship.

"You did it again," Kyle said much later as he set a log on the fire. He turned to look at Shana, who was staring at him. "Slept with me again, I mean." He stood and brushed off his hands. "After that, I can't even give you the opportunity to refuse to have coffee with me. It doesn't seem right."

"Ah, but I can give you the chance to refuse a cup of tea." Shana stood and stretched.

"Tea?"

"From my stash." She got her purse.

"You've got a tea stash?"

"I always have tea bags when I'm on the road. Motels have coffee, but they don't always think of tea drinkers." She placed a small plastic bag from her purse on the table and got her overnight bag. "I've got sweetener, too. After I make myself look decent, we can share some caffeine." She smiled and went into the bathroom.

"I think you look pretty decent right now," he mumbled after she was too far away to hear. "I hope this is going where I want it to go." He stared at the blanket, then went to the boys' bathroom.

When he came back, he got some cups and washed them. Then he waited for Shana.

As they drank the tea, they talked about camp, school

and basketball. They didn't talk about their growing re-lationship; but both knew it was there. A little later, they restored order to the room, gathered their things and left.

Kyle slowed when they got to the bridge. He thought of what had happened between them after they had turned back yesterday. *How do you thank a body of water?*

The only evidence that the creek had overflowed was the thick layer of mud on the bridge and the gaps in the gravel on the road.

"I wonder how long before it's back to the way it should be." Shana stared at the swollen creek. The water had to be skimming the underside of the bridge.

"It accomplished its mission. Now it can go back to normal."

"What mission?"

"It got us off dead center, didn't it?" He smiled at her as he eased across. "How can I show my gratitude to a creek?"

Shana smiled back. "Let me know if you find out." She stared at him. "I want to do the same."

He stopped on the other side of the bridge. "It sounds as if you're ready to move on."

"It feels like it, too." She met his gaze. "I feel as if a huge weight has lifted from me, as if the past is just that—past." She took a deep breath. "I like the feeling of a new slate."

"I think it's good that we're going home. If we had had this conversation last night, I'm afraid taking things slow would have been the last thing on my mind." He smiled at her. Then he put the car in gear and continued down the road.

They stopped by the motel on their way, prepared to pay for the reservations they had made, but were told that since the storm had knocked out the power and the motel had had to close, there was no charge.

Soon they were on their way back home. Each was grateful that they weren't back to the way they had been. Both were looking forward to the future.

Chapter 18

The mood when Kyle and Shana reached her house was the complete opposite from when they had left. Something had started forming between them. It was as if their world had been off-kilter and had finally gotten back on track. Neither could find a thread of conversation to take them home. Each was lost in thought.

Kyle parked and took Shana's bag from the trunk. He followed her up the steps.

Is she going to regret our last conversation? Is she going to take a step back and undo what seems to be happening? Could she possibly be as interested in moving our relationship forward as I am? Is she even interested in having a relationship with me? He frowned. *This seems like junior high all over again.* He took a deep breath and set her bag down. *Only one way to find out how she feels now.*

"Have dinner with me tomorrow," Kyle blurted. He stared at her, a frown creasing his forehead. "I…" He frowned. "Man, this is gonna sound weird, like something out of the sixties. You know, vibes and stuff." He shook his head. "I don't know if you're sorry for what you said after we crossed the bridge. I don't know if you regret saying it, if you've changed your mind. You were quiet on the ride home, we both were. What I do know is that I don't think this is all that's meant to be between us." He touched her arm lightly. "Please. Take a chance on us. Give us a chance."

Shana stared at him. She felt as if her options were having a wrestling match and she didn't know which one to root for. *Don't go backward,* she urged herself. *If you back away, you'll regret it for the rest of your life. Listen to your heart.*

"Okay." Her voice was weak, but he heard it.

"Okay? You said okay? Really?"

"Why not?" She shrugged again. "We already slept together." She laughed. "Want to come in and I'll see what I can find for lunch? Or is it an early dinner?"

"Doesn't matter."

"Not at all."

Kyle picked up her bag and was close behind her when she went inside. It was as if he was afraid she would change her mind and close the door on him.

"Come on out to the kitchen. Leftover chicken okay? Not from last night, of course."

"It's not from last night? Oh. That's right." He smiled. "You spent last night with me, didn't you?"

"Funny."

"But true."

"Would you rather have something else?"

"Leftovers are fine."

I'd rather have something else, but I don't dare tell you what. I'd scare you off before we even get started. I don't dare tell you that what I want is you. You in my arms. Me inside you, you wrapped around me, holding me inside you. Me making you forget everything bad that happened in your past. The two of us in a world of our own. He sat at the table.

This feels right. I could get used to this. Shana fixing a meal in our house... Yeah. This definitely feels right. His mind moved to this morning, back to when it had still been dark outside.

She had felt so right in my arms. Soft in the right places, pressed against me, against my hardness. He shook his head slightly as his body responded to his re-membering. *Stop. Get yourself under control and hope you don't have to stand up for anything before you are back to normal. You don't want to scare her off. Not now. Not when you're finally off dead center.*

He shifted, grateful that the table was hiding what his imagination had caused to his body. He leaned back and watched her, enjoying her smooth movements in the kitchen, once again imagining how different movements could be used between them. Her slacks molded to her hips as she bent over to take something from the refrigerator and his imagination took off again. *Is she thinking about the same thing that I'm thinking about?*

Something wonderful is happening, Shana thought. She closed the refrigerator, but opened it right away to take out the bag of salad she had meant to take out before. Her memory went back to work.

She remembered being pressed against him this morning when she'd gone back to bed because it had still been dark. She grinned. Now she was grateful for the darkness. It had sent her back to him.

A piece of plastic and a blanket, that was all their bed had been. Her grin faded. It had felt so right being in Kyle's arms, as if she belonged there. She closed her eyes and the memory sharpened. *I am finally ready to move on.*

"Is something wrong? Do you need help with that?"

"No, thank you." Shana looked at the knife resting against the chicken on the platter. How long had she been frozen in place? She sighed as she placed the pieces of chicken on a plate and put it into the microwave. Then she smiled.

As they ate, they talked about nothing, about everything—everything except how they felt about being together. That seemed to be a given.

"Coffee in the living room?" Shana stood after they had eaten.

"You have coffee?"

"Tea drinkers always take care of coffee drinkers. It's the coffee drinkers who ignore us."

"No one would ignore you. At least I wouldn't." *I know how I would take care of you. First I'd kiss...*

He forced the rest of the sentence to stay back. Instead, he fixed her with a stare, hoping she could guess what he was going to say, but also hoping she wouldn't be scared off.

"How am I supposed to respond to that?"

"Just take it as it is. Go with the flow. Ride with the tide. Play it as it lies. It ain't broke, so don't try to fix it." He grinned. "I can't think of any other appropriate clichés."

"Good." She smiled and shook her head.

Then she put the kettle on the burner. As she took out a package of chocolate-chip cookies, she decided to take his advice: go with the flow and see what happens.

Kyle still grinned as he carried the tray holding the coffee that he didn't want. It would probably keep him up all night, but it was worth taking that chance. He wasn't ready to leave her just yet; he was enjoying the magic spell too much.

They talked, but the conversation didn't matter; the company was what was important.

"Oh, man." Kyle glanced at his watch later and stood. "I'm sure I overstayed my welcome. It's midnight."

"I didn't realize it." Shana stood, too.

"That's 'cause time goes fast when you're not looking."

"Too true. It's okay. I don't have anyplace to go tomorrow until dinnertime." She grinned at him.

He went to the door and turned to face her.

"I'm going to miss holding you tonight. Only one night with you and I feel as if we belong together." He took a step to her. "Tell me you feel the same way."

"I do. I…" She smiled. "I do."

Kyle's head lowered to hers, slowly, so she could stop him if she wanted to. This felt like that other time. She hesitated, then closed the rest of the gap between them just as she had before. *No,* she thought as she closed her eyes. *This is better. This time I'm sure that I want this.*

Their bodies touched from knees to chest. The warmth created by the contact rivaled the fire of last evening when it had been at its best. Kyle's hands were on her upper arm, gently so she could leave him if she wanted to. Her hands rested on his chest, as softly as a butterfly lighting on a blossom. She wasn't going anywhere.

His lips touched hers once as if testing. He eased his head up enough so his gaze found its mate in hers. His head dipped and again his mouth met hers. The kiss moved from soft to firm, but quickly got to "this is what was meant to be" level.

Shana pressed insistently against Kyle. His stance widened and she moved into the space he made for her. She pressed against him and he insistently pressed back. His arms went around her, meeting at her back, holding her even closer. His hands stroked her body below the waist, stoking the fires.

Shana moved her hands up around his neck. She felt his hard chest against her sensitive breasts. He shifted his chest against her and her tips hardened to agonizing life. His hand moved up to the side of her breast, brushing a fire to life there as well. His fingers found her fullness and slowly stroked up, stopping short of the tip, which was now in full bloom. Shana gasped as heat flew to the sensitive spot between her legs, but the sound never reached the air. Kyle swallowed it as he tasted her sweetness yet again and continued to brush magic with his hands.

What was I afraid of? The question flitted through Shana's mind, but even that thought was erased by Kyle's kisses.

Slowly, agonizingly slowly, he kissed beneath her ear, along her jaw, the side of her neck. She leaned her head back and he took her invitation and kissed her throat, starting another fire and making her pulse leap.

If Shana had had the strength, she would have opened her eyes and looked for the smoke coming from her, the proof of the fire smoldering within her. Instead she kept her eyes closed and enjoyed what Kyle was doing to her, for her.

Her hands tightened against his back as if there were any more space left to fill. She opened and closed her fingers against his back, trying to find relief, but knowing she wouldn't find it there. Only he could give that to her.

Kyle found her mouth and claimed it all over again. Then he slowly leaned away.

"I'd better go before our running joke about sleeping together becomes reality, but the truth is, I don't think there'd be much sleeping going on." He brushed his thumb across her swollen lips. "I can't tell you how much I want you, but I'm afraid we got here too fast for you—zero-to-ninety in ten seconds flat. When we make love, I want you to be sure it's right for you. I don't want you to have regrets afterward." He stared at her, then touched the side of her face. "You are so totally beautiful, so desirable, so tempting. I already proved how kissable you are." Slowly he eased away from her and smiled. "See you tomorrow night."

Shana could only nod. Of course he was right. This was too soon. She frowned. *But why does it feel as if it's overdue?*

Kyle placed one last, quick kiss on her mouth, then touched his fingers to her lips.

"Tomorrow," he rumbled. Then he left.

She was still standing in front of the open door when his car pulled away.

"Wow," she said as she finally closed the door. "Wow." Despite shaking legs, she managed to take the tray into the kitchen and set it on the counter. She touched her still-sensitive lips and smiled. "Double wow." Smile still on her face, she went upstairs.

Before she got into bed, she stared at it. It was softer, bigger, prettier than where she'd slept last night. The room was comfortably warm and no fireplace was needed. She sighed as she slipped between the covers.

It was also lonelier. She pulled the covers up around her neck and frowned. *How can I miss him after one night?*

She shifted, trying to get comfortable. She'd never had trouble falling asleep before. Now it was as if she were trying to find Kyle to sleep against. She smiled.

I think, after tomorrow night, when we talk about sleeping together, we'll mean it in every sense of the word.

Chapter 19

When Shana awoke, her back was a few inches from the far edge of the bed. It was as if, in her sleep, she had tried to find Kyle. She smiled and stretched. *One night and I'm looking for him in my sleep.* She shifted her position. *Tomorrow morning at this time maybe I'll have better luck. I'll wake up with Kyle's arm around my middle like at the camp. I won't scoot away from him, tomorrow, though. I'll turn toward him. It will be morning, but I won't be in any hurry to leave him. I'll caress the side on his face.* Her grin widened. *Will he have stubble? I'll find out.* She closed her eyes. *He'll touch my lips, first with his finger, then with his mouth. Then his hands will repeat the wonderful things in the morning that they did the night before. I'll explore his body, too. I'll find out where his sensitive spots are, besides the obvious ones. We'll...*

The phone rang. Smile still in place, Shana picked it up.

"So what are you doing this fine morning?" Kyle's low voice rumbled over her.

"Waking up." She propped a pillow behind her back. Now she knew what he sounded like in the morning.

"Still in bed?"

"Sure. It's only..." she glanced at the clock "...ten o'clock? Is that right? Is it that late?"

"I'm hurt."

"Why?" She leaned closer to the clock as if that would make it be earlier.

"I was calling to see how well you slept without me. I guess the answer is fine."

"Aww. So sorry to hurt your feelings. I did miss the..." she hesitated on purpose "...piece of plastic." What she really missed was a lot harder than a flimsy tatter of plastic, but she wouldn't tell him. At least not right now. She moved to the middle of the bed. "How long have you been up? Or are you still in bed? You can tell me anything since I can't see you."

"I guess that's my fault, but that's for another discussion. To continue my quest for sympathy, despite the lateness of the hour when I got to bed, I had trouble falling asleep. Something was missing. My arms were cold from being empty."

Shana shifted as she remembered the feel of his arms

around her. She let the memory stay as she continued. "They have pillows made just for that. They're called body pillows, I think."

"Are you saying that you can be replaced by a pillow? Where can I find a pillow that feels like you against my body? One warm that fits perfectly in my arms? One that smells like tropical sunshine and fresh rain? One that I can kiss awake?"

"You never kissed me awake."

"Not yet, but be patient. Besides, that's *your* fault. You're the one who rushed out of bed. If you had stayed, we could have discovered pleasures a pillow could never provide."

"I am definitely changing the subject for the good of both of us. It's much too early in the year to turn the air conditioner on. What are you doing?"

"You mean besides missing you?"

Shana released an exaggerated sigh. "Don't go back there. Yes, that's what I mean."

"I already worked out. Then I had a bowl of cereal, an orange and a cup of coffee."

"You already had breakfast."

"Yes. And with every bite, with every sip, I thought about you. Every other bite and every other sip, I looked at my watch to see if it was late enough to call you."

"You waited so long because you figured I'd sleep late."

"I got desperate when time wouldn't move forward fast enough, so I went for a run. I just got out of the shower."

"Oh. Just now?"

"Umm-hmm. I still have the towel wrapped around me."

The image of Kyle with a towel draped around his body planted itself in her mind and brought company. The image of Kyle's chest glistening with a few drops of water. Water sliding down to his waist, slipping beneath the towel, finding...

His voice nudged her again. It went lower still and a sexy rumble eased out. "If you were with me, we'd probably still be in the shower. I have one of those showerheads that simulate the gentle rain in a tropical forest. Of course, if I was doing a proper job, you would forget all about the showerhead, the water, about everything except me and you and what we were doing to each other."

"Oh." She could only find that one word and it had trouble crawling out.

Shana flung the blanket aside. Heat settled in the part of her that was covered by her nightgown. Her breasts peaked and ached as if waiting for Kyle to stroke across them. As if she and he were taking each other higher. Then Kyle would...

"Are you a shower or a bath person?"

"What?"

"Did you drift off to sleep just now?"

"You're kidding, of course."

"Way serious."

"Of course I didn't." Shana took a deep breath. *Sleep is not at the top of my to-do list right now. Not when you're talking that talk.* She frowned. *That seems so calculating. Her face relaxed. But it's honest. I'm being honest about the way I feel about him, about what I want from him.*

"Well? What I asked isn't a hard question. It ranks right up there with 'paper or plastic?' and 'Do you want fries with that?'" He waited for her to answer.

First she had to struggle to go back to the question. That was no easy thing considering how far her mind had traveled from it. *I can do this.*

"Okay. Bath or shower. It depends. If I'm in a hurry, it's a shower. If I want to relax, it's a bath."

"Candles or not? If so, big or little? Scented or not? What's your favorite bubble-bath scent? How about music? Do you listen to music as you bathe? If so, what kind?"

"Are you taking a survey or something?"

"Or something. I don't have you within reach, so I'm trying to build something my imagination can use."

"Okay. I love jasmine and tropical scents, wild ginger, plumeria, anything Hawaiian. As for candles, I have all sizes around my tub and on my vanity. The scents can be anything that won't clash with the bubble bath. For music, I pull out my old, old real albums and turn the volume up so the sound can wash over me. Nina Simone, Etta James, Nancy Wilson, any of the sultry old, old-school singers."

"That's a waste."

"What is?"

"Playing that romantic music when you're alone. It's meant to be shared."

"Is that right?"

"Absolutely. I hope I can prove that to you soon—very, very soon."

Shana closed her eyes and tried to imagine them together. She didn't have a bit of trouble. "Maybe you'll get what you hope for."

"Have lunch with me."

"Yesterday you asked me to dinner."

"I'm moving the timetable up."

"You have something planned for this evening?"

"If I'm lucky."

"Oh." She took a deep breath. "Okay." Again images of them together appeared as if impatient to be seen.

"I'll be there in forty-five minutes. I would ask if you like cheesesteaks, but that's a given. They wouldn't allow you to live in Philly if you didn't."

"You have a place in mind?"

"Sure. Yours. I'm bringing lunch with me."

After Kyle hung up, Shana sat for a while.

I'm ready for this, she thought later as she stepped into the shower. She smiled as she picked up the plumeria-scented bath gel. She worked hard not to imagine it was Kyle's hands rather than the washcloth soaping her body. It didn't work one bit.

She looked at then discarded everything in her closet. Then she went back and took out a two-piece dress. The wild splash of colors matched her turmoil.

She looked through her underwear drawer carefully before choosing matching bits of lace and putting them on. Then she looked in the mirror. Bra, panties and a half slip—and still her skin peeked through. She sat on the edge of the bed and closed her eyes.

I have never done this in my life. I have never before planned a seduction. She smiled. *Is it a seduction when both parties know what's gonna happen?* She took a deep breath and stood.

As she changed the linens on her bed, she grinned. *If things work out the way I think they will, this bed is only gonna get messed up again.* She stared at it for a second. *Next time I'll have company, though.* She grinned as she flicked the covers back into place.

By the time the doorbell rang, she had gone through the house fluffing pillows, putting away the dishes from the drainer, straightening things that didn't need it, as if any of that mattered to what was going to happen.

Kyle kissed her when she opened the door. The kiss was soft and short, over almost as soon as it started; but it was full of promises.

The cheesesteaks were probably tasty, but neither Shana nor Kyle could swear to it. Finally, with more than a half sandwich left on each plate, their gazes met. As if following some silent signal, they stood.

"I'm ready for dessert." Kyle's gaze burned into hers. "I hope you are, too."

"What—what do you have in mind?"

"Something that I hope will be mutually satisfying."

He left his side of the table and stood in front of her. Only his gaze touched her, but she felt as if his hands were on her. Already.

"Yeah?"

"Um-hmm."

His heat reached her before his hands even touched her, even before he brushed slowly along her arms from the shoulders to the wrists, disturbing the tiny hairs along her arms. Then they moved back up again and reached under her sleeves.

His touch moved as if lack of speed were necessary to make sure he reached her, as if his fire hadn't already started a smoldering deep within her. "Something low carb," he rumbled. Then he kissed the side of her face. "And low fat," he added just before his mouth found her forehead. Her hands found the front of his shirt. "Even low protein." He kissed the other side of her face. Then he trailed a finger down her cheek and to the top of her blouse. "In fact, what I have in mind will burn calories in the most mutually desirable way." His mouth finally found hers and pressed a kiss there.

Shana's hands slid up to his neck. Her fingers played with the hair waiting for her fingers.

Kyle drew her closer. He widened his stance and pulled her between his thighs so she rested against him, his hard fullness against her softness. He teased her lower lip and she opened her mouth to allow him in. He tasted the hint of cheese on her tongue mixed with her sweetness.

His hands slipped open first one button of her blouse,

then another. His hand pushed the blouse aside and found her breast. There he stroked along the side near the center, then back again. All the while his mouth was fastened to hers. Shana pressed harder against him, wanting even more.

His hand left her breast and trailed to her waist. Before Shana could protest, he eased her even closer. Then his magical hands inched to her bottom and brushed tiny circles over the fullness there.

Shana moaned and shifted against him as desire shot through her before settling in her softness. She rubbed against him slightly, seeking release. She shifted her weight from one foot to the other, lightly marking a short trail against his groin.

Kyle moaned as his hardness pressed even more insistently against her softness searching for a way through the clothes, trying to reach her. He rubbed his hands along her bottom and pressed her more thoroughly against him as if she weren't already aware of how persistently he was pressing to get inside her.

"I want you," he said as if words were needed to state what was so obvious. "You are torturing me. I hope you'll put me out of my misery and soon." He captured her mouth before she could answer.

Her hands came to animated life, stroking down his back, along his waist, brushing along his bottom, answering better than words could.

"I want you, too," she managed to whisper. "Come with me."

"Anywhere you lead."

Shana took his hand. He held hers, but his thumb stroked over the back of it. Her desire soared, but she managed to find the way to her bedroom without getting lost.

Once there, he eased her back against him, her back against his chest. His hands found her breasts again and slowly stroked along the sides, then underneath, then across the top, creating a large circle of fire. He never touched the tips, although, tight and swollen, they waited, ached for him.

If Shana had opened her eyes, even through her clothes, she could have seen how her breasts were ready for his touch. Instead she felt them swell even more and press against her blouse as if wanting to get free of the clothes covering them, as if they were trying to reach Kyle. But she didn't need to look at her body. She could feel her need radiating through her, growing, begging for relief.

She was torn: should she press back against him, trying to make more of him touch her? Or should she push against his hands to make him soothe her aching, hard tips?

Kyle's mouth was busy at the side of her neck, tasting the spot where her nerve endings met, making her pulse jump. She tilted her head to allow him more access.

His hands cupped her breasts as his mouth tasted the little soft spot beneath her ear. His teeth gently tugged on her earlobe, showing her another sensitive spot, sending messages to every part of her body, but the strongest message found the nub hidden beneath her soft mound and throbbed there. She moaned and brushed restlessly against him.

Finally, moving at an agonizingly slow speed, Kyle's hands traveled up her front until his thumbs brushed lightly against the tips, hardening them even more. Her legs, already weak from what he was doing to her, threatened to let her fall. She leaned completely against him, giving him all of her weight. And he took it.

She arched her back, trying desperately to make him touch her breasts harder, yet wanting him to find the waiting moistness in her lower body, to do whatever was needed to give her relief from this ache burning her, threatening to consume her until she was nothing except a pile of ashes.

Kyle turned her in his arms until she faced him, but she was still within his shelter, still touching him. Their gazes met and they got lost in the promises they showed each other.

Kyle's fingers found the buttons on her blouse and opened the first one. He marked the new exposure with a kiss. Slowly he made his way down her chest until he could push the blouse down her arms and out of the way. Both were glad there weren't more buttons.

At the same time, Shana's fingers busied themselves with Kyle's shirt. She had to keep forcing her mind back to what she was doing because Kyle was distracting her with what he was doing, yet she managed to open every button, though none of them on the first try. Her hands stroked across his bare chest and back to the center. She slid a finger down a centerline to his waist, and followed it to his side, dipping below his belt. He moaned and pressed a kiss on her forehead. His hands slid her skirt and half slip down her body. Then it was her turn.

She shoved his shirt down his arms and to the floor. She brushed her hands across his belt buckle, but didn't open it. She smiled as he moaned when her hands skimmed below his waist. Then she moved her hands back up and opened the buckle. She paused, then slid his zipper down and pushed his jeans off.

His mouth found hers again and they wrapped now bare arms around each other.

Kyle eased from her mouth and allowed a little space between them. He smiled down at her. If he hadn't already had her, her smile would have done it.

"Beautiful. Sweet chocolate peeking through cream lace." His husky words rumbled over her as he gazed at her in her bra and panties.

He tweaked a hard tip through the lace cup and Shana gasped. He lowered his mouth and flicked his tongue across it, but the heat jumped to her lower body. Then he lifted his mouth away and blew lightly across the still encased, now moist, tip. Shana rewarded him with a moan. He lifted his head and his gaze found hers.

"Too much lace, though. Way too much." His hands found the clasp at her back and opened it. The lace dropped to the floor and her heavy, sensitive, aching breasts sprang loose. "Better, much better." He flicked his tongue across the tip and smiled at her new moan. His hands went to her waist. "Still too much lace. I think we should get rid of this, too. Don't you agree?"

"Uh…"

She frowned. Neither her brain nor her mouth was working right. What she was feeling was blocking all words.

"I'll take that as a yes." Kyle inched the bit of lace passing for panties from her body.

Shana eased against him, her fullness finally free to feel him against her bare skin.

"Not fair." She managed to get out. She brushed up his thighs. Her hands barely touched the side of his maleness, but it was enough to make him groan and clutch her. She smiled and pushed his shorts down his legs. His hardness sprang free and poked insistently against her before finding the place where it belonged.

Kyle picked her up and placed her on the bed. Then he lay beside her. His mouth found hers again. He kissed his way to her throat, to the hollow between her breasts, all the while his hands were busy with the lower part of her body.

Finally his mouth found her breasts again and kissed and tugged on each. His hand found her mound and stroked the curls. Then his finger dipped inside her, came out and found the hidden nub. Shana writhed.

"Please," she whispered.

"Yes, baby, yes."

"No," she protested when he left her instead of satisfying her.

"Only for a second, baby," he promised. He returned and quickly opened the foil pack. He rolled it on then straddled her.

His mouth found hers yet again. The first kiss was gentle, but the next held promise of what pleasure was to come.

He poised above her, then slowly lowered himself to her. His hardness pushed against her, seeking entry. Then he eased inside her until she held all of his fullness.

She closed around him and together they sought relief.

Chapter 20

Eyes still closed, Shana smiled. She shifted, an arm tightened around her middle, and her smile widened.

Not déjà vu all over again, she thought. *Much better. This is so much better than the first time I awoke with him.*

She and Kyle had shared love twice during the night. *I could get used to this dessert,* she thought. She adjusted her back against Kyle's chest.

"Woman, are you always so fidgety in the morning?" Kyle pressed his lips to the side of her face.

"Are you always so cranky in the morning?" She tilted her head to allow him access to her neck.

"Only when a beautiful woman tries to move from against me." His leg covered hers.

"I wasn't moving away from you." She elbowed him slightly. "I appreciate being called a beautiful woman, but any beautiful woman will do, huh?" She poked him again.

"Uh-uh. There is only one gorgeous woman in the world." His hand made slow circles on her bare midriff. "That's many steps up from beautiful." He placed a kiss on her neck. "And I'm lucky that she has chosen to be with me." His circles, still slow, grew wider and longer. "Right now."

"The luck is mutual." Shana traced patterns of her own along Kyle's thigh. She felt his muscles bunch beneath her hand. She warmed as a different part of his body pressed against her from behind.

Kyle's hand smoothed up from her waist and cradled her full breast. He thumbed across the tip, startling it awake. Shana found that the heat from last night hadn't disappeared; it had been waiting for Kyle to coax it back.

He teased and stroked first one, then the other, as if trying to decide which he liked best.

Shana reached behind her and found his hardness. She gently stroked down its length, but her touch was firm enough to encourage it to swell. She stopped only long enough to turn in Kyle's arms.

He groaned as she found the reason for her pleasure. She touched his sensitive tip and his groan deepened in his chest and she felt that, too.

"Baby, if you keep that up I'll be the only one to get satisfaction from this." He eased her hand from him. "And I want us to come together again."

He put enough space between them so he could grab a foil pack from the nightstand where he had thrown the extras the first time he'd prepared to love her during the night. She took it from him and fumbled it open.

"Allow me," she whispered as she quickly rolled it into place.

"I'd say…" Kyle took a deep breath. "I'd say my pleasure, but I know from fantastic experience that the pleasure is yet to come." He lifted her until she was on top of him, until she was lying between his thighs, pressing her mound to his shaft. "Soon, please."

His covered hardness prodded her impatiently, seeking entrance to where he had been welcomed much too long ago. He smiled as she moaned when his hand found her moist and waiting for him. He guided himself into her, making himself go slowly when what he wanted more than anything right now was to push home.

Her arms tightened around him as her body closed around him. He rolled her onto her side. Then they began another journey that was the same yet gloriously different. The only sameness was that they would end up soaring together again. And they did.

Slowly Shana opened her eyes. The clock said twelve-thirty, but she smiled. She moved and Kyle's arm tightened around her. Her smile widened.

Like before again, but again so different. She felt her

face warm as she thought of what they had shared. Again. She inched away from him. His arm tightened once more, then relaxed. She slipped from beneath his arm and out of bed.

She looked down at him and resisted the urge to place a light kiss on his forehead. *I don't want to waken him, even though he did with me twice during the night. I was already wide awake this morning when we came together. Again. Wow.*

She stared at his strong face, relaxed in sleep, for a few seconds longer, then she got out clean underwear and quietly left the room.

Her shower over and wearing the red terry robe she kept on the bathroom door, she paused outside the bedroom. If she didn't know better, she would have thought the room was empty.

She continued to the kitchen, trying to remember what she had on hand for breakfast. The grin returned. *Late lunch is more like it. I can't top the breakfast we already had.*

She pulled eggs and cheese from the refrigerator. She hesitated then took out a can of biscuits, opened them and put them into the oven.

"Beautiful scene," Kyle said a few minutes later as she set the dishes on the table. He smiled at her from the doorway. She smiled back. Her stomach grumbled as if trying to persuade her to take care of it first.

He walked to her and wrapped his arms around her. "Of course, any scene with you in it would be beautiful." He kissed the side of her face and rocked her gently. "I would complain about you leaving our nest, but I'm hungry—for food this time. Clothes? You put on clothes?" He slipped his hand inside her robe and stroked her breast. "That doesn't give me much hope for the afternoon."

"It's already afternoon." Shana swatted his hand and tightened the belt back. Kyle kissed her quickly, then took a step backward.

"Oh, but what a sweet way to spend a morning." He pinned her with a stare. "And a night, too." His stomach growled. "Sorry."

"Worked up an appetite, did we?"

"*We* is the correct choice of words, but *worked* is not. Nothing as pleasurable as what we shared could be called work."

"You're right. My mistake." Shana broke eggs into a bowl.

"We'll think of a way for you to make up for it later. What can I do to help?"

"If you like mushrooms, you can get a can from that cupboard over the microwave."

Kyle opened the can and drained it as Shana slipped the eggs into the pan. She sprinkled shredded cheese over them a short while later.

We work well together in the kitchen, she thought as she added the mushrooms. She smiled as Kyle took the biscuits from the oven and she slid the omelets onto plates. *Of course, we work well in the bedroom, too.*

Soon they were sitting across from each other, legs touching under the table. They gave almost as much attention to the food as they did to each other.

"Good breakfast. Good biscuits," Kyle said later as he laid his napkin beside his empty plate.

"The best money can buy. I don't ever make them from scratch. I figured, those companies spend a fortune perfecting a recipe. How could I hope to top them? So I don't try."

"That leaves you time for more important things."

"That's right."

Their thoughts on the same thing, they stood and walked arm in arm back to their love nest again.

"Don't you have to go to work?" Shana asked Friday night after they had cleared away the last of their dinner.

"Tired of me already, huh?" Kyle tried to frown at her, but the sparkle in his eyes gave him away.

"You know better." Shana kissed his chin.

"One perk about being the boss is I don't *have* to go to work at any particular time." He tucked her head under his chin. "The downside is that there are things I *have* to do. There are times I have to go places. I have a conference in Los Angeles starting on Monday so I have a flight Sunday evening. I'm on the committee and I have to be there early."

"Sunday?"

"I know I should have told you before, but I didn't

want to put a damper on what we have going." He brushed his hand down her arms. "I'll be gone until late Friday afternoon."

"Five days. We have to be apart five whole days."

"The conference ends after lunch on Friday. I was coming back early evening, but I'll change my reservations to the earliest flight I can get. It didn't matter before. Now I want to get back here before I even go." He kissed her. "See what you do to me?" He kissed her again. "I'd skip Friday's luncheon, but I'm the speaker. We fought hard to get one of us of the darker persuasion in visible positions. I don't want to mess up."

"I understand. I'll be back at school next week, anyway."

"Nice try and thank you, but we both know that school isn't 24/7. We could have given new meaning to the term *after-school program*."

"But we couldn't let the kids know." She laughed. "Too many of them engage in grown-up activities as it is."

They spent the rest of their time together loving, trying to learn all about each other, enjoying time together and falling asleep in each other's arms. Sometimes they remembered to eat.

After one lovemaking episode, Shana thought as she drifted off to sleep snuggled in Kyle's arms, *I've found the most pleasurable way to lose weight. Not only are you not deprived, you have the most exquisite pleasure imaginable.*

* * *

Kyle left as late as he could on Sunday. After he was gone from her house, Shana stared at the door until the sound of his car told her that he was really leaving. Then she went back into the house and tried not to notice how empty it was.

How did he get so far into my heart in such a short time? she wondered as she got ready to face reality the next morning.

Chapter 21

"Mrs. Garner?" Andy, a fourth-grader came to her room after school. "Here. This is for you." He pushed a small plastic bag at her as he stared at the floor.

"What's this?" Shana looked inside. Balled-up paper money and coins were jumbled together.

"I didn't believe it could really work. Honest. I heard Darryl and his homies talkin' 'bout it, but they're always talkin' stuff."

"*About.* And it's *talking.* Don't drop the *g* from the end of words," she corrected automatically. "Who is Darryl?"

"My big brother. He's in ninth grade. I heard them talking."

"What does that have to do with this money?"

"I know it's not enough, but I'll give you some more when I get my allowance on Friday. It cost you a lot of money to fix it, didn't it?"

"I think you'd better start at the beginning."

Andy took a deep breath. Then, still frowning, he explained.

"Darryl and his homies were talking about cars and how an ordinary house key can make a scratch on it." Andy finally looked at her. "I didn't believe it. A car costs a lot of money. How could a key scratch off the paint that easy?"

"You scratched my car?"

"I didn't mean to. Honest. I didn't think it would work. And I didn't pick it because it was your car." He shrugged. "It was..." He took a deep breath. "It was just there." His eyes got moist. "When I saw the metal after I did it, at first I thought it came off the key." His voice got lower and shaky. "My—my stomach felt funny when I touched the scratch. The key really took off the paint." He wiped his eyes with the back of his hand. "I ran home. I told Darryl and he talked to me. Then he told me I should come tell you. I didn't tell you before because I knew you would tell my mom and we were going to Disney World for vacation and I didn't want her to make me stay home with my aunt Yolanda." He wiped his face again. "Plus, I don't want my dad to lock me up. He's a cop."

"Your father won't put you in jail." Shana handed him a tissue from the box on her desk.

"But I broke the law and he's a policeman. He locks up bad people."

"Andy, he still won't put you in jail. Okay?"

Andy nodded slightly. "If you tell me how much more I owe you, Mrs. Garner, I promise I'll pay you all of it." He swallowed hard. "This morning Darryl said I still have to tell our parents." His sigh sounded grown-up size. "I'll—I'll tell them, but I wanted to tell you first." His eyes looked too large in his kid's face.

"You go talk to your parents, Andy. They'll handle this. I'm sure they'll punish you, but you won't go to jail."

"Aren't you mad?"

"Yes."

"Don't you want to kill me?"

"No. We don't kill people over things." Shana held back a smile. "Go talk to your parents. Let them handle this." She patted his shoulder. She smiled as she heard him run up the steps.

That solves a mystery, she thought. *I feel guilty for accusing Daisy even though she doesn't know I did.* Shana shook her head as she left school.

"Girl, where were you?" Martie was waiting on Shana's porch. "Where have you been?" she asked before Shana came up the steps. "I tried to reach you by phone from the time I got back from vacation late Sunday afternoon until it was too late for even a best friend to call. Then I started to call you this morning when I remembered that we weren't carpooling today

and that we couldn't have this conversation until now."
She put her hands on her hips. "If I *had* remembered that
last night, I would have burned up that redial button
then. Come on, sister girl. Where were you? More importantly, what were you doing? Did you decide to go
away after your visit to that camp? Where did you go?"
Martie stared at Shana as if expecting the answer to be
written on her face.

"I was busy." Shana tried to control it, but a slight
grin spilled over her face.

"Busy planning lessons, busy scheming how to get
out of the track-camp thing, or busy in ways I can only
imagine? Scratch that last as wishful hoping for you on
my part." She frowned at Shana. "Well?"

"What I was doing had nothing to do with camp."
Her grin widened. "Well, maybe it did in a round-
about way."

"Unlock your door so we can take this inside. I've got
a feeling this is gonna take a while. I also think, from the
look on your face, it's gonna be worth the time it takes."

Shana laughed as she opened the door.

"You don't have to wait until we get inside to start,
you know," Martie said as Shana put her key in the lock
in what seemed like slow motion.

"Patience, my friend." Shana opened the door,
stepped aside and waved Martie in.

"Okay. Give. I know this is juicy from the way you're
dragging it out."

"Want a cup of tea?"

"See what I mean?" Martie sighed. "If it will make you hurry up, yes, I'll have a cup of tea."

She followed Shana into the kitchen. She had the mugs on the table before Shana got the tea bags out.

"All right already. What's up?"

"Kyle and I went up to the camp. We were coming back, when we couldn't cross the bridge because it was flooded. We had to turn back and spend the night at the camp."

"You spent the night with Kyle?"

"It wasn't like that."

"Then what was it like?"

"We had to sleep on the floor." Shana filled the mugs.

"Nothing wrong with the floor."

Shana shook her head and laughed.

"Girl, you are something else. We slept on the floor. Emphasis on the *slept*. Then we came home."

"And? That doesn't explain why I couldn't reach you."

"We got to know each other better on the way home. He's not so bad." She took her tea bag from her cup.

"Not so bad. Uh-huh." Martie put sweetener in her cup and stirred. "What does that mean?"

"I decided it was time to move forward in my life."

"Thank goodness for common sense. Better late than never." Martie took a sip.

"Are you going to let me talk or not?"

"Talk on, girlfriend, talk on."

"Promise to listen calmly without interrupting."

"I promise." Martie made an X over her heart.

"We got together." She stared at a wide-eyed Martie and smiled.

"Do you mean what I think you mean?"

"Yes."

"You mean to tell me that you got together from just putting in time until the program was over to…" She frowned again. "Exactly what did you get to?"

Shana told her how she and Kyle had gotten to know each other on the ride up. Then she skimmed over the flooded bridge and having to spend the night at camp. She sketched in that they spent the time until late Sunday together, but she kept the details to herself. That was too private to share even with Martie, and Martie understood. Long ago they had made an agreement to keep details about relationships to themselves.

"You didn't," Martie said after she had finished.

"I didn't?"

"Wow. You did, didn't you?" Martie said when Shana had finished. "I guess you got to see that crooked smile." She laughed. "I guess you got to see a lot more than that." She ducked when Shana threw a balled-up napkin at her.

"He'll be away until Friday night. It's gonna be hard waiting until then to see him again."

"Yeah, but it sounds like he's worth it."

"Oh, yeah." Shana sighed. "He is so worth it that it scares me. You know, coming so soon after…"

"Don't say it. Don't let that other name part your lips."

"You're right. Tell me about your cruise. Meet anybody interesting?"

"Remind me to do more research before I book a cruise during spring vacation again. There were enough kids running around—" she stared at Shana "—and I do mean running around—for them to have school onboard." She shook her head. "And they should have. That would have kept the wild things under control." She sighed. "Some cruise line has got to have an adults-only cruise."

"I'm sorry." Shana patted Martie's hand. "If I had some sweet-potato pie, we could eat away your misery."

"You could probably afford the calories. I'll bet you were so active through yesterday evening that you burned yourself into a caloric deficit."

"Stop." Shana felt her face heat up. "I'm changing the subject. The mystery of the scratch on my car has been solved." Shana explained about Andy. "I'd apologize to Daisy if she knew I was blaming her."

"Don't worry about it. She probably would have done it if she had thought of it."

"Forget her. Back to the cruise. Did they have a decent band? Was the food good? How about the places where you stopped?"

Martie told Shana details about the cruise. When they were still talking at dinnertime, Shana pulled out two meals she had frozen. They talked some more after they ate.

"I'm going home before I wear out my welcome," Martie said about ten o'clock. "I'm sure you still have to catch up on your sleep." She stood. "Are you driving tomorrow or am I?"

"I'll drive." They walked to the door. "See you at the usual time."

After Martie left, Shana cleaned up the kitchen. *One down and three more long days to go,* she thought as she went upstairs.

The phone rang and she settled into bed and talked to Kyle. After talking for an hour, they both agreed that words were no substitute for touching each other. She fell into a fitful sleep hugging her pillow. It wasn't a substitute for flesh and blood, either.

Monday at track practice when Shana explained that Kyle was away, the track team was disappointed. They couldn't have been as disappointed as Shana was. They had been told at the beginning that Kyle would have to miss a meeting from time to time, but it was as if they hadn't believed it.

Monday night she got ready for bed. After Kyle's call, she tried not to notice how large the bed felt when she slipped between the covers. It was just as lonely as Sunday night had been. *Three even longer nights to manage,* she thought as she turned out the light.

Tuesday passed slower than kids going into a classroom to take a test. Kyle called again, but it wasn't the same as having him where she could touch him. And where he could touch her.

On Wednesday, she and the team boarded the bus for the field. As she sat alone in her seat, it seemed even wider than she had wished for at the beginning of the program.

* * *

Finally, Friday had mercy on her and showed up. Shana stopped at the store on the way home to get what she needed to cook dinner.

She smiled as she prepared the meat to marinate for the pot roast that Kyle had said was his favorite. She shook her head. She had figured him for a meat-and-potatoes guy, but she would have guessed steak.

The doorbell rang as she put the dish into the refrigerator to set.

"Yes?" she asked as she looked through the peephole at the woman standing on her doorstep.

"Shana Garner?"

"Yes? How can I help you?"

"I have to talk to you."

"Yes?"

"It's about Kyle."

"Kyle?" Shana flung open the door. "Did something happen to him? Is he all right?"

"May I come in?" She brushed past Shana without waiting for an answer.

"What's the matter with Kyle? What happened?"

"Oh, nothing unusual happened." She laughed. "Kyle is just being Kyle."

"What do you mean?"

"I'm Rita. I'm sure Kyle didn't tell you about me."

"Rita? Kyle's ex-fiancé?"

Rita laughed again and shook her head. "Oh, that man. He's being bad again. When will he behave?" She frowned. "Look, my dear, I don't know how to put this in a better way. Kyle and I are still engaged." She shook her head again. "From time to time he gets these urges to sample outside our relationship."

"He told me he called the engagement off."

"Does this look like it's off?" Rita held up her finger. Light glinted off the large ring that gave proof to her words. Shana stared at it as if willing it to disappear. Rita continued, "We're getting married in a few months. I wanted to wait until the place I want us to buy was available, but that's not until September and Kyle said he can't wait that long to make me his wife." She laughed. "He's afraid I'll find somebody else. Silly him. As if anybody could take his place." She batted her eyes at Shana. "Isn't that something? Being married didn't make any difference with your husband, but to Kyle it is sacred." She released a tiny giggle.

Shana flinched at the reference to Elliot. She shook her gaze from the ring and looked at Rita.

"If—if he's engaged to you, why has he been with me?"

"You know how men are. They see a piece of tail and they think they have to have it." Rita's stare narrowed. "They seem to know which woman is willing to have a fling."

"If he cheats on you, why do you want him?" Shana's voice was weak.

"I love him." Rita's stare hardened. "I'm not like you. I can't let a good man go because he found a new temporary plaything. The novelty wears off and they always go home."

Shana thought about Elliot. That was true about him. Was Kyle like him after all?

"I see I've shocked you. You didn't know he was still mine." Rita smiled, but only her mouth showed it. "I know you have a lot to digest. I'll see myself out."

She shut the door behind her. A grin showed on her face and stayed in place as she went to her car.

This is way more fun than spattering yellow paint on a black Rolls. Way more fun. Too bad I won't be around when she confronts Kyle.

Shana stood rooted in the hall. Then she stumbled to the living room and plopped onto the couch.

This can't be. Kyle is not like Elliot. She shook her head. *Rita has the ring to prove it. Why would she do this if it isn't true?* She swallowed hard. *They have a wedding date. Am I just Kyle's latest fling? Was my opinion of him right when I first met him?* She rushed upstairs.

"I can't be here when he gets back. I—I'm not ready to face him. Not yet. Maybe not ever."

She threw some things into a small suitcase and hoped she had everything she needed. In a few minutes, she was back downstairs.

She paused in front of the phone. Then she picked it up. She punched in Kyle's home number wondering how long it would stay in her memory. Another thing to worry about.

"I've gone away," she said after the beep. "I—I don't want to see you. Or even talk to you again. One cheater was more than enough for me." She hung up, wiped her eyes and left.

She wasn't sure where she was going, but she knew she wasn't going to be home when Kyle got back.

Chapter 22

Shana struggled to keep her mind on her driving. How did people deal with the distraction of a cell phone when this kind of internal struggle was almost too much by itself?

She had no place in mind; her only destination was away. Maybe distance could dull the hurt. *How could he?* How could Kyle do that to her? He knew how much she had been hurt by Elliot. She wiped her eyes. *Kyle talked about his ex-wife and his ex-girlfriend. He said they hurt him.* She shook her head. *He must have been lying. If they hurt him so much, how could he turn around and do the same thing to me? Why couldn't he just leave me alone?* She wiped her eyes, then tightened her grip on the steering wheel.

She drove toward a place she hadn't been to in a long time. It was far enough away to dull the memories of Kyle, but close enough to reach in a few hours.

She changed her mind when she got to the outskirts of town. The huge logo of a chocolate kiss announcing the town was not what she'd had in mind when she'd thought to escape from memories of Kyle.

As far as she could see down the road, lights shaped like the same kisses lined both sides. No, she couldn't handle this. Kisses of any kind were out. Kisses were the last thing she wanted to think about. Her eyes filled with tears.

Against her will, she thought of how Kyle's hands had felt on her; of how they'd teased her usually quiet parts awake; of how he could ignite a heat in her like she had never felt before, despite having been married. She remembered how he had made her forget all about Elliot.

She pulled to the side of the road and turned off the motor. Then she lay her head back and closed her eyes.

Kyle came to mind so clearly, it was as if he were with her. As if she could feel his arms around her, his sensuous mouth kissing her. She swallowed the lump of tears that rose in her throat. His kisses had always been sweeter than any candy—even chocolate—and so much more pleasurable.

She tightened her hands into fists as they itched at the memories that the word *pleasure* brought up. Memories of her and Kyle, touching each other. Kyle awakening parts of her that had never been awake before. Kyle creating a need in her, taking her to the edge of torture and pinning her there as her desire mounted before he filled her, completed her. She sighed at the memory of Kyle leading her to their own pleasure place, loving her until she was satisfied. Then loving her all over again. *No, not love.* Shana shook away that thought. *He loves Rita and she wears his ring to prove it. He even had her move up their wedding date because he couldn't wait to marry her, to make her his wife.* Shana grabbed the tissue box from the backseat.

I didn't make him wait. I went to him eagerly. I didn't even need the first ring to get me into his bed. A tear slid down her heated face. *Not his bed—mine. I set out to get him into my bed and I succeeded.* She wiped her eyes again. *The only thing between us is lust—basic, simple lust. At least on his part.* She shook her head. *I thought I had found love, real love, at last.* She sniffed. *As for what he thought of me, I was just his next target, his next conquest. He saw me, took the challenge and won. I didn't even make it hard for him.* She swallowed hard. *I wonder who will be next? I wonder if the next one will feel her heart break the way mine is breaking right now.*

She wiped her face once more, then started the car and drove away from signs that mocked her, that made her think of other, sweeter kisses. Kisses that satisfied at first, then led to pain. As she drove, she tried to decide where else she could go that was far enough from Philadelphia to escape, at least for a little while, the memories there.

Someplace where she could regroup so she could be ready for the confrontation with Kyle that was sure to come.

I'm not going to the Poconos, she thought. *There are a lot of places in the mountains, but the first part of the trip is the same as the one I traveled with Kyle and I'm not up to traveling those roads yet.* She frowned as her mind sifted information, looking for a safe place.

Harrisburg. Harrisburg is safe, she thought as she found her way to the turnpike. *I won't find any memories of Kyle there.* She got on the turnpike and headed west. Anything she experienced in Harrisburg wouldn't have any memories of Kyle attached.

When she got close, Shana parked in front of a motel on the outskirts of the state capital. She checked in, stumbled over the word *one* when she told how many would be staying. *Get used to that,* she told herself as she took her bag to her room. *This is your life from now on—safe and, if you're lucky, boring.*

She placed her bag on one of the beds, then she sat on the other and stared at the screen of the television as if it were turned on. Finally, she opened her bag and looked inside to see what she had packed. She sighed and picked up the phone to ask for directions to the closest store. She didn't question herself; she knew how she could have forgotten something as basic as a toothbrush and toothpaste.

When she got back to her room, she curled up on the bed. Finally she allowed the tears she had been holding in check for a while to flow. By the time she drifted into a disturbed sleep, time was well on its way to morning.

Midmorning she remembered to go get something to eat. The rest of the time she spent staring at whatever was on television when she remembered to turn it on. It still didn't drown out her thoughts, though. Finally checkout time came.

She hesitated when she reached the road, knowing she had to be at school tomorrow morning. Then she ignored common sense and turned the opposite way from home.

She went into the city and drove as if she were a tourist and somebody was going to make her draw a map when she got home. Then she parked her car in the small neighborhood across from downtown and walked over the bridge. The slight breeze was like midsummer, but Shana didn't appreciate it. She didn't appreciate anything. She was busy trying to understand how someone with a broken heart could still walk around and act alive.

When it got so dark she could no longer pretend to see anything, she walked back to her car and drove home.

Shortly before midnight she stopped when she reached the street just before hers and hesitated. *Please don't let him be waiting for me. I'm not ready to face him. Not yet. Please.*

She took a deep breath and drove to her house. She breathed easier when her empty driveway greeted her. *Empty. Just like after Elliot got his stuff,* she thought as she pulled into the garage.

She got ready for bed, but when she got back to her bedroom, she just stood in the doorway. Then, for the second time—a time too close to the first—she went to the guest room.

Tomorrow, she thought as she slipped between the sheets. *It will be better tomorrow.*

A little after dawn, Shana got out of bed. Now she understood the significance of the phrase "one day at a time." Right now, making it through the next five minutes seemed an overly optimistic goal.

She got ready for school and was glad to leave the house. Maybe some of the memories lurking there would have dissipated by the time she got back home.

What are the chances of that? she wondered as she backed out of the garage. *Memories of two no-good men in one house.* She frowned. *I hope this is unusual. I'd hate to think of anybody else going through this pain.*

She parked, managed to fake a smile and went into the office. She must have made the correct small talk because nobody gave her strange looks. She left messages for the teachers to bring the kids outside. After what seemed like hours in the office, she escaped to her gym, got what she needed, then went to the yard. She was coping until her second group came out.

"Mr. Kyle is back, right?" Carl stood in front of her.

"Track after school today, right?" Joel left a little space beside Carl. "Mr. Kyle didn't diss us, did he?"

"We'll have practice after school as usual," she answered. "Let's line up for a relay."

"But will Mr. Kyle be here?" Julie asked. "He didn't get tired of us, did he?"

"As far as I know, he'll be here." She blinked hard. She should have known they'd recognize a nonanswer when they heard one. She took a deep breath, then continued. "Are we going to stand around the whole period, or are we going to play?" *Not you,* her mind answered Julie's question. *He didn't get tired of you, just me.* She frowned. *No.* She shook her head slightly. *I ended it before he could tire of me.*

The kids stood in place for several seconds, then they lined up. The lines were more like a snake than a ruler, but Shana didn't notice. Her attention was still stuck on Kyle.

He hadn't left a message that he wasn't coming, so she had to assume that he'd be there. She was happy for the sake of the kids. As for herself, she had to find a way to cope. *How am I going to face him?*

"Mrs. Garner? We're ready." Karen's voice interrupted Shana's thoughts. "Should we start?"

Shana glanced at the two lines. *Focus,* she told herself.

"Ready?" she asked even though it was obvious that they were. "Go." She managed a slight smile as the kids dribbled the ball to the other side of the yard and back, and passed it to the next person in line. For the rest of the period, she almost forgot about Kyle.

She got through the next two groups better than she had the first. By then she was ready for the questions about Kyle.

She had just walked into the gym after her last morning class when Martie came in.

"Girl," she said as she hugged Shana. "I would ask you where you've been, but I think I know." She laughed. "You should have put some makeup on those circles, though. They give away the fact that you didn't get much sleep. So, how are you gonna play it when he comes today?" Martie asked as she went to the table at the back of Shana's office. "Are you gonna act like you haven't seen each other since before he went away?" Martie looked up from her lunch that she had unpacked. "Hey, Shana. What's wrong?"

"I don't know where to begin." Shana plugged in the hot pot. She frowned. "It's over."

"What?" Martie forgot about her lunch. "What do you mean it's over? You just got started good."

As Martie ate, Shana, stumbling over words from time to time, told her what had happened, ending with her drive to Harrisburg and back. "I feel like I've been on a roller coaster nonstop for the past week," she said after she finished.

"What did he say when you confronted him?"

"I didn't."

"You didn't talk to him about this? Why not?"

"I haven't talked to him at all. I didn't have to. I saw Rita's ring." She wiped her eyes. "I swore I wasn't going to cry about this again." She released a little laugh that held no happiness. "I also swore, after Elliot, that I wasn't going to let anybody hurt me again." She wiped her face again. "It's sad when you can't keep a promise to yourself, isn't it?" She glanced at Martie. "This time I get to play Ingrid."

"This is not the same thing. Kyle is not married. He might not even be engaged. You only have that woman's word. You have to give him a chance to explain."

"He'll probably have some lies ready."

"Give him a chance." Martie squeezed her hand. "If not for him, you owe it to yourself."

"I probably won't have a choice. He'll be here today for the after-school track program." She sighed. "At least nobody told me that he's not coming."

"Maybe that's a good thing," Martie said softly. The bell rang and they stood.

"Hang in there," she added. "It has to get better."

"That's what we said after I threw Elliot out."

"Give Kyle a chance to explain. He is not Elliot." Martie hugged her and left.

Shana threw away the rest of her lunch, grabbed the bag of volleyballs and went to the yard to meet her next class.

Too soon, the regular school day was over. With mixed feelings, she went to check her box for messages.

She didn't want to see Kyle, but the kids did. She chewed on her bottom lip. *What I want doesn't make a bit of difference, anyway.* She sighed as the empty box greeted her. *The kids will be happy,* she thought as she went to the yard.

He was waiting at the fence with Carl and Jennifer. Shana's heart seemed to jump before it realized that this was not like the last time she'd seen Kyle. Still, it was slow to drop the beat back to normal.

As she got near to him, her gaze traveled over him, looking for some outward sign of his cheating nature. She frowned. Just because she didn't see any didn't mean there wasn't any. Maybe her problem was that she didn't know what to look for.

She stopped a good distance from him. He closed most of the gap. But not all of it. Not the way he had the last time they'd been together.

"We have to talk." His voice was low.

"We don't have anything to talk about."

"Oh, yes we do. We…"

"Did you visit the camp?" Carl rushed over to them. "I was just fixing to ask Mr. Kyle when you came out. What's it like? Are we all set for July?" The other kids waited for the answer.

"Do you want to tell them about it?" Kyle's gaze told her that he wasn't through with the other conversation. Her gaze answered that she was.

"You can tell them."

She moved to the fence. She looked at Kyle as he spoke, but her attention wasn't there. It had wandered off on its own, second-guessing what had happened between them as if it were possible to change the past. How far back would she go if she could? What would she undo?

"Do you want to add anything?" Kyle jerked her attention back to the present. It was a good thing that they had discussed and planned the camp program. She had no idea what he had just said.

Shana looked at the faces surrounding them. Even her health-test finals hadn't held the kids' attention this completely.

"I described the camp and filled them in on the probable dates and the program," Kyle added.

He knows my attention wasn't on the camp. He's covering for me. Her mind tried to go to what had happened between them at the camp, but she didn't let it, so it jumped to Rita. *Too late for him to score points.* She took some papers from her clipboard and distributed them.

"Here are the details of the camp. Make sure you give them to your parents. Let me know if they have any questions. Also let me know as soon as you can if you can make it. We need to have numbers as soon as possible."

"I will be there no matter what," Carl said.

"So will I," Joel added. The others echoed his words and nodded.

"We don't have much time left today. Let's run through some exercises. I know it's been a week since some of you did this."

The looks on their faces told her which kids hadn't run for the past week.

What was left of the time passed quickly. Shana dismissed the kids. *There goes my buffer,* she thought as she watched the last of them go.

"We need to talk." Kyle stepped closer, but he didn't touch her. He didn't even kiss her cheek. She tried not to miss his touch.

"We don't have anything to say."

"How about an explanation for that message you left?"

"What happened between us was a mistake."

"It didn't feel like a mistake." He took a step closer to her as if he weren't already close enough for her to remember their time together. "It still doesn't feel like it now. The only mistake I can think of is your message."

"That wasn't a mistake." She glanced at him and caught a glimpse of a group of kids not too far away. They looked as if they were watching a television show.

Just what I need. Giving them something else to talk about on their way home.

"I'm not discussing this here."

"Then where?" Kyle glanced at the kids then back at her.

"I—I can't discuss this with you at all. There's nothing to discuss." She turned, but not before he could see the tears in her eyes.

What is wrong with her? Kyle watched Shana leave the yard. *It can't be that I did something wrong. I wasn't here and when I left, things were fine between us.* He frowned. *Things were better than fine, better than I ever imagined they could be when I first met her. What the heck went wrong while I was gone?*

He walked to his car, muttering to himself. *It can't*

be that I left. I told her about the conference and she seemed all right with it. He reached his car and slipped behind the wheel. *Did she take Elliot back? Is that it? She told me the divorce was final. Did she lie? Did she dump me because he's back in her life?* He ignored the jealousy that knifed through him at the thought of Shana with somebody else, in somebody else's arms, loving anybody else.

He drove down the street, making himself stay under the speed limit. He never minded that she had been Elliot's first. That was before he'd even known she existed. What she'd done back then had nothing to do with him. He'd had a life before then, too. He frowned. *I don't care what she says. She owes me an explanation. After what we've shared together, she owes me more than an "I'm through with you" message.*

It was difficult, but he forced his attention to stay on the curves of Lincoln Drive. *She never gave us a chance. Rita wouldn't let go and Shana won't stay. Somebody else might find humor in that.* The last thing he felt like doing right now was laughing.

She's gonna talk to me, he thought as he parked in the dealership. *She has to see me on Wednesday because of track. I'm not leaving her alone after practice until we sort this out.* His frowned deepened. *This is too important to me to just let it go.*

He thought of how she had felt in his arms. His lower body remembered. He wanted her back there. He wanted her right now.

They hadn't had much time together, but it was enough for him to know that he wanted more.

Wednesday rushed past for Shana as if it were one of the track kids going for the gold. No way could she stop time from moving. She looked at the clock, sighed and stopped fooling with things on her already neat desk.

"I came to help carry the stuff." Carl stood in the doorway. "Everybody's already waiting at the bus."

"Okay." Shana handed him the box of sticks and blocks. She smiled. "Because you are so helpful, you may sit beside Mr. Kyle on the bus." She didn't feel guilty for using him. This was something he wanted. She blinked hard. *I'd want it, too, if things were different. If…* She managed to smile at Carl.

"Really? No fooling? All right." He bobbed up and down. "Wait till Joel hears this." He laughed and, despite the heavy box, almost skipped up the steps.

Shana ignored the guilt that tried to creep into her. *No harm no foul. Carl got something he wanted and I got out of a situation that I don't need.*

"Guess what, y'all. I get to sit next to Mr. Kyle," Carl announced before he reached the others.

"No way."

"Yes, way." He laughed.

Shana glanced at Kyle, who was staring at her. She let her glance slide away. Then she let the kids board the bus.

Because of her change in the seating, she let the

others choose their own seats. She ended up beside Julie in the seat behind Kyle.

"Did you have a good holiday, Mrs. Garner?" Julie asked. "We went to visit my grandma in Virginia," she continued before Shana could answer. "My grandma doesn't live far from D.C. We went up there on Wednesday and visited the museums. My brother thinks he gonna be an astronaut, so he just had to visit the Air and Space Museum. My mom loves art, so she visited the African Art Museum. My dad wasn't particular, so we spent a little time at a few of the others." She finally stopped. "What did you do? I know you visited the camp, but what did you do the rest of the week?"

"I did some things."

"You shouldn't spend your vacation doing work stuff. You're supposed to have fun." Julie moved the conversation back to her trip. "At this one museum…"

Shana was stuck on her own week. *What a composition I could write:* "What I Did On My Spring Vacation," By Shana Garner.

I made a fool of myself. I let Kyle Rayburn get too close and now I'm hurting. We spent most of the week making the most fantastic love imaginable. She shifted in her seat. *I was stupid enough to let him into my heart and he ripped it apart.* She blinked hard. *Maybe the scar will be hard enough to protect me from other pain in the future.* She frowned. *First it has to get over this hurt.*

"Do you want me to carry this box again?" Carl stood in front of her.

"I'll carry it if it means I get to sit beside Mr. Kyle on the way back." Tyrone grabbed the box.

"Mrs. Garner didn't say you could." Carl tried to wrestle it from him.

"Joel, will you carry this?" Kyle stood and took the box. Joel grabbed it before Kyle could change his mind.

"Does this mean I get the seat next to you?"

"If you want it. It seems to be up for grabs." He glanced at Shana. "Let's get going. You all know the procedure by now," he said to the kids. "Is that all right with you?" He stared at Shana.

"Yes." She stood. "Get with your teams. We'll take it a bit easy today until your bodies get used to working out again."

She glanced at Kyle. Was he thinking of the workout they had put themselves through?

It was good that she had done this so many times before. Not even half of her mind was on it. The rest was struggling to find a way out of the mess she was in.

Finally practice was over. The kids shifted seats again, but Shana still sat beside Julie. During the ride home, she heard about the White House and other government buildings. They seemed to get back to school faster than usual.

The kids went home as soon as they got off the bus. They walked in their usual groups. Shana heard bits of conversations about their activities of the past week. Her mind tried to sneak back to what she had done, but she yanked it away.

She left Kyle without saying goodbye. Maybe he watched her. Maybe not. She didn't look back to see. As she left the yard after they'd finished, the only thing she could think of was: *No almost-kiss today. Not ever again.*

Shana got through Tuesday even though she knew Wednesday was waiting for her. She even struggled through practice.

Martie was waiting after they got back from the field.

"Let's all go for something cold to drink. You both look like you could use it."

Kyle looked at Shana. His eyes dared her to refuse.

She took the dare. "Not today. Maybe some other time." She left them standing together at the fence.

Chapter 23

Shana walked from the garage, but stopped before she reached the porch. Kyle was walking toward her. *He must have been right behind me.* She sighed. *I should have known it wasn't going to be that easy.* She reached deep inside for the strength she was going to need. *Just for a short while,* she hoped. *You have to get this over with. May as well do it now.*

"What are you doing here?"

"You know the answer to that. We have to talk."

"We don't have anything to talk about."

"Contrary to what you women think, men are not mind readers. You want us to know something, you have to tell us." His jaw tightened.

"Go away."

"That's telling me the end, but you left out the part that comes before that. You have a choice—we can talk out here in your driveway. We can talk on your porch. We can talk with you inside your house and me on the porch shouting through the door. Or we can talk inside."

Shana looked around. She didn't need to put on a show for whoever happened to pass by. The neighborhood was probably still talking about the last incident, the one where Elliot's things lined the driveway.

She walked past him, careful not to brush against him, acting as if she would find his touch repulsive. A whiff of his aftershave made her fumble a little with the key, but she finally got the door open.

"I don't know why you don't let this go." She refused to look at him. Afraid one glance would break the thin thread holding her together. "You may as well come inside."

Kyle followed her. Neither spoke until they were inside.

"Okay. What do you want?" She turned toward him, but still didn't look at his face.

"A little over a week ago that would have been obvious since you wanted the same thing."

Shana's keys clattered to the floor. She didn't mind picking them up, since that let her hide the sudden rush of color that blanketed her face. *Why won't he let it go?*

"I guess a few days do make a difference," he continued. His jaw tightened. "An explanation will do for starters."

"What's to explain? My message was clear."

"Uh-uh." He shook his head. "Your words were clear, but you left out the why."

"You already know why." Shana sounded as if the volume of her voice would make up for the lack of explanation.

"I still don't read minds." His voice was louder than hers, but he didn't try to touch her. Instead he kept his hands to himself by crossing his arms.

Shana felt her gaze drawn to that action. She remembered not so long ago when he'd held her within those arms. She thought of the feel of his hard chest against her back, the feel of his strong hands as they did wonderful, magical things to her breasts. She crossed her arms. Maybe that would quiet the tingle in her hard tips. Maybe it would make the ache go away.

If they had still been outside, in spite of the fact that Shana's house was a single on a large lot, her neighbors would have come out to see what the noise was about.

"You don't have to read minds." She was at full volume now.

"I don't understand." His voice reached top decibels, too. "I thought we had something growing between us." He leaned toward her. "I know you enjoyed our time together. You can't deny that you got pleasure from making love with me."

"I—I didn't say I didn't." Her voice matched his. She didn't have enough energy left to ignore the heat now filling her body, the need making itself felt just at his words. He didn't have to touch her to stir up the desire, but her body ached for his touch anyway.

"Then what's the matter?" Kyle didn't even pretend to have his temper under control.

"Ask Rita."

"Rita?" A puzzled look appeared on his face and Shana was tempted to wonder about it. But this time she didn't give in to temptation.

"Yes, Rita."

"I told you I had been engaged to Rita. She's history. What does she have to do with you and me?"

"As your *fiancée* she has a lot to do with it."

"What?"

"She came to see me. I saw the ring. I know about the wedding coming up soon. I know how you got her to move the date up because you couldn't wait to marry her." She glared at him, but quickly looked away. Tears wouldn't go with her shouting. "How long were you going to keep that from me? Was I going to be your last fling before you got married or did you intend to keep it going afterward?" Shana swallowed hard. "I was easy, wasn't I? Did you laugh at how easy it was to get me into bed?"

Kyle stared at her but he didn't say anything. He just stood still in front of her, staring at her.

"Rita told you that we're getting married." His stare hardened. He crossed his arms again. "And you believed her. A stranger comes to you with a way-out story and you believe her over me. After what we shared, you believe I would do something like that to you, that you're just a fling for me? You think that's all you are to me?"

A finger of doubt crept into Shana, but she couldn't find any words that would fit. When he put it that way, it sounded so unfair.

"I guess you meant more to me than I do to you," he said, his anger gone. Then he turned quietly, but deliberately, and walked away. He paused at the door and turned to face her.

"I'm not Elliot." His words were barely a whisper, but they were strong enough to get through. She watched as he turned away from her.

He closed the door softly behind him, but it was a slam in Shana's mind. It was the closing of the door to something wonderful that she had been allowed to taste. Just a small taste. Her eyes filled. She shook her head. *That's not true. I could have had it all, but I threw it away. It was precious, but I didn't value it.*

It was her doing, but she felt the hurt. This hurt was deeper, stronger than any she had ever felt.

She stumbled to the living room and flopped down in her favorite chair.

Kyle was right. I never gave him a chance to explain. I was so quick to accept what somebody told me about him, so eager to believe that he's like Elliot that I took a stranger's word. She shook her head. *I can't blame Rita. I didn't have to believe her. I didn't have to think the worst of Kyle. How could I treat him that way? How could I do that to the man I love?*

At the thought of the word *love*, tears flowed as if a dam had broken inside her and the pent-up water was escaping.

She would have sat in the living room forever if the doorbell hadn't rung. She got up slowly. She knew it wasn't Kyle; she didn't deserve such good luck.

She looked through the peephole from habit; right now she didn't care who it was or what happened to her. She sighed and opened the door to Martie.

"Where have you been? I tried to reach you yesterday. Don't you check your messages? I would have come over, but…" She stared at Shana. "What's wrong? You look awful."

"He's gone." Shana went back to the living room.

"Who's gone? Kyle?" Martie followed. "What do you mean he's gone?" She sat opposite Shana.

"I can't blame him. It's my fault. I chased him away."

"Why would you do that?" Her forehead wrinkled. "I thought you were going to patch things up. What happened?"

"We just had a big blowup. It's all my fault."

"Tell me."

Martie listened quietly as Shana explained what had just happened. It didn't take but a few minutes and she stopped after nearly every word to dry her face, but she got to the end of her story.

"I lumped him with Elliot even though, deep down, I know that's not true. He's nothing like Elliot. He's sweet and considerate. He has a sense of humor." She wiped her face again. "He cares about the kids. He's…"

"He's a whole lot more than all that and a bushel of chips," Martie added.

"Yeah." A dreamy look came over Shana's face, but quickly disappeared. "I can't believe I messed up so thoroughly. He never wants to see me again and I can't blame him." She didn't try to stop the tears. Maybe they would take some of the pain with them.

"Do you love him?"

"More than I ever thought it possible to love." Her sobbing increased. "I just admitted it to myself too late."

"Then you'll just have to find a way to get him back."

"I don't know if I can."

"Do you want him?"

"More than anything."

"Let him know." Martie stood and hugged her. "This is something you have to work out for yourself. If he loves you, too, it's not too late to fix things." She squeezed Shana's shoulders, then left.

Shana leaned her head back against the chair and closed her eyes. *How am I gonna do that?*

I have to congratulate myself, Kyle thought as he let himself into his house. *I saw Rita, got her straight, and didn't strangle her to keep any more lying words from coming out of her sorry mouth.*

He threw his keys into the basket on the hall table. Instead of picking them back up as he was tempted to do, he stared at them. Then he walked into the living room and sat.

How could Shana accuse me of doing something like that? He shook his head. *Uh-uh. She didn't even accuse me. She assumed the worst without even asking me. If she cared deeply for me, she couldn't have dropped me like that. She couldn't have just left a "bye, see ya" message on my phone. I don't know what game she's playing, but I don't like it. I didn't deserve to be treated like that. I thought we had something developing between us.*

He stood, stomped back into the hall and picked up his keys. *Might as well salvage some of this workday,* he thought as he left for the dealership. *Shana wants me to leave her alone. Well, she's got it. She got over me, I can get over her. She's just another woman. I can forget her. I knew she was bad news from the first time I saw her. Why didn't I leave her alone? Her behavior told me that was what she wanted. But no, I had to push myself into her life.* He frowned. *You can't make somebody love you.*

He hesitated at the garage door and his frown deepened. *I am not in love with her.*

As he got in the car and started it, he dared his heart to disagree.

Chapter 24

Dark had taken over the living room a long time ago and Shana still sat in the same spot.

What am I going to do? She took in a deep breath and released it slowly, but it didn't pull up a solution with it. *"I'm sorry" seems so lame. Those words can't begin to make up for what I did to him. I hurt him.* She blinked rapidly. *Probably as much as Elliot hurt me.* She tried to control the doubts rising in her, but they popped up anyway. *Was he just hurt because I wrongly accused him or is love mixed in with his feelings?* She frowned. *Is he hurt because he loves me and I hurt him?* She shook her head. *I don't have a way to know.* She trudged upstairs still wondering what to do.

You don't just come right out and ask somebody if he loves you. I can't do that. What if he says no? What if he tells me that he's moving on? What if he says he's sorry we ever got together? What if I hurt him so badly that he can't forgive me?

She spent the night in bed, but she didn't sleep. Maybe if she had, an idea of what she should do would have come to her.

She made it through the next day, glad she had a routine to follow and she didn't have to think about what she was doing. Friday moved Thursday aside, but it didn't bring an answer with it.

Shana got home after school at her usual time, but instead of planting herself in the living-room chair as she had done the past two days, she picked up the phone. But she didn't make a call. Instead she walked around downstairs with it as if she were holding a baby and trying to quiet it down.

After her third circuit around, she punched in a few numbers, but didn't complete the sequence. *What am I going to say?*

She broke the connection and stared at the number pad as if she didn't understand what she was looking at. Then she sighed and started over.

While she was waiting for a voice to answer, she would have rehearsed what she was going to say, but she didn't know. Kyle's voice came on and she thought of how, except for during the track practices, this was the only way she'd ever hear him again. The beep ending her chance to leave a message sounded before she said a word. She took a deep breath and pressed the numbers again. How do you go about eating crow?

"Kyle," she said after the voice told her to leave a message. "This is Shana." *As if he doesn't recognize my voice.* "I—I'm sorry for the way I acted, for what I said to you. I know I don't deserve it, but please forgive me. I was wrong in so many ways." She hesitated, then stepped out onto the limb. "I love you."

The closing beep sounded, but that was okay. She didn't have anything else to say. She placed the phone back in the cradle and stared at it as if that would make it ring.

Ridiculous. He's not even home to get the message. She chewed on her lower lip. *When he gets home, he still might not call me back. I'm not sure I would in his place.*

She turned on the television to help fill the quiet. Still she couldn't help glancing at the phone too many times. She had just looked away from it when the doorbell rang. Maybe Martie could make her stop staring at the phone and hoping like crazy.

She flung the door open and stared at someone more interesting. She gazed at the answer to her hope.

"You gonna let me in or you gonna make me stand out here?"

"Oh. Yes. I mean, no. I mean…come in."

She stared at Kyle, hoping to see how he felt, but his face gave nothing away. *Maybe he came over to tell me to quit calling him, that he agrees with what I first said, that what happened between us was a mistake. That we should both consider it an experience and move on. Or maybe...*

"Did you mean what you said?"

His stare was intense, but it still didn't give anything away. Maybe he was going to throw her love back in her face. *What can I say? No? I changed my mind? It was all a mistake?* She frowned. *I don't believe that what we had was a mistake, anymore. I'm not sure I ever believed it.*

"Yes. I—I guess I had to lose you to admit to myself how I feel about you." She stared at the floor.

"You didn't lose me. You kicked me to the curb. You seem to be good at that."

Something in his voice made her look at him. She relaxed when she saw a twinkle, when she saw the warmth in his eyes.

"I—I tried to unkick you when I called." *Please let me see that smile.*

"*Unkick*. Is that a word?" *No smile yet.*

"It is now." She swallowed hard, then went on. "I can't think of another word that would mean the same thing." She swallowed hard. "Kyle, I am so sorry for my behavior." She stared at him, struggling to keep from reaching to him. If she did, what if he shrugged her off? What would she do then? She shook her head. "I know 'I'm sorry' doesn't make up for what I said to you, for what I did to you, but I don't know what else to do."

He stared at her, but he didn't move. It seemed to

Shana as if they held the distance between them for hours. Then he spoke in the low, warm voice she loved.

"I can think of a few things." He began closing the space between them, one agonizingly slow step at a time. Then he smiled. He showed her his gorgeous, sexy, crooked smile. "You can start by coming here." He opened his arms and she was there before he finished, before he could change his mind.

His mouth found hers. Their arms wrapped around each other as they let her kiss apologize to him and his accept her apology. Glorious seconds—or was it minutes—later he eased his mouth from hers.

"Are you ready for the next thing you can do?" he said as he pressed his lips to the side of her face. His hands brushed along her back, pressing her to him, making her aware of his desire, of his need.

"More than ready," she whispered.

They kissed their way up the stairs and into her bedroom. They separated only to remove the clothes that were keeping them from touching each other's skin completely.

Their hands explored each other's body as if they had been apart for years and they had to learn each other all over again.

Each hard in their own way, they melted onto the bed. Protection quickly in place, they began to show each other how much they had remembered about pleasuring each other while they sought new ways to demonstrate their love.

* * *

They showed each other two more times during the night and again in the morning. After breakfast, they repeated the showing.

It was Sunday evening before they bothered to get fully dressed.

"You don't know how much I hate to do this." Kyle rubbed his hand down her thigh.

"You didn't seem to feel that way last night and all of the other fantastic times you did that."

"You know by now that's not what I meant." He kissed the top of her head and stroked the mound of her breast. "I have to go and you have to get ready for school tomorrow." He brushed across the now hard tip and she moaned. He skimmed over it again. "Maybe I don't have to go right now."

She turned to face him and they kissed as if it were the first time after they'd realized their love. Then they shared love once more.

From the time she woke up on Monday morning, then as she got ready for school, and still as she walked into the building, Shana knew the widest grin possible was on her face. And she didn't care if it looked silly. She was going to see Kyle in a few hours. She giggled. Again.

"You saw Kyle. Right?" Martie asked when they met outside the office. "That's the only way to explain the look on your face. Actually, the look seems to be all over you. You patched things up, right?"

"So right."

"From the looks of you, that crow tasted a lot like chicken cooked your favorite way." Shana laughed and Martie chuckled with her. "You know you gotta tell me later." She grinned at her. "At least a little part about your reunion. I'm sure you gave new meaning to the word *re-union*." She laughed as Shana reddened. "See you at lunch. My room." She went to her classroom and Shana went to the gym.

At lunchtime, still amazed that her life was as it should be, Shana told Martie of Kyle's forgiveness. She kept the details private as they always did.

After school came at the usual time, but it still took too long to get there.

"Good afternoon, baby." Kyle stood in the doorway of her office looking sexier than she remembered. Then he was in front of her and they were in each other's arms. Their kiss was long and deep, as if they were making up for months apart rather than hours.

"This is totally inappropriate behavior for a school building," she managed to get out as they ended the kiss.

"Then I guess we'll have to hurry through the rest of the day so we can take our action someplace more appropriate."

He gave her one more quick kiss, then grabbed the box of equipment. "This is to keep me from grabbing you again," he whispered to her as they went outside.

She laughed, but managed to cut it off when they reached the kids.

Both she and Kyle were able to keep enough of their minds on the practice, but after it was over they hurriedly put away the equipment.

"I would ask 'my place or yours?' but I'm afraid you'd pick mine and yours is much closer," Kyle said as they went up the stairs arm in arm.

"It has been so long since we've seen each other."

"Too long, but I warn you, I won't be satisfied with just seeing you." Kyle kissed her after they reached the parking lot, but the kiss was quick and soft for the benefit of a group of kids playing across the street. "I won't say 'last one there is a rotten egg' because I don't want either of us to have an accident." He opened her door for her, then got into his own car.

They met on her porch and the kissing started right there. Once they got inside, the loving started.

Later that evening, Kyle, as contented as Shana was, lay with her in his arms.

"I hate to say this, but I have to go. I have neglected my business lately."

"Are you blaming me?"

"Baby, I'm giving you the credit. Nothing nor nobody has been able to take my mind off the business in a long time." He squeezed her hip gently. "We still on for tomorrow afternoon?"

"I have a feeling you're not talking about a repeat of

this. I…" She sat up quickly. "Oh. The assemblies. I forgot."

"I guess you had something else on your mind."

"You think?" She stroked his thigh. "We have you on the schedule. Two assemblies back-to-back after lunch. Lower grades first." His hand lightly stroked along her thigh and she had to search for the rest of her sentence. "The—the upper grades will be so hyper, they wouldn't be able to concentrate on their classes if we did them first. Are you ready?"

"I'm always ready for you."

"You know that's not what I meant. Besides, don't you have to go?"

"Not yet. I have more important things to do—like making love one more time with my woman."

Two hours later, Kyle left, although he admitted that it was too late to go to the dealership.

"If I don't leave tonight, we'll go through this scene in the morning and you'll be late for school," he explained as he dressed.

"You're right." Shana sighed. "See you at twelve forty-five."

"Yes, ma'am." Kyle buttoned his shirt. "Don't look at me like that or I won't go anywhere except back to you."

"I have no idea what you mean." Shana got out of bed slowly and walked to the closet. She looked over her shoulder, wiggled her hips, then winked before she took out a robe. She turned to face him as she slowly pulled the robe closed and tied the belt.

"Baby, you could teach torture procedures to spy-wannabes."

"Consider that just a preview of what's to come."

"I like the sound of that. It's better than calling it a recap of what already took place."

After Kyle got dressed, they walked to the door as if neither one would have cared if it had disappeared and there was no way out of the house.

The next morning, Shana awoke with a grin on her face just as she had the morning before. It widened as she looked in the bathroom mirror.

"You look like a woman who has been thoroughly loved," she said to her image and grinned. "I guess that's because it's true."

She sang as she showered, found another song to take her through breakfast, put a Nina Simone CD in the player in the car and sang about her baby just caring for her.

By the time the first assembly began, she felt as if she hadn't seen Kyle for months.

This love thing is something else, she thought as she watched him come into the hall outside the auditorium.

Cora introduced Kyle and thanked him for coming. Next she thanked Shana for arranging the assembly. Then Shana moved to the end seat of the first row and let Kyle do his thing.

Even if she didn't have a relationship going with him, she would have admired the way he related to the kids. She was also amazed at the knowledgeable questions they asked.

Everyone laughed when a third-grader asked if they practiced their scoring celebrations.

"You can tell which ones practice," Kyle answered and the staff as well as the kids laughed again.

The kids protested when Shana announced the end of the assembly.

The upper grades rushed in next as if afraid somebody was going to call the assembly off. The track-team members made it a point of speaking to Kyle.

"Our attendance is at one hundred percent," Cora said to Kyle and Shana as the kids took their seats. "Too bad we can't have you here every day." She smiled. "Of course, the students wouldn't pay attention in their classes, so maybe that's not such a good idea after all."

The three of them laughed. Then Cora stepped forward and repeated the introduction she had used for the first assembly.

Kyle's presentation went into more detail and the questions were more sophisticated, but the general topics were the same.

"Any more questions?" Kyle asked at the end. The kids had asked everything they could think of. "Well, I have one." He turned to Shana, who was sitting in the front row. "Ms. Garner, would you please come here?" His crooked smile was in place, but it was a little tentative.

Shana frowned and walked up on the stage. The hush in the auditorium let her footsteps echo off the walls and ceiling.

"I have a question for you."

Shana watched as Kyle reached into his pocket.

"Yes?"

"You haven't heard the question yet."

"Oh. Sorry." She smiled at him.

"Shana Garner," he said as he dropped to one knee. "Will you do me the honor of marrying me?"

Shana stared at him with wide eyes. Her mouth was open just as wide. It was so quiet that no one would have guessed that an auditorium full of upper-school kids was assembled. In the hall somebody walked past and the footsteps sounded too loud. Still Shana and everybody remained frozen in place.

"You gonna leave me down here?" Kyle asked.

"Say yes, Mrs. Garner," Carl yelled.

"Yeah," a lot of the others added. "Say yes."

"Yes. I mean no." Shana shook her head as she stared at Kyle. She took a deep breath. "I mean, no…I'm not going to leave you down there." She reached for his hand. "And, yes, I'll marry you."

The auditorium should have burst from the noise that erupted as Kyle took her in his arms and kissed her.

"That's so romantic," Jennifer said with a sigh from the front row.

Everybody cheered again when Kyle slid the engagement ring onto Shana's finger.

After the noise died down, Cora dismissed the kids. Then she dismissed them again. It was the first time that anybody could remember having to practically shove the kids out the school door.

Shana and Kyle left together, reluctantly separating so they could drive their own cars.

Kyle stopped for takeout since he knew neither one of them would want to take time to cook, much less go out to eat. He'd take her to a restaurant to celebrate on Friday. When they got to the house now, they'd have a different and very private celebration.

"I guess you want a big wedding, huh?" Kyle asked later that evening.

"I already had that and look how it turned out." She smiled. "I'd send Elliot a thank-you note if I knew where he was."

"He's not at the university?"

"He brought scandal on the school. That's a no-no."

"Too bad. I'd like to thank him, too." He stroked her thigh. "About the wedding, do you know you can get married in three days in Pennsylvania?"

"I didn't know that. But—" she slowed his hand "—I need more than three days."

"I don't guess you're talking about four, huh?"

"We have to find a place for the reception."

"I know somebody."

"We have to send out invitations and it takes a long time to get them printed."

"I know somebody who will do a rush job on the printing."

"We still have to mail them—and no, we will not send them by overnight mail."

"How much time are we talking?"

"If we can't find a place the Saturday after school is out for the summer, we can try for the earliest Saturday after that. Is that okay with you?"

"I guess it will have to be." He kissed her. "Now I have an idea."

"What's that?"

"Let's practice for the honeymoon."

"Kyle." Shana shook her head. "I'd ask what I'm going to do with you, but I think you're about to show me."

He took her hand and led her upstairs and proceeded to do exactly that.

Chapter 25

"How was school today?" Kyle asked as he picked Shana up after the last day of school.

"As hectic as it is every year at closing." She laughed. "Of course, the way the kids have been behaving since you pulled your stunt at the end of the assembly, the board might as well have closed school that day."

"My *romantic* stunt, thank you." He kissed the side of her face and opened the door for her.

"Oh, yeah, your most romantic stunt." She grinned as she slid into the seat. "The kids hadn't quit talking about your proposal, when they received their invitations. Every member of the track team thanked me every single time they had gym." She laughed. "The girls had to describe their dresses to me and ask me about mine."

"I know that's a girl thing. I'll bet not one boy described what he was wearing." He got in and drove toward her house.

"What's to describe?" Shana said as they neared the corner. "A suit is a suit. Everybody knows that males are just decorations at a wedding. As for the groom, he's just arm candy for the bride so she can show off her beautiful dress." She laughed but Kyle was silent until they got out of the car in her driveway.

"I don't think candy could do this," he said as he eased her to him. He kissed the spot beneath her ear and was satisfied by the jump of her pulse.

"Okay," she said breathlessly. "I'll concede that point." She sighed. "I'm still having trouble believing that we're getting married on Saturday," she said as they walked onto the porch.

"You are ready for our big day, right?"

"I don't know how you found a place available for the reception in mid-June on such short notice," Shana said.

"I told you I knew somebody." He pulled her close and kissed her again.

"It took more than that."

"Somebody else's misfortune is our good fortune. Somebody canceled a party." He kissed the side of her face. "It also means that my buddy, Alonzo, will get the deal of a lifetime on his next two cars."

"Why would somebody cancel at the last minute?"

"I don't know, but their loss is definitely our gain. Are we all set?" He held her loosely in his arms.

"Well, actually, no. My dress doesn't fit right, the band backed out and the florist can't deliver the order. On top of all that, Martie and I had a big argument and she doesn't want to have anything to do with me. I can't get married without Martie as my bridesmaid—it's bad luck to change bridesmaids, you know. We'll have to set another date. Maybe in a few weeks we can…"

"What?" Kyle backed up against the porch railing. "What are we going to do? You can wear something else, right? Make up with Martie. The rest doesn't matter. We'll think of something. We can…"

"Relax, Kyle." Shana laughed and put her hand on his arm. "I'm kidding you. Everything is fine."

"How could you joke about something like this?" He shook off her hand and stepped away from her. "You know I've been uptight about this coming off right since we started planning. See, if we had eloped, we'd already be married and I wouldn't be stressing like this. How could you think this would be funny?"

"Oh, honey, I'm so sorry." Shana closed the space between them. She stroked her hand along the side of his face. "You have been so tense about this. I shouldn't have joked like that. Nothing could keep me from marrying you on Saturday." She wrapped her arms around him. "The bride is the one who's supposed to be nervous. Poor baby. You've taken on my role."

Kyle relaxed his muscles. He put his hands on her arms, but he didn't pull her close.

"Kyle, I love you." She pressed her body against his. "The only thing that could happen to make me not marry you is for you to decide that *you* don't want to marry *me* anymore." She pressed her lips to his chest. "I love you," she repeated. "More than I ever thought possible."

"I love you, too, baby. I love you so much it scares me. I'm so afraid something will happen to keep us from marrying." He tightened his arms around her.

"Nothing can do that. If everything falls apart, we have what we need—you, me, a marriage license and offices all over the city with officials qualified to perform the ceremony." She lifted her face to him. "Come here. Let me apologize properly."

Kyle lowered his mouth to hers. The kiss lasted until a driver passing by blew the car horn.

"That is not a proper apology," Kyle said as their gazes held them in place.

"Then I guess you'll have to demonstrate what is."

They went inside and "apologized" to each other several times throughout the night.

"Time to go, sisterfriend," Martie said. "Much longer and poor Kyle will pass out from stress." She adjusted the bit of scalloped lace framing Shana's face. "Besides, you can't get any more beautiful."

"Why, thank you, Miss Martie. You do know the right thing to say."

"I know I do. Besides, I want to get closer to that fine creature serving as Kyle's best man. Until after the ceremony, he has to keep Kyle together."

"And after that, I have a feeling that you intend to try to pull Mr. Fine apart."

"But only in the nicest sort of way." Martie and Shana laughed.

"Are you two ready?" Paula poked her head into the small room off from the banquet hall. "Gloria said she has played through her entire repertoire of appropriate songs and is getting ready to switch to show tunes. Some of those are not meant for an occasion such as this."

"We're ready." Shana smoothed her hand down her dress.

"Tell her to hit it," Martie added as she moved in front of Shana.

The cue sounded and Martie patted Shana's arm, winked, then left her. Shana smiled.

If I knew where he is, I'd certainly send Elliot a thank-you note without any pizzas attached, she thought after Martie had time to reach the end of the red carpet. *Without him, I would never have had a real chance at happiness.*

She took a deep breath, then began the walk to take her to her future husband, to the man she loved more than she ever thought possible, the man with whom she would spend the rest of her life.

She wanted to run, but instead she moved slowly down the aisle to take her place beside her Kyle.

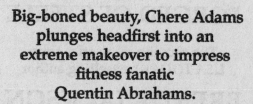

Big-boned beauty, Chere Adams
plunges headfirst into an
extreme makeover to impress
fitness fanatic
Quentin Abrahams.

But perhaps it's Chere's curves that
have caught Quentin's eye?

All About Me

Marcia
King-Gamble

AVAILABLE JANUARY 2007
FROM KIMANI™ ROMANCE

Love's Ultimate Destination

Available at your favorite retail outlet.